Monsterman

Monsterman

Joseph J. Curtin

Five Star • Waterville, Maine

First Edition
First Printing: September 2006

Published in 2006 in conjunction with Tekno Books and Ed Gorman.

Set in 11 pt. Plantin.

Printed in the United States on permanent paper.

Library of Congress Cataloging-in-Publication Data

Curtin, Joseph.
    Monsterman / by Joseph J. Curtin.—1st ed.
      p. cm.
    ISBN 1-59414-365-X (hc : alk. paper)
     1. Teenage boys—Fiction.   2. High school athletes—Fiction.
   3. Football—Fiction. 4. Muscle strength—Fiction. I. Title.
    PS3603.U775M66 2006
     813'.6—dc22
                                                 2006012781

This book is dedicated to my father, Neil Curtin, a force on the high school football fields of Chicago when facemasks were a novelty. By example, he taught me the nuances of the game and more importantly, how to conduct myself as a man. Thanks, Dad—for everything.

Acknowledgments

Writing, by its nature, is a solitary endeavor, but with my family surrounding me it is never a lonely one. Thank you, Karen, Tonimarie and Jodi (the bear), for your patience and support throughout the long nights.

Also, a special and sincere thank you to Mort Castle, friend, mentor, and one hell of a banjo player.

And to John Helfers and the gang at Tekno Books and Five Star Publishing, thank you one and all.

Prologue

July 4, 1987

Growing up in nearby Shelbyville, Tom Fenner had regarded Talbot-Hyde Laboratories with the reverent awe usually reserved for more cryptic local legends, like the haunted Miller house, or Bachelor's Grove, the abandoned cemetery off 135th street.

In the full light of day, driving past the high chain-link fences along Route 83, one could sometimes catch a glimpse of the white deer that were exclusive to the lab's twelve hundred acres of wooded grounds. Rumor had it that the deer were genetic mutations grown from petri dishes, quirky experiments from the same mad scientists that had given the world the atomic bomb. Tom's father had told him that was nothing but tavern scuttlebutt, but shortly after taking the job here, Tom had seen the rabbits.

The rabbits.

They were green—neon green—and they glowed in the dark, created just to see if such a thing could be done. The Talbot-Hyde P.R. team had their hands full explaining that one, 'fessing up only after the little monsters had escaped from a lab in Sector C into the neighboring countryside. The fact that they were cute and fuzzy did little to ease Tom's anxiety as he motored into the nearly deserted parking lot and parked in a well-lit spot, exactly one row back from the reserved spaces near the lab's main entrance.

Tom lingered a moment, letting the last bars of the Clash's *My Sharona* fade into the night air before gathering up his clipboard, flashlight, and nightstick—standard issue of the rent-a-cop's trade. He stole a glimpse of himself in the

Impala's tinted window as the car door swung shut, more impressed with the figure that he cut in his navy blue uniform than he had any right to be. He seated the nightstick through the loop on his Sam Browne belt and stood on the tarmac, peering past the few cars dotting the expansive lot, into the surrounding woods.

White deer, glow-in-the-dark bunnies, and God knew what else.

He turned his back on the things shuffling beneath the warm rhythm of the crickets' song and strolled with exaggerated indifference to the shadowy mouth of the administration building. Bobby Conroy's Mustang was parked illegally in its familiar spot in the handicapped zone and he could make out the silhouette of the painter's van at the far end of Sector D. All well and good. The guard at the front gate had told him to expect the painters. They were working a double-shift, trying to finish up before the plant re-opened after the long holiday weekend tomorrow morning at seven sharp. He didn't recognize the Chevy Blazer sitting a few rows back, but the reflective blue tape of the Talbot-Hyde windshield sticker glittering in his flashlight beam put his mind at ease. It was a company vehicle.

Tom plucked the master from the sheaf of keys on the oversize chrome hoop and stabbed the keyhole on the massive steel and glass door. He was inside with one full twist and punching in the security clearance code on the sentry box before the door had a chance to close. The only light burning was the reading lamp on the check-in desk in the center of the lobby. Tom braced himself, waiting for Conroy to jump out of the darkness and scare the shit out of him, as he was apt to do.

"Quit screwin' around, Bobby," he announced as he made his way behind the desk. "I got a headache and I ain't in no mood for you!" That much was true. Tom had been at a Fourth of July barbecue for the better part of the day and the three hours of sleep that he had managed to squeeze in did not allow him to forget the nine beers he had put away.

Tom thumbed the switch on the control panel seated flush in the dark oak finish of the reception desk. The recessed spots in the drop-ceiling tiles came to life, lending a soft blue glow to the lobby, and Tom felt better immediately. Just enough light to eliminate the long shadows and allow him to holster his flashlight. He scanned the sign-in sheet, his stubby finger traveling down the page to the lone blank rectangle in the checkout column.

Dr. Von-os-o . . . *Vonosovich,* had neglected to sign out Thursday night. Didn't surprise Tom. He'd never met the man, but from what he'd heard, the guy was your typical absent-minded professor. Still, that was pretty sloppy security work on Conroy's part—you make a guy sign out when he leaves a secure area, big shot or not.

Tom Fenner hitched his belt up and began his rounds. A quick check of each sector, some minor paperwork, and he'd be able to dive into the new Superman/Spiderman crossover, maybe even catch a few Zs on the couch in the women's bathroom—the nice one in D Sector.

Tom saw the light creeping out from under the door at the far end of Sector C as soon as he rounded the corner, and stopped dead in his tracks. He fumbled for his clipboard and flipped through his paperwork, looking for a reason—any reason—why someone would be working a "hot" zone at this hour. Tom drew the nightstick from his belt and walked resolutely down the dim hallway, the rubbery squeak of his shoes suddenly very loud on the linoleum tile.

"Spider sense is tingling," he whispered with nervous candor as he sidled up alongside the wall. He stopped short of

11

lab 612 before the light seeping from under the door could touch his shoe tips. Tom stood there for a long moment, steeling his nerve before he rapped on the heavy door.

"Frain Security," he announced in his deepest voice. Nothing.

He rapped again. This time with the nightstick.

"Bobby?" Tom drew the red key from the smaller of the two hoops and inserted it into the lock of the oversized door. "Bobby, you best not be messing with—"

The shotgun blast cut him off just as the door swung open, making for the grandest entrance of his young life. Tom Fenner would have run, but the spectacle of the bloody panorama splashed across the bright green tiles of lab 612 froze him where he stood.

What little remained of Bobby Conroy lay in a tangle, caked to the floor in a black pool of dried blood. His exposed rib cage protruded from the purpled tatters of his uniform shirt like a rack of lamb, picked clean to the bone and void of the internal organs it had once protected. He stared at Tom through wide, terrified, eyes, his mouth frozen in a silent, unfinished, scream. More blood, quite fresh and still dripping, smeared the opposite wall above an oblong vat isolated atop an elevated platform. The arm of a Talbot-Hyde lab coat dangled over the side, above a still-smoking Remington 12-gauge shotgun. The hand protruding from the sleeve almost looked human.

Tom willed himself over to the cast-iron trough. He looked at the headless remains of the thing bubbling in the vat of corrosive acid.

When the first painter arrived nearly seven minutes later, Tom Fenner was still screaming.

PART I

INCEPTION

Chapter 1

June 22, 1999

The football drifted off its high arc in a loose spiral, the only blemish in the cloudless blue of the late June sky. Streaking along the near sideline down below, Matt McGee recognized the safety blitz and broke off his post pattern a split-second too late. He sliced across the midfield hash mark into traffic, silently praying that McAllister had made the same read. With a quick look-behind, he spotted the pill falling high and fast—too fast, over his left shoulder. He leaped in a last-ditch effort to salvage his starting job, almost smiling as the ball dropped onto the tips of his long fingers. He gathered it into his—

Matt McGee did not remember the collision when asked about it in the hospital the next day but the horrific impact was something that most sideline observers would never forget.

"Whoa. . . ." Coach Mangan whistled.

"Where the hell was McAllister?" Coach Houghwat growled, his tactician's eye immediately noting the missed assignment. "He's supposed to provide support."

Coach Minot only stared straight ahead, his dark eyes narrowing as he watched the defensive back who had delivered the hit, standing dispassionately over the crumpled receiver.

"Number 47," Minot mumbled. "Again. Who is that kid? He really brings the wood. What's he doing with the second unit?"

Coach Mangan sniffed. "Vonosovich. Kid's a dog. Slow—no stick. Must have gotten lucky. He's been riding pine for three years. Barely made the cut last year."

Coach Houghwat watched the trainer gingerly removing

15

the McGee kid's helmet. It took two caps of smelling salts before the boy lifted his head off the grass. "Making the cut won't be a problem this year," he said, watching the wobbly receiver being helped to his feet. "That dog has learned to bite." He ran his fingers through the last loyal wisps of silver hair atop his balding head. Try as he may, he couldn't remember the kid from last year's varsity squad. *Vonosovich.* Didn't ring a bell. Getting old really was a bitch.

Coach Minot spoke up. "Let's give him a shot with the first unit," he said, more of a demand than a suggestion. "The boy plays with bad intentions. We need him on the field."

Mangan frowned and scratched his chin. "Where we gonna put him? The defensive backfield is set. Halloran and Webber are our best cover men. You think he's big enough to play linebacker?"

"Nothing is set," Minot said, matter-of-factly. "This defense ranked last in the conference last year. Everyone is playing for a job."

Houghwat bristled. He was still trying to get a take on his new defensive coordinator—trying very hard to like him. Not a bad guy, you understand. A man's man for sure, but the type who would never pass up a mirror. The athletic department had brought him in just before the summer sessions had started and placed him on the varsity coaching staff, rather than move him up through the frosh-soph ranks, as was standard procedure. Houghwat considered it a big P.R. move at the time. Mike Minot had spent two nondescript seasons with the Kansas City Chiefs as a strong safety before blowing out a knee. They probably figured it would help recruiting— young, good-looking ex-NFL player and all that, but as it turned out, the guy came in with a very inventive scheme and a good eye for talent. Although he was hired as a defensive specialist, the A.D. had anointed him "Assistant Head

Coach," the first such title in Ridgewood High's history.

Houghwat could read the writing on the wall. He'd been head coach of the Ridgewood Redskins—er, RedHawks (he'd never get used to the politically correct name change) since the school opened in 1971. In his twenty-eight years, he'd brought home eleven division titles and two state championships. Not bad for a small school from the far south suburbs of Chicago. Still, they had missed the playoffs for the last three years. People were starting to talk.

That was all right. He had two years left on his contract and then he could retire with a fat thirty-year pension. He had put three sons through this school and into college. The youngest, his daughter Melanie, was a senior this year and an all-state volleyball player with a free ride guaranteed to just about any college of her choice.

It would be nice to go out with a bang, though. After just one week of summer two-a-days, he could see that this year's crop of juniors would fill a lot of holes. A few of the returning seniors, especially this Vonosovich kid, had moved their game up a notch or two. A winning record and a shot at the playoffs were certainly not out of the question. With Minot taking over the defense, he would have more time to fine-tune the wishbone offense the RedSki—Hawks had been running so seamlessly for twenty-eight years. He still had a few tricks up his sleeve.

Coach Houghwat looked at his eventual successor. The former pro from Fresno State was drumming a Sharpie off his clipboard, his large biceps moving rhythmically up and down his arm like a cantaloupe on a pulley. He seemed to be unaware of the action.

"I think you're right, Mike," Houghwat said, stepping in between the two assistants. "We've got to get the boy more time on the field." He liked the fact that he was a bigger man than Minot, that he carried his weight on a larger frame. Although he had never played at the pro level, Tom Houghwat had been an All-American center at Michigan and had started in two Rose Bowls. That counted for something. Besides, everyone knew that offensive linemen made the best coaches. He peered over Minot's broad shoulder at the intricate diagram of X's and O's. This was still his team and he would have final say on all personnel matters. "Where do you see him playing?"

Mike Minot stared straight ahead, seeming to ignore the older man. After a long moment he turned to his boss with an easy smile full of movie star white teeth, almost dazzling against his perpetual five o'clock shadow. It was this smile that had wrested women off of barstools in countless nightspots across the country with ridiculous ease and now it made Tom Houghwat forget that he had been waiting just a little too long for an answer.

"We're going to plug him in where he can do the most damage, Tom," he said before the smile melted into the hard set of his jaw. He scrawled the boy's name beneath the lone red X on the defensive schematic and lifted his cold eyes to the field where number 47 was taking his spot in a three-deep zone. "Roving free-safety. The Monsterman."

Chapter 2

August 26, 1999

Sergei Vonosovich breathed deep, enjoying the tight flutter of his pectoral muscles as his chest expanded with the intake of the crisp morning air. He crossed beneath the canopy of old elms at the corner of Homan Avenue that had stood for over a century, young when the street was laid with brick and cobblestone. Dappled bursts of sunlight filtered through the broad leaves and rolled over his arms and shoulders, dancing across his face and through his thick black hair with every step. His gait, a casual, confident lope, hinted at the boundless and explosive energy intrinsic to the young and perfectly fit.

He felt none of the anxiety normally associated with the first day of school, only the hungry anticipation a wolf would feel when approaching a hen house. The acne that had ravaged his face since seventh grade was a distant memory, as were the scars and the pitting it had left in its wake. Gone also was the gaunt hollow under his prominent cheekbones, a ripple effect of the thirty-five pounds of new muscle he had added to his frame since school had let out only three months ago. It was a summer of discovery—self-discovery and otherwise—that had led him to this pinnacle of physical well-being. The cockiness in his step owed as much to what he had learned about himself in the long hours spent pumping iron in his basement and hauling drywall up endless stairwells for McGann Construction.

A burgundy Mustang convertible with the top down rolled to a stop directly in front of him as he emerged from the leafy tunnel at the intersection of Homan and Pearl. He recognized the girl sitting shotgun and relished the startled look on her face as she turned and took notice of him. After recovering from her nearly comical double take, Jackie Wells gestured frantically for the Mustang's pilot to turn and look also. Brandi Brewer's rake of honeycomb blonde hair rolled back with the perfect synchronicity of falling dominos as she turned her head and saw Von standing patiently at her passenger side door.

"Hi, Jackie . . . Brandi," Von said, looking down into the tan cockpit of the Mustang. Beneath the Passion cologne worn by Jackie Wells and the Opium sported by Brandi Brewer, his keen nose picked up the one-of-a-kind smell of new leather upholstery. It was a good smell—a smell he had only been able to borrow at this point in his life. "Nice car," he offered, listening now to the perfect hum of the motor. "You get the V-8 or the V-6?" He knew from the muted growl that it was the V-8.

Brandi Brewer recovered first. "Hi Von—um, V-8 I think." Her eyes moved over him boldly and she made no effort to hide her approval. Jackie Wells seemed to have lost her ability to speak, which in itself was remarkable. "How was your summer?"

"Good," Von answered. He smiled. "Summer was good. How about yours?"

"Too short," Brandi answered, just a little too chippy. "Aren't they all? I barely—"

The irritated blare of a car horn cut her short. She turned to see a Dodge Ram pick-up idling behind the Mustang's rear bumper. A thirty-ish woman, looking forty-ish without her morning make-up, sat in her bathrobe behind the wheel, a smoldering Winston tucked angrily in the corner of her mouth. Her husband sat alongside, honing his silent, angry glare through his own cloud of carcinogens, oblivious to the well-being of the toddler strapped into the plank seat behind them.

Brandi rolled her eyes at Von. "Sheesh! I think the gene pool could use a little chlorine. You need a ride to school?"

Jackie Wells's jaw dropped, astonished that her friend would cross class boundaries so casually.

Von considered just a moment before begging off. "Uh, thanks, but it's a nice morning. I think I'll walk."

"Suit yourself." Brandi smiled, a sly saucy smile, meant more for Jackie than him. "See you in school." She pulled away and stepped on the gas as she veered left onto Homan, eliciting a chirp from the wide, high-performance radials.

Von stood on the corner watching her taillights grow small before stepping off the curb, catching himself as the Dodge pick-up rumbled abruptly into his path. The man sitting shotgun looked defiantly at Von over the top of the half-open window as his shrewish wife waited for the drizzle of on-coming traffic to clear. Von stared back, sizing him up, as men will do. A hard hat rested on the seat beside him atop a large metal thermos and lunchpail strung together with a frayed bungee cord. A Harley-Davidson tattoo peeked out from under the sleeve of his white T-shirt, adorning an arm hard with muscle from years of manual labor.

Von could take him.

They both knew it.

The man surrendered his gaze and motioned for his wife to proceed through the intersection. It was not cowardice, but a wary respect the younger, more powerfully built man had instilled in the hard-hat. The dance was almost as old as time itself, played out on mating grounds and watering holes long before the dawn of man.

Von smiled inside, knowing that as little as three months ago he would not even have raised his eyes to the challenge. He began to whistle as he strode toward Ridgewood High School.

It was going to be a good year.

Chapter 3

The student body of Ridgewood High milled about the campus in varying clusters of size and substance. Incoming freshmen, bewildered and apprehensive, dotted the perimeter, searching for familiar faces from the local grammar schools and junior highs that bottlenecked into the mammoth diploma factory. Upperclassmen gathered in well-established cliques, ranked by social stature and lifestyle affiliation. A small pocket of goths compared facial piercings and hair dye a few yards away from the metal-heads and stoners in their black concert T-shirts and blue jeans, blinking through the fog of an early morning joint. Standing a safe distance away, a small but growing number of re-born Christians, dubbed the *God Squad* by students and faculty alike, looked on with pious indignity. The jocks, blue chippers like Sean Graham and Ward Starret, held court near the row of glass doors that marked the entryway, coupling up with the cream of Ridgewood's female population. On the outer fringe of this group, Jason Jankowski was leaning against the hood of his beater Chevy Beretta, chatting it up with Donny Musconi, when he looked up to see Von make his way across new Western Avenue and onto the campus grounds. Donny Musconi, nicknamed "horse" for his unfortunate resemblance to Mr. Ed, followed his gaze. He let out a low whistle as they watched him approach.

"Wow, is it my imagination or did he get bigger since two-a-days?" Donny asked, referring to the grueling summer practices that had ended just two weeks ago.

Jason said nothing, watching the heads turn and the stares of disbelief as his friend strode through the parking lot toward them.

"You think he's on the 'juice'? " Donny prodded, noting Jason's silence.

"Nah," Jason said quickly, "Von's too smart for that. It's just a late growth spurt—happens all the time."

"You know," Donny continued, motioning toward the doors where several of the interior linemen stood milling around quarterback Ward Starret like Neanderthal bookends, "Jake and Lally-gags are juicing."

Jason looked at Dan "Jake" Jacobson and Frank Lally, snorting and laughing as they compared the girth of their respective forearms. He wondered, not for the first time, if their brains shrank in inverse proportion to their biceps. Jake was no body-beautiful but he was an imposing physical specimen nonetheless. The doughy blubber that had always adorned his large frame had grown harder since taking up with Frank Lally, a weightroom monster, in his sophomore year.

"Yeah, I figured as much," Jason said. "Jake's still a fat-ass but he's hauling it around with a little more authority."

"He's puffy," Donny observed. "He's got that puffy, bloated look that comes from steroids. It's not natural. It's—"

"What's not natural?"

Donny turned to see Von standing at his elbow.

"Hey, Von," Donny said, hoping the big defensive back didn't think he was talking about him. "Jake and Lally-gags—they've been practically living in the weightroom."

"Word is out that they're on the juice," Jason said, more to the point, looking directly at Von. "Steroids."

Von didn't flinch. "Those things will jack you up," he said distastefully. "Wildcards have no place in this game, gentlemen. You have to play the hand that nature dealt you." He punched Jason in the arm. A playful shot, but it carried more than just a little sting. "Hey, bud, where you been hiding all summer?"

"Hey," Donny Musconi piped up a little too excitedly, "there's Haley."

Von said nothing as he watched Haley McBride talking with Kerri Wheeler and Melanie Houghwat. Haley McBride was somewhat of an enigma to the male population of Ridgewood High. She had politely but firmly fended off the many requests for dates that she had been bombarded with since transferring from Luther South last year. Her refusal to date had raised all sorts of speculation and innuendo, none of it of course, remotely close to the truth. Looking at her now, Von felt a tug on his heart that could not be suppressed by endless bench press repetitions or the lonely but satisfying grind of writing late into the night. He'd had crushes before— he even thought he might have been in love with Courtney Chute, a girl he had dated for nearly three months in his sophomore year. He thought they had a good thing going until the night she got drunk and fell into the arms of Lou Krystakos. Lou was an upperclassman who drove a new Trans Am and supplied coke and X to all the raves south of Merrionette Park. Last he'd heard, old Lou was doing a ten-year hitch in Statesville, and Courtney—well, Courtney had dropped out of school after coming up preggers. Rumor had it the baby could have been Lou's or any of the guys he ran with. Funny thing, she had really torn his heart out, but looking at Haley now, he had to wonder what all the fuss was about.

"Whoa, dude," Donny yelped, pulling Von back into the here and now, "check this out!"

Von turned to see the red Z06 Corvette gliding through the parking lot and docking in one of the reserved Faculty Only spots near the gym doors. Mike Minot sat behind the wheel, seemingly indifferent to the multitude of eyes suddenly and totally cast upon him. He dialed the volume on the six-speaker stereo system down to a respectable level and lightly goosed the accelerator, savoring the LS1 motor's own sweet music before cutting the ignition.

He hefted a duffel bag from the passenger seat, pausing just a moment to offer a nod to the cluster of jocks, hooting and waving near the main entryway as he made his way toward the gymnasium doors.

"Yo, Coach," Ryan Amberson yelled from the crowd of blue-chippers, "grand theft auto is a felony in this state!"

Mike Minot smirked and discreetly scratched an imaginary itch on his temple with his middle finger, drawing overdone laughter and guffaws from his loyal subjects. The smirk broke into a genuine smile when he spotted Von standing off to the side with Jason Jankowski and Donny Musconi. He veered toward the group of boys and fished a clipboard from the bag thrown over his shoulder.

"New car, Coach?" Jason asked, noting the small crowd gathering a safe distance away from the sleek red rocket.

"Better than new," Minot said, answering and ignoring Jason at the same time. "This is a new twist for the 4-5-2," he said, plucking a sheet from the clipboard and handing it to Von. "Look it over and let me know what you think."

With that, the former pro turned and strode toward the gym, his broad back and narrow waist well defined under the white cotton polo shirt. A press of bodies, many of them female, greeted Von as he turned again to his friends. Kerri Wheeler stood staring over Von's shoulder, dropping her eyes to him only after the gymnasium doors closed behind the defensive guru.

"*That's* the new coach?" Kerri asked incredulously, turning to Melanie Houghwat. "Melanie! I thought you said he was a major league tool!"

"Trust me," Melanie said, a strange smile dancing in her Nordic blue eyes, "he is."

Chapter 4

Tall and whippet thin, Eugene Kroc paced the narrow aisle between his desk and the blackboard. His hands, which would gesture wildly as he lectured, were folded behind his back, laced together with spindly fingers yellowed with seven years of chalk dust. With the peal of the second bell, he stopped pacing and dropped his bony rump into the familiar wooden chair like a prizefighter heading to his designated corner before the first round. He adjusted his ridiculously long frame in the seat, adapting a casual attitude as the first wave of students filtered through the hallways outside his door. The butterflies seemed larger and angrier this year—nothing like the leathery bats that had invaded his gut when he was plucked from his very comfortable curator's post at the Temple's vast library and placed in front of other people's children with the order to teach and *watch*. Much to his surprise (and his wife's amusement), Kroc had found that he enjoyed teaching more than he would ever care to admit, but the first day of school never failed to fill him with a nervous anticipation culled from equal parts of hope and dread.

The freshmen were the worst, scared and immature, they would snicker nervously and roll their eyes when they first saw him. His face was sculpted in graceful lines that might have been considered beautiful perched atop anything other than his skinny neck, and crowned with an unruly shank of wavy hair, still jet-black as he stood on the threshold of forty. He'd grown a mustache as soon as he was able, to diffuse his feminine features, most notably the cupid bow of his lips, but it only served to accentuate the ultra-long lashes that framed his wet brown eyes.

They called him, among other things, *The Stork,* but if they only knew what he was capable of.

It usually took a week, maybe two, for them to come around and fall under his spell. Eugene Kroc was born to teach and his passion for the written word (just one of the attributes that had first caught the attention of the Elders), infected all but the most jaded (and let's face it—*stupid*) of his students. He hated that word and never allowed himself to say it out loud, even to himself, but he could think of no other term to aptly describe someone who flat-out refused to learn of the inherent joy that comes from reading a good book.

The true numbskulls were few and far between, thank God, and every once in a while a truly gifted student would come along and supply him with some small measure of satisfaction. He'd seen a few move on to careers in journalism and teaching. One student, Wayne Allen, had gone on to become a somewhat successful science fiction writer, with a novel and dozens of short stories on the market (and didn't he feel a bitter sting of jealousy as his own novel sat unfinished in the closet?). All in all, it wasn't a bad life. He enjoyed working with the kids, most of whom really wanted to learn, and the gratification he received from nurturing a real talent was its own reward.

As if to underscore that point, Sergei Vonosovich stuck his head in the doorway, separate and distinct from the swell of bodies buzzing through the halls.

"Hey, Mr. Kroc—you got room for one more in here?" he asked peering into the empty classroom.

Kroc pressed a long finger to the pursed lips beneath his caterpillar mustache. "Hmm," he snorted, pretending to scan his student list, "I don't know. Did you have reservations?"

"Yeah, but I came anyway," Von laughed, stepping

through the doorway and into the room.

Eugene Kroc recovered quickly enough so that he did not fall out of his chair, but just barely. The physical transformation the boy had gone through over the summer was that amazing. Kroc had seen some dramatic growth spurts from May through September in his time but this . . . this was—no he wouldn't allow himself to think it. He blinked twice in rapid succession, just to keep from staring.

"So how was your summer, Von?" he asked, back in control now.

"Pretty good, Mr. Kroc," Von answered as he plopped his stack of books onto the arm-table and worked himself into the narrow seat. "How 'bout you?"

"Terrible," Kroc replied. "I missed coming in here every morning and seeing all your smiling faces. Seriously though, it was okay. Took the family up to Michigan. Trish's folks have a place on the lake. Did some fishing." He paused, recalling the night he and Trish made love under a blanket of stars while Carolyn was sleeping soundly in the cabin with her grandparents. "It was nice."

"That's cool," Von said, noting his teacher's goofy grin.

"How's the writing coming along?" Kroc asked. "Did you join that workshop I told you about?"

"Eh . . ." Von mumbled, "no, I didn't. Kind of busy. Football and all . . ."

"Yeah, I know. It's hard to find the time," the teacher replied, thinking again of his incomplete manuscript gathering more dust with each passing year. The demands of the Order had made it all but impossible for him to write. "Don't let it get too far away, Von. It's tough to come back." He forced a fatherly smile. "Take it from someone who—"

"Yo! Mr. Kroc."

Dale Summers sauntered in, followed by Jason

Jankowski—another one of Kroc's favorites—and Ward Starret.

"Mr. Summers. Mr. Jankowski." Mr. Kroc nodded politely to the golden boy. He had only had the quarterback and resident Big Man on Campus in his class once before, freshman year—English Fundamentals. He seemed like a good enough kid, almost too good to be true.

The final bell sounded and the crowds lingering in the hallways dispersed and filtered into their various homerooms. Eugene Kroc watched his students take their seats, making mental notes, sizing up the year in store. Kerri Wheeler and her crew—chatty but no real discipline concerns. Haley McBride, Coach Houghwat's daughter Melanie, Jonathan Howell . . . pretty good group all in all. He was glad to have a senior homeroom. Ridgewood was college prep and although there were plenty of trade and shop courses, most of the students would go on to higher institutes of learning.

Frank Lally and Dan Jacobson lumbered past him just as he was closing the door. Frank was not the sharpest knife in the drawer, but the kid had a good sense of humor and they would, on occasion, engage in some good-natured ribbing. Jacobson was a stranger to him, but the word from the faculty grapevine was not encouraging.

"Gentlemen," he said, holding the door open with an exaggerated sweep of his arm, allowing the big tackles to step past him, "so glad you could make it. I hope we didn't put a crimp in your busy schedule."

"Nah—we figured we'd make it in here sooner or later," Lally wisecracked as he looked around the crowded classroom. "You know, the least you could have done was save us a seat."

"Oh, but I did," Kroc replied, indicating the two remaining seats on opposite ends of the front row. "Right up front here. Better to take advantage of my vast expertise of *Contemporary American Literature*—a subject near and dear to my heart."

"Aww . . ." Lally moaned as he shambled over to the window seat.

"I thought you said this guy was cool," Jake sneered, looking at the gangly teacher with a sort of amused disgust.

The disrespect was not lost on Kroc and he moved in quickly, crossing the room in three long strides.

"Kroc's first rule for a healthy learning environment," he said, bending low and placing his large hands on Jacobson's desk, "is *punctuality*. It is of course, a matter of *respect*." The teacher's face grew hard as he accentuated the key word. It was a face he saved for moments such as this. A mask smelted from years of childhood ridicule suffered at the hands of oafs and fools. "Any student not seated by the final bell is considered tardy. Three tardies constitute a jug. If you value your Saturdays I would suggest you make it in to my class on time. I'll give you both a pass on this one but it is the only one you will receive. Understood?"

Jake backed off, surprised and momentarily unnerved by the flash of anger (and what else?) he saw in the teacher's eyes. "Understood," Jake mumbled.

"Excellent," Kroc said, addressing the whole class now. The flint was gone from his eyes, replaced by the familiar gleam. He took attendance and strategically rearranged a few seating assignments to better insure a *healthy learning environment* before moving on.

"The class is *Contemporary American Literature*, contemporary, meaning anything written in the latter stages of this century." He walked among the rows distributing the class syllabus as he talked. "In addition to the short stories contained in your anthologies, you will read one novel of your own choice from the list on page three. As a bonus, I will allow you to read one novel of your own choosing by any contemporary author. I want it to be a writer you enjoy reading. That is the only restriction. Any questions? Good.

"We're going to jump right in with a little gem from Shirley Jackson entitled *The Lottery*—page one twenty-four in your copy of *Selected*, which I trust you all have. *The Lottery* has traditionally been viewed as a scapegoat metaphor, but I stand before you today with the truth. *The Lottery* is in fact a fertility allegory and this is how you will—"

"My uncle won five grand on the Lotto quick pick last year," Jake piped up suddenly.

A few muted gasps and a brief titter of nervous laughter preceded the awful silence that followed.

It took a moment for Eugene Kroc to collect himself. "I'm sorry, Mr. Jacobson, but I don't recall seeing you raise your hand."

"That's 'cuz I didn't," Jake snorted. He looked around for support. Even Frank Lally had lowered his head. "It just sorta' came out."

"Kroc's *second* rule for a healthy learning environment— and maybe this is my fault for not laying out the ground rules for those of you unfamiliar with basic classroom etiquette—is *never*, under any circumstances, interrupt Kroc while Kroc has the floor. If you feel you have something pertinent to add, raise your hand and I will allow you to speak when I have finished. Do you understand, Mr. Jacobson?"

"Yeah," Jake frowned. "Sorry. Go ahead, Mr. *Kroc*."

Kroc ignored the petty jab, steeling himself for the trouble he could smell brewing like a first pot of morning coffee. "As I was saying, there are two basic ways to interpret this story and although you—"

"He didn't tell my aunt about it," Jake said turning to Jonathan Howell, who was nothing less than mortified. "He blew off work and went to the gambling boat in Marquette. She found out after—"

"Jacobson!" Kroc seethed, fighting to keep his composure. "On Friday you will present to me, a one thousand word essay entitled *The Lottery, A Contemporary Fertility Allegory.* Failure to do so will result in a Saturday jug wherein you will complete said assignment. If you choose to interrupt me again I will double it."

Dan Jacobson could feel the hot color rising in his doughy cheeks. Who did this skinny little twerp think he was, talking to him like that? He was sure he would have no problem picking him up and breaking him clean in half like a pretzel stick. No problem at all.

"Do you have a problem with that, Mr. Jacobson?" Kroc asked.

"No," Jake smiled. "No problem at all."

Chapter 5

The lunch sack landed next to Jason's elbow with a crinkly thud, the considerable bulk nearly bursting though its brown paper confines.

"Touch the Ho-Hos and you're a dead man," Von said without breaking stride as he made his way to the bank of vending machines on the cafeteria's west wall. Jason considered the bag a moment, thought better of it, and turned his attention back to the drawing taking shape in his sketchbook.

Jason was a talented artist, maybe the best ever to pass through Ridgewood High, and together with Von, he had developed what he thought was a pretty damn good comic book character. *NightHawk* was a semi-vampiric antihero. A disembodied soul, the former priest prowled the night, administering a swift and final justice to the city's criminal element. More shadow than substance, he would drain the life force from his victims, regaining the essence of flesh and blood before being driven back underground by the rays of the rising sun. It was an interesting concept but still in its infancy stage.

"I'm thinking of giving him a cape," Jason said, tapping his pencil thoughtfully on the open sketchbook.

"Capes are gay," Von quipped as he settled in next to his friend with two ice cold cans of Mountain Dew. "Nobody wears capes anymore." He paused for a moment, waiting for the blare of the second bell to fade. "Except *Spawn*. Spawn can get away with it because he's such a bad-ass."

"I was thinking more like wings," Jason said, "a cape that looks like wings."

the draft at all?" he
asked, watching Von empty the vast contents of his lunch bag
on to the table. "We've got a lot of holes to patch regarding
his origin."

Von blanched at the mention of the NightHawk script.
"Uh—yeah," he lied. "I wanted to talk to you about that.
Why don't you come by at the end of the week and I'll show
you what I've got and we'll toss it around?" He had been
meaning to get some work done on that but he always seemed
to end up doing something else—like lifting weights. "Hey,
check this out," he said, eager to change the subject. Von
pulled Minot's defensive diagram from his pocket. "Coach is
giving me total liberty on all nickel packs between the red
zones."

Jason eyeballed the schematic as Von worked his way into
the first of three sandwiches. It was quite a departure from
the strict zones and standard man-to-man coverages that
Ridgewood had deployed for years. He wondered how it
would fly with Coach Houghwat.

"Basically, I just follow the ball," Von said, already into
his second sandwich. "I only have zone responsibility if there
is a four receiver set. It's a license to kill."

"Is that a *Fluffernutter?*"

Von looked up in mid chew, delighted to see Haley
McBride looking down at him from across the table. Haley, in
her faded jeans and tight-fitting top. Her wild mane of straw-
berry blonde hair rolled like velvet wildfire over her shoulders
nearly igniting the clutch of textbooks cradled against her

34

breasts. Incredibly, she set the books down on the lunch table directly across from him and sat down. "I haven't had one of those in years," she said, eyeing the remaining sandwich at his elbow. "I didn't even know they still made the stuff."

Von couldn't swallow the sticky mouthful quickly enough. "You want it?" he blurted, just a little too loudly.

Jackie Wells nudged Haley and added an eye-roll for dramatic effect. "Come *on*, Haley," she moaned, looking around the rapidly filling cafeteria. "We won't get a seat."

"That's tempting," Haley said, ignoring Jackie. "But I really shouldn't. Maybe I could have a quick bite of that one?"

Jackie Wells sat down next to her, secure now in the knowledge that something interesting was about to transpire.

Von nodded mutely and handed the half-eaten sandwich across the table to Haley.

"Mmmm . . . that's good," Haley said, taking a healthy bite. "Wonder Bread, right?"

Jason smiled to himself as he watched Von nod stupidly in agreement. He knew how Von felt about Haley McBride.

"So," Jackie piped up, having gone long past her limit without speaking, "you guys ready for Saturday night?"

Von looked at the creamy dab of peanut butter and Marshmallow Fluff on Haley McBride's lower lip. For a moment he forgot all about football.

Chapter 6

"Dude, she took a bite of your sandwich!" Jason Jankowski poked his head through the netted practice jersey and worked the tattered garment over his bulky shoulder pads. "Think about it, man. That almost qualifies as an exchange of bodily fluids."

Von laughed and pulled a thick tube sock over his foot, doubling it over his muscular calf. It was a joke, but his friend was onto something. Haley could have just as easily asked for one of the untouched sandwiches. But she wanted that one— the one he had his *mouth* on. "Yeah, right," he said, trying to make light of it. "I'm lucky she didn't ask for any of my Mountain Dew—then I'd have to marry her."

"Yeah, like you wouldn't love that," Jason said, pulling his headgear down from the top of his locker. "Sex with Haley McBride night after night."

"Think we'll scrimmage today?" Von asked, eager to change the subject. He was not keen on discussing Haley McBride in the boys' locker room. There was no place for the mention of her name among the swearing and the farting and the lewd horseplay of the testosterone-charged clubhouse.

"Sex with Haley McBride? Isn't that a contradiction in terms?" Ryan Amberson chimed in.

Too late.

"To boldly go where no man has gone before . . ." Owen Daniels laughed. Daniels and Amberson were the weak and strong side linebackers respectively. They had made the *Chicago Tribune*'s list of Prep Players to Watch in a pre-season write-up and were the only bright spots on last year's porous defense. A couple of bad hombres to be sure, but they were stepping rather lightly here—being careful not to bust his chops too hard. It was a matter of respect. Von was a starter now—an integral part of what was shaping up to be a very solid unit.

"You can forget about that broad," Dan Jacobson snorted, sticking his big head over the bank of lockers. He sneered down at Von. "She swings the other way. Hell, everyone knows that—"

Von glared at the big offensive lineman, hate flashing in his dark eyes. It was true hate, dark and deep as the bottom of the Black Sea, and just as old.

Jake recovered and pressed on, his loud voice containing the slightest bit of a croak. "I got one thing to say to her kind—thanks for nothing!" He laughed—a loud braying laugh that cut to Von's last nerve. "They need to know what it's like to be with a real man!"

Von rose up off the bench and squared himself up. "Well then why don't you clue her in, fat boy? You sound like you speak from experience."

The locker room, noisy and boisterous, fell silent as a tomb.

Von could feel Jason and the others backing slowly out of the cramped aisle between the bench and the banks of lockers. He could feel his accelerated heartbeat pumping oxygen-rich blood into his tightening muscles as his body readied itself for combat.

The near-comical look of astonishment on Dan Jacobson's face twisted into a mask of rage. "I'm going to kill you, Vonosovich. I'm going to rip off your head and—"

"Jacobson!" Coach Minot's voice boomed through the locker room like a thunderclap. "Get your fat ass down offa' there and get those cleats off that pine!"

The small crowd that had gravitated toward the confrontation was already dispersing as Minot elbowed his way through the narrow aisle. Dan Jacobson stepped down and looked sheepishly at the defensive coordinator, their faces only inches apart.

"This is a locker room, not a playground," he said, somehow a more imposing presence in his polo shirt and shorts than the larger teenager in full battle gear. "You better pray you bring some of that attitude to the field with you on Saturday!" He turned away from Jake, addressing all of them now. "Eisenhower is coming in here looking to kick our ass. So unless you want to get lit up for forty-one points like you did last year, I suggest we focus on the real enemy. Understood?"

Jake nodded solemnly. "Yeah, Coach, sorry."

"Good," Minot said checking his watch for effect. "Practice starts in two minutes. Anyone not on the field will be joining Jacobson for extra laps. Let's go."

Jake glared at Von and swore silently to himself. *Coach's pet. We'll see about that.*

The few stragglers hurried to pull on their gear and trotted toward the door, not wanting any part of extra laps in the oppressive heat. Minot paused at the door, under the sign that read: "Home of the Ridgewood RedHawks State Champions 1985, 1989."

He'd handled that with kid gloves solely for the benefit of Coach Houghwat. The two of them had been watching the whole scene unfold from inside the three glass walls of the coaches' office tucked against the east wall. He knew the old war-horse was big on discipline and all the old school, rah-rah crap, so he broke it up before any leather could fly. If it was his team (and it would be, soon enough), he would have let them mix it up a little before stepping in. He'd been in enough losing locker rooms in his life to know that an occasional fight was a necessary evil—good for clearing the air. Besides, this one would have been interesting. He would have bet on his free safety to lay the big lineman out before the second bell. Jacobson was a big boy, but he was slow and stupid. The Vonosovich kid was a little smaller, but was quick as a cat and had a real love of violent contact hidden beneath his quiet demeanor. The *Neanderthal gene* is what Coach Konrath used to call it back in Fresno State. It couldn't be taught and all the great hitters possessed it: Butkus, Singletary, Nitsche—hell, he could have added his own name to that list if he hadn't sheared his ACL in that godforsaken downpour against Oakland two years ago. He was silently cursing the fates that had brought him from the bright lights of the NFL to coaching a mediocre high school football team when he saw Von hanging back by his locker.

"What's the hold-up, Vonosovich?" Minot laughed. "Jacobson scare you?"

"Hell no, Coach," Von said, forcing a grin. "I'll be out in a minute." He shrugged and nodded toward the toilets, slightly embarrassed, "I gotta take a dump."

"You'll be runnin' laps with your buddy," Minot said.

"Yeah well, when you gotta go, you gotta go," Von said heading for the stalls.

"Suit yourself." Minot opened the door to a bright blue August sky. "But hurry it up or you'll be running laps until tomorrow morning."

Von waited until the door closed with a decisive click before he toed back to his locker and pulled the small leather satchel from the depths of his gym bag. With a careful look around, he skirted across the gunmetal gray of the concrete floor and slid into the second stall in the bank of five, opposite the showers. He waited a moment, his ears picking up nothing but the slow drip of the leaky showers. Von closed his eyes and extended his range, letting his preternatural hearing seek out the most distant hint of an intruder. The noise crept in slowly at first: the double blasts of Coach Houghwat's whistle to start practice, the voices of his teammates counting out the cadence of the calisthenics, Coach Mangan yelling at them to step it up. Now the sounds were rolling in like an approaching avalanche; the pounding of their feet on the turf as they ran their warm-up lap, even their labored breathing, roaring in his ears like the engine of a 747. He shut it down, satisfied that he was alone, and zipped open the satchel. Inside was a portable med kit, familiar to many diabetics. Von carefully extracted the syringe from its Velcro loop and screwed on a disposable needle, bringing it flush with the hypo's barrel. He pulled the vial from its recessed compartment and held it up to the light. A twinge of guilt tickled the hairs on his neck like the first hint of winter in an October breeze. He'd never fixed in school before, and this was of course an aberration on his scheduled routine, but the confrontation with Jake had left him feeling the need for a boost. Knowing Coach Minot, he had a pretty good hunch that he would be paired up against Jake in the "nutcracker" drill and he wanted to be ready for the worst. He lowered the vial, bringing it just inches from his face, and stared at the green elixir, fascinated and just a bit unnerved by its covert turbulence. It seemed to shimmer with an inherent energy, like a film of algae deceptively working the surface of a pond.

Von jabbed the needle through the soft cork topping the vial and carefully drew out four milliliters of the tacky elixir. He pumped his left fist twice, accentuating the ropy network of superficial veins feeding the impressive musculature of his arm. The hollow at his elbow looked the most inviting, which surprised him, considering he had used that very same vein not two days ago. There was no trace of the previous entry, not a blemish. His body's regenerative and healing capacity of late was nothing short of remarkable. Working through a grimace (Von never was much for shots), he poked through the semi-resistant protest of his skin and stabbed the needle into the stout vein. He worked the plunger down patiently, giving the tacky liquid ample time to enter his body, where it thinned, matching the viscosity of his own lifeblood. Once diluted, its camouflaging nature took hold, aping the size and shape of the red corpuscles and rendering itself undetectable to his body's immune system.

Von steadied himself but was still caught off-guard by the intensity of the rush as the elixir hit his adrenal glands. He jerked spasmodically, clutching the chrome handrails along the stall walls, his knuckles glowing bone white until the initial charge leveled off to a delicious hum. His entire neuro-muscular system thrummed with vitality, and the urge to simply sit and bask in the lush sensation of it all was replaced by the need to unleash it. The slack set of his jaw grew harsh and the euphoric glaze in his eyes turned steely cold.

He was ready.

Oh God, he was ready.

Chapter 7

Lorelei Vonosovich emerged from the basement of her modest bungalow on Ridgewood's East Side, and elbowed the door shut behind her. The soft click of the door was muted by the sigh that escaped from her pursed lips as she set the basket of laundry on the kitchen table. That she had found nothing was of little surprise since she was not really looking for any one thing in particular. She'd lost track of time down there, wandering around amongst Von's things, poking—as the mother of any teenager is apt to do—through his drawers, under his bed, and generally taking stock of the world where her son seemed to spend so much time.

He had partitioned the basement off into three sections in June, using supplies and skills he had picked up from his summer job with McGann Construction. His bedroom was now actually a separate room, but the door to it would remain, under her insistence, unlocked—this was, after all, her house. His "den" separated his bedroom from her laundry/utility room and this was where his computer hutch, his weight-training equipment, and that damned iguana tank were strategically located.

It was a very nice arrangement, one any seventeen year-old boy would envy—almost like his own apartment. Maybe *too* much like his own apartment, she thought.

Pouring herself a cup of coffee from the fresh pot, she settled in for a quick smoke before sorting and folding. She fished her glittery gold cigarette pouch from the purse slung over the chair and frowned. Only two left from the pack she had bought last night before work. Damn Salems. Almost four dollars a pack but she'd be damned if she was going to switch to one of those generic brands just to save money. She'd quit first.

She lit up with a twinge of guilt, knowing how Von hated the smell of her cigarette smoke. She tried not to smoke in the kitchen where they ate supper—one of the few times her schedule allowed them to spend time together—but hell, she was entitled to some minor luxuries. Raising a teenage boy without a father in this day and age was no cakewalk; she could tell you that, mister.

The money from the modest trust that Alexei Vonosovich had set up for them had run out long ago. There was an on-going, but futile, battle with Liberty Bell Mutual over a very large life insurance claim that she would almost certainly never see. The "strange and extenuating" circumstances of her husband's death were still officially under review, but Liberty Bell would consider his death a suicide until she could prove otherwise.

Strange and extenuating.

Indeed.

She took a long drag of menthol deep into her lungs and expelled that last thought in a cloud of cigarette smoke. Pulling herself out of her chair, she mashed the Salem out and began to sort through the pile of whites. She still had to fix her son a hot supper before her shift at the *LadyLuck* and it was already getting on five.

She didn't mind hustling drinks to the rubes on the gambling boat. In fact, she liked the job much more than she let on. Oh sure, she had to hustle but the tips were great as long as she kept her skirt high and her neckline low. Lorelei Vonosovich was the senior cocktail waitress on the LadyLuck Casino. She was there for its inaugural "voyage" three years ago, after Illinois lawmakers had finally legalized riverboat gambling through some very creative legislation. The small town of Marquette had greased enough palms to land one of the precious vessels on the banks of the Des Plaines River and she had stood in line with hundreds of others for the privilege of filling out an application to work the floating gold mine. When she got the call, she had kissed her job at Ken's Chop House goodbye and had promptly ended her affair with Ken Caulfield, restaurateur, family man, church deacon, and general louse.

Still trim and very fit at thirty-seven, Lorelei had no problem holding her own against the younger girls who worked the tables on the big boat. Most of them were ditzes or college kids just passing through, getting by on jiggle and bounce, with no clue of how to really waitress. It kept her busy and the modest benefits package included a 401K and decent health insurance for her and Von. She could do a lot worse, she thought, rolling up a pair of tube socks and tossing them into the green-latticed plastic bin.

She was heading into the dining room with the basket of clothes when she heard the car pull up outside. Peering through the front room window, she saw Von emerge from a late-model Chrysler Sebring. She watched him bend low, laughing at something the boy sitting in back had said before it pulled away with the stereo blasting. He waved them off and turned toward the house, his face brightening even more upon seeing his mother in the window watching him.

She saw him as a man for the first time, confident, secure, and happy with himself. He was—and she knew this was more than maternal pride—handsome to the point of being almost beautiful. His face, growing even more striking as he closed the distance between them, bore the smooth, angular finish of a Donatello sculpture but his body owed more to Michelangelo. A fluid and natural grace imbued his every move and as he burst through the door and laid a kiss on her cheek, she saw Alexei drowning in the depths of his dark watery eyes. An overwhelming sadness gripped her and she shook it off, refusing to grant flesh to ghosts long dead and buried.

"Hey, Mom," he said, letting the sack of books fall to the floor with a clunk. "What's for supper?"

"My day was fine, thanks for asking," she replied, pleasantly surprised by the peck on her cheek. "Someone's in a good mood. So tell me, how's it feel to be a big-shot senior?"

"Top of the world, Ma," he said, doing a serviceable Jimmy Cagney, from *White Heat*. "Top of the world!" He was already making his way toward the kitchen, nosing around for a meal she had yet to start. "Hey, what gives? I thought we were having stuffed flank steak tonight?"

"I forgot to take it out of the freezer last night, honey," she lied. Truth is, she had slept in late this morning (depression will do that to you), cheating herself out of the time she needed to prepare her son's favorite meal. "It's not defrosted yet. I'm sorry. We'll have it tomorrow, okay? I promise. How about an omelet? I've got those *Ore-Ida* hash browns you like."

"All right," he sighed, making no attempt to hide the disappointment in his voice. He had been thinking about the meal, steak covered in bleu cheese, rolled tight, and slow roasted with vegetables and Mediterranean potatoes, since fourth period study hall.

She felt like a real shit.

"You know what?" she said. "Screw the omelet. Let's order a pizza. Deep dish—from anywhere you want. I'll go pick it up."

Von beamed. Pizza was a close second to rolled flank steak. "Faustini's sausage and pepperoni?"

She winced. The pepperoni was so damn greasy. "Sure,

but order one quarter mushroom only for my side. And a bowl of minestrone."

"Thanks, Ma," he said, coming up behind her and giving her a hug. "You're the best."

"I know," she lied again.

Chapter 8

Von waited until he heard the exhaust note of his mother's Honda Accord grow faint and disappear before closing the shiny cover of McCrimmon's *Writing with a Purpose*. He sat for just a moment, savoring the silence of the empty house before rising from his chair.

Finally.

His stocking feet whispered across the cement floor, finding the carpet of his bedroom in four long strides. He checked, as he always did, for any signs of disturbance, any indication, that the sanctity of the hiding place may have been violated. Satisfied that his mother's snooping had not lost its superficial nature, he methodically extracted two acoustic tiles from the drop ceiling and laid them gingerly on his bed. Raising himself up on the balls of his feet, Von reached up over the rafters. His hand slid blindly along the short edge of the two-by-four, letting his fingers find the pebbled surface of the book beneath the roll of pink insulation just as they had done for the first time nearly eight months ago.

He would never be able to explain, least of all to himself, how he knew it was there. In the beginning he didn't even know exactly what it was he was looking for, but he had woke one chilly December morning last year with the obtuse certainty that this gift, this legacy, awaited him, hidden in the bowels of the house. After little more than an hour of searching he had found it, driven to it as if by some internal compass. The discovery was an epiphany of sorts, a manifestation of all the fuzzy hunches and abstract notions that had plagued him since early childhood. He had stared at the cover a long time before opening it, and when he did, the sight of his father's beautiful cursive script on the pages had brought tears to his eyes.

Memories of his father were few but extremely precious. Bolstered by old snapshots and a few home movies, they were stubbornly recalled and enhanced, restored like old paintings under the guardianship of a doting curator. He had died when Von was only five, too young to begin to comprehend the bleak finality of it all. Perhaps it was a child's inability to understand the concept of death that had made it so hard for the boy to let go. He had continued to talk to his father as though he was still alive, to carry on conversations with his empty chair at the supper table, driving his mother to the point of tears. The phantom dialogues had ceased abruptly and altogether when Von was six.

Just as he was learning to read and write.

That his father would leave him a journal was appropriate, given the boy's love of the written word. He had never, much to his mother's relief, spent his idle time entrenched in front of a TV screen, watching cartoons or playing video games, preferring to lose himself in the pages of a book for hours on end.

He had mentioned the discovery to no one, not even his paternal grandfather, who was the closest thing Von had to a father figure, despite the somewhat shaky relationship "Papa" had shared with his mother. Things had softened between the two since the old man's stroke a few years ago, but Von still thought it best that this secret was his and his alone.

Especially considering what lay inside.

He took it now and padded back to his study hutch, drawing a tangible comfort from the feel of its sturdy leather binding and the substantial heft of its page count. It was a robust volume, meant to hold off the ravages of time, with

pages pressed from 60-pound rag and ruled in fine 2-point line from top to bottom.

Much of it read like a textbook, formulaic and concise, while other entries were stream of consciousness, almost rambling, lapsing at times into his father's native Romanian. It was both a testament to the man's scientific vision and a gut-wrenching account of his father's—and these were his own words—"struggle to wrest the key of Divinity from the hand of God Himself."

Such colorful language was indicative of the paradoxical nature of Alexei Vonosovich. The almost visionary scope of his hard research, groundbreaking and lauded by his colleagues, was, upon closer inspection, grounded in the medieval schooling of alchemy (although, Von would learn its roots went as deep as second-century Egypt). Peppered in amongst complex, hand drawn schematics of DNA strands and cell structures, were cryptic references to the *Balm of Azoth* and the *Vinegar of the Sages*.

Indeed, obscure texts such as *A Suggestive Inquiry into the Hermetic Mystery*, 1850, and *Mirror of Alchemy*, 1597, were footnoted alongside James's *Regulation of Cell Growth and Activation*, 1979 and Bruce's *Cytoskeletal-Membrane Transduction*, 1982. Von had found these former volumes, along with a handful of others, at the Newberry Library, a wonderful reference source on Chicago's north side, known for its eclectic collection of obscure and ancient texts.

Although the "art" of alchemy had become defunct in the eighteenth century with the advent of chemical science, its practice had been widespread throughout Europe with remarkably little variation for nearly fifteen hundred years. Alchemy, Von had learned, held at its core three basic goals: the transmutation of the baser metals into gold and silver, the discovery of an elixir by which life may be prolonged indefi-

nitely, and the manufacture of an artificial process of human life. The keystone for this three-fold quest was the discovery and fabrication of a powder or liquid universally referred to as the *Philosopher's Stone*. With the Philosopher's Stone, a seasoned alchemist could conceivably not only transform lead into gold, but also distill the *Elixir of Life*, "the spiritual fluid which forms the wellspring of human existence."

Modern science was quick to debunk such notions as astrophysical mumbo-jumbo, but his father saw little difference between the quests of the ancient *philosophers* and the microbiologist. Was not the betterment of the human condition the common goal of both? While the alchemist may have been without the benefit of supercomputers and the electron microscope, Alexei Vonosovich thought today's scientists lacked the soul and vision of their predecessors.

It was clear from the more impassioned entries in the journal that his father, a tireless technician who had headed the Microbiology Department at Chicago's world renowned Talbot-Hyde Laboratories, lacked neither.

Von propped a pillow behind his head and settled back on his bed with the precious volume and randomly opened it to one of many book-marked pages.

I cannot help but feel a sense of wonder when looking at a living cell from within. The most simple unicellular organism shares with man a sequence of highly ordered matter, precisely shaped and faultlessly arranged to perform coordinated functions. From where does such order originate? What separates a living organism from nonliving matter? It is of course, the ability to maintain order against the constant disorder of the universe. It is in this "organizing principle," this abstract entity that manages to maintain order in the liquid pandemonium of atoms and macromolecules that we can begin to search for the breath of God.

50

Recorded history would tell us that this quest for the touchstone of existence first came to light during the remarkably enlightened cultures rising up from the Mediterranean basin some five hundred years before the birth of Christ. It is my belief that its roots run much deeper, to our earliest ancestors, and my direct kin, the tribes of Irad, some three thousand years earlier, upon being granted refuge by King Zoser in the Old Kingdom of Egypt. It was their familiarity with the transmutant powers of photosynthesis inherent in all plant life that spawned the quest for eternal life.

Is this where my ancestors stumbled? In their misguided—but well-intentioned—attempts to keep safe the Fruit of Creation (pilfered as it was), did they succeed in only corrupting the perfection fashioned by God on the Sixth Day? I am afraid this is so. It is up to modern science then, armed with gifts unimagined by the ancient philosophers, to restore the Divine Birthright of the Chosen Tribe. Like a repentant thief, I steal back to the scene of my crime, intent on reparation and absolution. I can only pray that God will look elsewhere as I lurk in His garden.

It was this vision, this passionate quest for the spark of life that had led Alexei Vonosovich to undertake the monumental task of sequencing the DNA patterns of human beings, strand by strand.

Deciphering the chemical letters of the genetic code will provide us with an essential blueprint, a map, of what makes us human. I estimate that there are approximately three billion base chemical pairs that make up human DNA in their proper order. If we were to start tomorrow, we are still perhaps two decades away from exact sequencing. My time is far too short for such an undertaking. Furthermore, even armed with such a map, we do not know the exact function of each gene or the role that it plays within the grand scheme.

51

Von paused, as he always did at this passage, mulling over the single phrase, *My time is far too short . . .* before moving on.

Therefore, we must concentrate all our energies on exacting the source of information exchange within the gene itself. INFORMATION—and I'm using the term here as a measure of ORDER—is a universal measure applicable to any system, any structure. Information's partner entity in physics is ENTROPY, the measure of the degree to which the energy in a closed thermodynamic assemblage or process has ceased to be available energy. The Entropy concept pertains to all natural events and once put in motion, cannot be undone: the turning of hot coals into cold ashes, the dispersion of a puff of smoke, the rotting of a corpse.

Viewed in its basest form, Entropy is a measure of disorder, just as Information is a measure of order. To further illustrate the Information-Entropy link, let us revisit, for the sake of simplicity, the puff of smoke. At its genesis, when the puff is expelled, the molecular structure of the smoke is tight and close to the source. At that moment, the system has substantial order—it has Information. As time passes the smoke molecules disperse, distributing themselves more evenly. The system has moved to the inevitable state of less order—less Information/more Entropy. This is the state of Thermodynamic Equilibrium, natural and irreversible.

This thermodynamic chain of events holds true for living as well as non-living matter. As complex as we are as an organism, we are continually losing Information. No matter how strong our chemical bonds, they cannot resist the thermal jostling of our molecules and the inevitable march toward equilibrium. Therefore, the only way to maintain an organism at its highest level is to infuse new Information.

Infuse new Information.

Von glanced at the crook of his elbow where the needle

track from his last injection, only four hours ago, was already beginning to fade. He flipped ahead to the next bookmark.

But how to restructure and reprogram the human genome outside the confines of the lab and the petri dish? Given the complexities of gene splicing, a complete revamping of the genetic blueprint in a multicellular, elaborately architectured organism such as man would seem to be unfathomable.

Our predecessor, the alchemist, shackled by his limited resources, could only wander blindly down this corridor, missing more often than not, through a futile series of trial and error. Indeed, only the recent classification of the diverse proteins and their functions has provided us a rudder with which to steer through the primordial swamp. Structural proteins, (see Cohabba extract), which determine an organism's physical form are easily altered. However, it is the regulatory proteins, the ENZYMES, (Trichosanthes root), those that act as switches, directing metabolic response and change WHERE APPROPRIATE, that are key to maintaining mastery of our chemical makeup. Only armed with a proper understanding of these proteins will gene sequencing—indeed, complete DNA blueprinting—be possible.

Isolating regulatory and structural proteins from various species of plant life, while laborious, was a relatively simple task. However, it was not until I was able to introduce a viral Integrase Enzyme into the mix that the application became practical. The Integrase enzyme snips a cell's DNA and splices the virus' own genes into the host chromosome. Pre-arming the Integrase with select proteins produces a stabilized and highly bioavailable systemic mechanism, which is rapidly absorbed into the bloodstream. This, I believe, is the elusive Philosopher's Stone, and its derivative is, dare I say, the Elixir of Life.

Von bookmarked his spot, laid the journal on the edge of

his bed, and ambled into his den where the row of potted plants lay atop the shelf directly over Ignatz's tank.

"How you doin', Ig?" Von asked as he pulled a large hibiscus plant off the shelf and set it on an end table. Ignatz the iguana considered her keeper with a wary indifference. She was a beautiful specimen, as green iguanas go—over three-and-a-half feet long with the tail, fat, healthy, and amazingly green. A small horn protruded from the end of her blunt gray snout above her nostrils, tagging her as a member of the *iguana iguana rhinolophoba* genus, a precious commodity among collectors. Her cold reptilian eyes darted from Von's face to the tasty, pink hibiscus petals the lumbering human was gingerly pulling from the plant.

"You hungry, Ig?" Von asked, stepping back from the tank and waving the treat in front of the neon-lime reptile. The tank itself was indicative of the care the boy lavished on the animal. About the size of a large screen TV, its three supporting sides were constructed of oak, with sliding glass doors in the front. A heater, purchased from a zoological warehouse, was set into the back wall, strategically nestled beneath the ersatz outcropping of rocks built from chicken wire and drywall compound. Several large tree limbs jutted out from the artificial landscape, giving the creature several points at which to bask under the industrial sun lamp. The heater, thermostat, and sun lamp were timer-activated, providing the animal with a controlled habitat on par with many zoo environments.

Von slid the glass door open and crouched down in front of the pen, waiting for trust to blossom in the lizard's primitive brain. Within moments, the miniature dragon was clinging to Von's thick forearm, snapping hibiscus petals from his fingertips in greedy mouthfuls. With the snack depleted, Von placed the animal on the ground and watched it scurry off. He would let it roam the basement from time to time, knowing re-capture was relatively easy. After an hour or so, the cold-blooded beast would grow lethargic and offer little resistance to being returned to the warmth of the cage.

Von enjoyed the animal a great deal. Its striking beauty and almost surreal non-conformity with the twentieth century fascinated him. He viewed it as an evolutionary quirk, not far removed from the dinosaurs, a living reminder of man's long crawl out of the primordial swamp.

As an added bonus, it provided him an opportunity to raise the various species of plant life necessary for cultivating the elixir, without drawing too much suspicion from his mother.

Von placed the hibiscus plant back on the shelf under the Gro-lite. He pulled the pungent cohobba plant down from its spot next to the amaranth shrub and inspected its progress.

Almost ready for a new batch.

Chapter 9

Mike Minot eased into the booth and set his beer down on the table with a wet slide. A plastic half-shell of artificial stained glass hung from a cheap brass chain overhead, casting a faint prismatic ellipse on the dark scarred wood. Tiny effervescent bubbles rose up from the bottom of the thick glass to lose themselves in the frosty head and Minot contemplated these for a moment before raising the beer to his lips.

Coldest beer in town.

The Velvet Hammer was a cop-bar—had been ever since Big John Rafferty, Chicago Heights' Chief of Police back in the fifties, bought it with kickback booty from the deep pockets of the Chicago mob. Of course, it wasn't always called the Hammer. It started out as *The Roost* and then became *Ringside*, when Nick Pecceni, the mayor's cousin by marriage, bought it in 1966. Dolores Middelbrooks picked it up in 1972 after little Nicky went to jail for embezzling from the firemen's pension fund. She'd owned it ever since, but because of her failing health, her son Randy had managed it for the last ten years. Strategically located at the junction where Chicago Heights, Mokena, and Ridgewood met at the apex of 191st Street, it attracted law enforcement personnel from all three villages along with the state troopers from the headquarters on 183rd. Cops were lousy tippers but they drank like fish and Randy never had to worry about the place getting robbed.

It was Mike's Uncle Teddy, a district commander with the Illinois State Police up in Rockford, who suggested that Mike come back east after his knee blew out. Uncle Teddy had promised to find a place for him on the state payroll and Mike had known his uncle well enough to know that meant more than coaching prep ball at Ridgewood High.

Minot looked to the door, where a small group of blue-shirts from the Heights was rolling in, fresh off their shift change. Young guys in button-down casuals and Dockers with their hair high and tight and their whole lives in front of them.

He hated them.

He wondered who they were going to send this time. He hoped it wasn't Ruhnke. The guy talked too much about things he knew nothing about, football being a prime example. On top of that, he talked to Mike as if he were some kind of bagman or something. Minot took a short sip off his draft and thought how nice it would be to take him out in the alley and show him what he could really do.

A tall brunette with a really short skirt walked in, giving Mike a long look before cozying up to her boyfriend at the bar—one of the young guys, sporting a cheesy regulation cop mustache and sideburns to match. Mike recognized her as a dispatcher from Mokena. The face was no oil painting but she was far from ugly and her legs would make a racehorse jealous. She looked again at Mike and he gave her a discreet smile. Her eyes returned the favor before she turned away and nuzzled closer to the rookie.

Tease.

He was filing her away for future reference when the door opened again and Andy Freeman walked in. He saw Mike immediately and headed his way, stopping briefly to exchange greetings with the group at the bar.

Mike genuinely liked Andy. Andy had played Division One College baseball and was a three-sport standout at Brother Rice High School in Chicago, but getting him to talk about it was like pulling teeth. He worked another job at a printing company after his graveyard shift in one of the Heights' worst neighborhoods. Mike had heard his boy had spina-bifida or one of those god-awful things that should never happen to kids. Poor bastard.

"How you doin', Mike?" Andy asked. He set a fresh draft down in front of Minot and took a short pull off a longneck Bud. "Sam Adams, right?"

"Yeah thanks, Andy," Minot said. "You didn't have to do that."

Andy waved him off. "No problem. Hey, how the Redskins lookin' this year?"

Minot laughed. "Red*Hawks*. I think we'll be all right. Got a few kids with some serious talent. I think we're going to surprise some people."

A short uncomfortable silence passed before Minot asked, "How's the family?"

"They're good," Andy replied with a sheepish grin. He extracted an eight-and-a-half-by-eleven glossy photograph from the smaller of the two manila envelopes at his side and flipped it over for Mike to see. "I was wondering if you could do me a favor and sign this for Andy Jr."

"Oh man," Minot sighed upon seeing the photo.

It was the publicity shot from his rookie year with the Kansas City Chiefs. Decked out in pads and eye-black, the face that stared back at him was young, determined, and full of promise. "Where'd you get this, Andy? They have an old has-beens file down at the station?"

"C'mon, Mike," Andy prodded. "The little guy's a big football fan. Andy Jr. will think his old man's a big shot, knowing a real NFL player."

"Yeah sure," Minot said, taking the pen from Andy. He scrawled: *To a real tough guy—hang in there, Andy. 24 Mike Minot.* It had been years since he had signed an autograph.

He missed it more than he would care to admit.

"Thanks, Mike," Andy said, reading the salutation. "I really appreciate it."

"No problem." Minot took a long swallow from his fresh Sam Adams, drowning the nostalgia welling up in his throat. He motioned to the thicker envelope at the policeman's side. "What you got there?"

Andy Freeman tucked his son's treasure away and handed the other packet across the table. All business now, he watched as Minot pulled the mug shot and rap sheet from the envelope. "Paul Knoll, scumbag of the first degree. He runs the dogfight operations on the entire south side. Used to be strictly Chicago but the blue heat was coming down and he mostly works the suburbs now. He was hard to nail down but we pinched one of his lieutenants on a coke bust. The guy was a three-time loser and looking at a long stretch in Statesville, so we squeezed him and he agreed to wear a wire."

Minot looked long and hard at the mug shot of the bearded man before glancing at the long rap sheet. He could tell more about a man by looking in his eyes than he could from reading his life story. This guy was a piece of shit.

"We thought we had an airtight case. About twelve hours of tape of this guy booking fights and muscling breeders—plus, we busted him on location at an actual fight—on video-tape! Anyway, his lawyer digs up this obscure 'previous' from 1972, starts talking, and I mean for two days, about entrapment—and the judge buys it! All the tape gets thrown out and we're left with a misdemeanor. The creep gets credit for time served and walks the very same day. This one really—oh," Andy stopped for a moment, watching Minot grimace as he pulled the remaining photos from the file. "Those are shots of the dogs and the conditions they were kept in. Nice, huh?"

Mike Minot was a hard man and not easily shaken, but he

found it hard to look at the grisly photographs. Soft, scared brown eyes looked up at him from mutilated faces sheared to the bone. Muscle and tissue, raw and exposed, where ears and noses should have been. One dog, a stout rottweiler, just like the one he'd had at Fresno State, sat panting and doomed, its lower jaw torn off and hanging by a sinewy thread.

"All inadmissible. Without the tape, it was all rendered irrelevant. Can you believe it?" Andy slid a fat A10 envelope across the table and Minot slipped it inside his jacket without counting the pad of bills inside it. "He's a bad, bad, man, Mike," Andy said, watching the hate burn in the coach's eyes. "A lot of the guys are really upset." He added softly, almost in a whisper, "There'll be a bonus for every month he spends in the hospital."

Mike Minot frowned as he gathered up the horrible color photographs and shuffled them behind the black and white mug shot of Paul Knoll. He said nothing as he stared down at the face of the man responsible for the inhumane carnage and suffering of animals for profit.

This one was going to be fun.

Chapter 10

Haley McBride kept telling herself that she would get used to the smell. It was an old smell. A diseased smell, terminal, and incurable, teetering midway between the sickbed and the grave. It permeated the hallways of the Regent like a fresh coat of paint, and unlike the feces she found herself cleaning more often than she would have thought possible, no amount of ammonia or bleach could wash it away. She hated the fact that she found the place so unpleasant, a vestige perhaps of the guilt so deeply ingrained into her consciousness since first grade.

It could be worse, Haley—it could be you lying there unable to control your bowels or feed yourself. How would you like that? At least you can go home at the end of your shift. You can walk outside and smell the fresh air. Just be thankful you can walk!

The yellow light flashed on the console just as she sat down (as it always seemed to do) followed by the inevitable beeping. Room 310. Helen Beach. Hard to drum up any sympathy there. Haley had only been working at Regent Extended Care Center for a little over a week but she was already wise to the ways of the crafty old woman. Drove two roommates out in three months, Angel had told her. Likes to have the room all to herself, you see.

Haley leaned over the counter of the nurses' station and peered down the hall, hoping someone else would grab this one. Angel was at the north end of the wing with the med-cart, doling out the final round of sleeping pills and pain-killers before lights-out. He looked up, caught her hopeful stare and shook his head with a knowing grin. The light over room 310 continued its angry flashing. Haley sighed and rose from her chair. She was halfway down the hall when the heavy security door at the end of the wing opened.

Von walked in, his face breaking into a smile upon seeing her standing there in her candy striper's uniform. She felt her own face light up and got a grip on it before she made an ass of herself.

"Hi, Haley," Von said. He gave her a quick look up and down. "When did you start working here?"

"Just last week. Work-study program. I wanted to get a jump on it before school officially started." She arched an eyebrow. "What are you doing here? You work here?"

"No," Von replied, shaking his head for emphasis. "I couldn't handle that. You people are saints. No—my grandfather is here. He's in A-wing. He's been here almost two years now. I usually use the main entrance but it's locked and they changed the code."

Haley felt a strange sense of relief upon hearing that Von was here to see a relative. She knew that was how it always started. They start coming by to see you at work. Dropping by your house unannounced. Waiting for you to come outside so they can just talk it over one more time . . .

"Your grandfather? I'm sorry. I mean—what—"

"He had a stroke two years ago," Von said, rescuing her. "Pretty bad one. He'll never walk again. Took away all the motor functions of his right side. He just got to the point where he could speak intelligibly last year." Von frowned. "It's real tough on him. He was a strong guy. Fit as a man half his age. Now he can't even get up to go to the . . ." He paused. "Well, he can't even get up."

Because she could do little else, Haley smiled a sad, condescending smile. "I know," she said. "It's so sad. And then no one wants anything to do with them. Like it's their fault or something. They're so grateful for the slightest bit of kindness or a—"

"Well!" Helen Beach appeared in the wide doorway of room 310 leaning on her cane as though she were trying to drive it through the shiny linoleum floor. "This is just fine!" She glared at the two teenagers. "Maybe when you're done talking to your *boyfriend,* you can help me out in the bathroom here." She winked and smiled at them like a demented Jack-O-Lantern. "I think I might have made a little mess."

Haley leaned close to Von and rolled her eyes. "Well, most of them anyway," she said under her breath. "Okay, dear," she said turning to Helen. "I'll be right in. I was just showing this gentleman how to get to A-wing." She took Von by the elbow and led him a few feet down the hall, out of the old woman's earshot.

"Up here and to the left," she said with exaggerated volume. "Then follow the yellow dots on the floor all the way." She turned in time to see Helen Beach disappear into her room. "I'll look in on your grandfather when I get a chance," she said to Von. "The help in A wing leaves a lot to be desired, especially on the night shift. His name is Vonosovich?"

"Yeah," Von said, genuinely touched by the offer. He knew all too well the slipshod attitude of some of the workers. "He was my father's—he's my paternal grandfather. Thanks, Haley. I really appreciate it."

"Don't mention it," she said, looking a little too long at his eyes. God, he was gorgeous.

They stood smiling at each other for a moment.

"Well," Haley said, rocking on her heels. "Duty calls."

Von grimaced. "Yeah. Good luck."

"See you in school."

"You bet. And thanks again."

She watched him disappear around the corner and then headed for the linen closet to get a fresh mop.

★ ★ ★ ★ ★

Drajac Vonosovich had smelled his grandson long before the boy had poked his head into the room as he always did before entering. The scent had pulled him from the light sleep he had drifted into and corrupted the lovely dream he had been enjoying. He was a wolf again in the dream, young and powerful, the forest racing by in a flurry of colors so sharp their edges seemed to vibrate with the contrast.

He broke into a clearing at full gallop and came upon the glade where he slowed to a trot before stopping abruptly. An odd smell, familiar but tainted, had reached his nose, giving him cause for alarm. His ears pointed forward as his brow knit in frustration, eliciting an uncharacteristic whine from his throat. He sat, as a dog would, awaiting a command from a human, until the foliage at the opposite end of the clearing stirred and his patience was rewarded.

Von walked upright into the clearing, tall and strong in the body of a wolf. In his forelegs, bent and distorted like the long arms of a man, he cradled the lifeless body of Drajac's only son, Alexei Peter Vonosovich. As they approached he could see, with sickening clarity, the horrible consequences of his son's tampering. Instead of the thick coat of silver fur that had made him such a noble wolf, his skin was covered in scales like those of a dragon and dotted with open lesions oozing pus and the stink of perversion. His eyes, once bright with the moonlight and the wisdom of the ages, stared through the cold, dead, crescent irises of a reptile.

Von laid his father's body down at his feet, shooing the horseflies away with his hairy paw before stepping back.

Drajac looked down at the abomination that had been his son and shook his shaggy head. "I tried. I tried to warn him," he said in a low growl.

"Forgive him, Papa," his grandson said, pleading to the

elder wolf for his father's absolution. "He was only trying to help. He was only trying to help, Papa. Papa, Papa . . ."

"Papa?"

Drajac awoke to find his grandson standing over him, a troubled look on his handsome face.

"You were having a dream, Papa," Von said, placing his hand on the old man's bony shoulder. "You all right? It sounded like a bad one."

Drajac straightened up in his bed as best he could, shaking the cobwebs from his head. "Bad-good. What makes the difference?" he asked. His broken English, further mangled by the stroke, made it difficult at times to understand him. "In dream, I walk again. How bad izzat?"

Von frowned. "Not so bad, I guess. You were moaning, though. Like you were scared. And look, you're sweating."

"Exercise." He pronounced it *egzorsise*. "Lots of exercise. In dream I *run*." Drajac eyed the boy. His grandson seemed to be growing more robust with each visit. So why should he worry about that? "How are you, Sergei?" he asked, invoking the boy's Christian name. "How is your football? You say you will play more this year?"

Von smiled, still a little giddy from his unexpected encounter with Haley McBride. "I'm starting, Papa—on defense anyway. I'm still second team fullback. We run the wishbone and we've had the same four guys in the backfield since freshman year. You develop a certain chemistry running the option. I don't think they want to . . ." He stopped, realizing his grandfather had no idea what he was talking about. The old boy seemed pretty sharp tonight, but he had never warmed to the game of American football. "Yeah," he said. "I'll play more this year."

"Fine for you," Drajac smiled. "You are growing so fast, Sergei. In no time you are a man." He motioned for the boy to come closer. "I need you to promise me something . . ."

"Yes, Papa?" Von asked, leaning forward.

"The first time you wake up in the woods—I want you to come and tell me."

Von laughed. "What?"

"You will be confused. Maybe you will have no clothes. You will come and talk to me, no?"

Von frowned. The old man was talking nonsense again. Conversation wasn't going to be so easy tonight after all. "Yeah sure, Papa," he said. "I'll come and talk to you."

"Good boy," Drajac said. The working side of his face attempted to smile, producing only a sardonic grimace. "Is nothing to be scared of. Only nature taking its course." The twisted grin disappeared from his face. "That was your father's downfall. He would not let sleeping wolves lie."

Von shook his head. "Sleeping *dogs*, Papa."

Drajac Vonosovich raised his good arm from his sickbed and waved at the air. He seemed all at once, very sad. "Whatever."

Chapter 11

The steady ticking of the clock on the wall only seemed to amplify the maddening silence of the room and the scrutiny of the eyes he could feel boring through him. As if on turrets like a Jackson's chameleon, Eugene Kroc's eyes darted up from the sheaf of papers that he had been correcting for the last half-hour.

Dan Jacobson was staring at him.

Kroc stared back, caught unaware by what he saw in the teenager's face. It was not contempt—or even hate. No, this could only be described as glee—the sick, detached amusement one might find on the face of a disturbed child torturing an insect. It was cold and soulless, born of low intellect, and even more disturbing, a total lack of conscience.

Jacobson had been at turns flippant or sullen all week, depending on his mood. He had walked in today just as the final bell had rung, and taken his seat while Kroc was passing out the pop quiz on last night's reading. He had taken it without a word, letting it flutter to his desk rather than accept it from Kroc's offering hand. As near as Kroc could tell, the insolent lout hadn't made a mark on it since he'd sat down.

Kroc recovered from his initial shock and smiled at the simpleton, knowing that looking away was tantamount to surrender. He could see a few of the other students had noticed the quirky stare-down, their eyes darting back and forth between the teacher and Jake with mild astonishment. The bell rang, mercifully enough, just as he was about to challenge the lumbering oaf—a prospect that he knew could only be ugly.

"Okay, people," Kroc barked. "Pens up. Drop your quizzes in the tray on your way out. We start Faulkner's *Barn*

Burning on Monday. If you're feeling motivated, by all means, feel free to look it over this weekend. Jacobson—I want to see you for a moment."

The lineman lingered at the edge of Kroc's desk as the class filed out. He plucked a small bust of Edgar Allan Poe from the desk and fiddled with it absent-mindedly.

Kroc pulled Jacobson's quiz from the pile. It was blank except for his name, simply signed *Jake.*

"Looks like you flunked, Jake," Kroc said. "I thought you would be a little more knowledgeable about this story, given all the extra research you did. Where's your essay?"

Jake looked down, still fingering the Poe paperweight. "Didn't do it."

Kroc sensed the eyes on him from the hall where students were taking much longer than usual to move on to the next class. He rose from his chair and snatched the paperweight from the boy's meaty fist. The movement was so quick Jake was left staring at his empty hand.

"No?" Kroc asked, inspecting the paperweight before setting it back down on his desk. "Why not?"

"Dunno," Jake shrugged. "Didn't have time."

"Well," Kroc replied, pulling a pink detention slip from the pad at the lip of his lectern, "we'll make some time for you. How's Saturday at seven A.M. sound? You'll need an early start because now you owe me two thousand words."

"Saturday's bad for me, Mr. *Kroc,*" Jake said, as if he really believed he was being offered a choice. "We got a walk-through in the morning. Big game Saturday night."

"Your walk-though's at eleven, Jake," Kroc said, not looking up as he filled out the detention. "Jug lasts from seven until ten. You're welcome to stay longer if you need more time to finish up." He handed Jacobson the pink slip. "And you probably will."

68

Jake stared, incredulous, at the detention slip. He couldn't believe the skinny twerp had actually jugged him. *He was on the football team!*

"Room 111. Mr. Blodgett has the honor this week," Kroc said, putting an end to the matter. "Better get moving, Jake. I'm not going to write you a tardy pass."

Jake turned to go, cutting a wide swath through the freshmen filing in for Kroc's next class. He stopped at the door. "This ain't over," he said, whirling around and pointing a fat finger at the English teacher before storming out.

Eugene Kroc watched the big teenager lumber down the hall. "This *isn't* over," he said to no one in particular.

How true that was.

Chapter 12

Jason was halfway down the short flight of stairs when he heard the doorknob turn behind him. Lorelei Vonosovich peeked out, her hair bundled high beneath a tight turban of fluffy blue towel in that manner that only women could seem to master. She smiled upon seeing Jason and pulled the door open wide.

"Jason Jankowski!" she said, cinching the belt around her robe a shade tighter. "Where have you been all summer? You stay up at the cottage longer than usual?"

"Hey, Mrs. V," Jason replied, somewhat embarrassed by her near-nakedness. "No, we've been back for a few weeks now. I called Von a few times but we haven't had a chance to hook up. He's been laying low."

Lorelei nodded. Aside from work, her son had rarely ventured from the basement. "Yeah, I know, hon," she said, offering up the standard excuse. "He's been busy. He'd put in a long day with McGann and then work on the basement." She brightened. "Hey! Have you seen it? Come on in before someone sees me standing here in a towel. What you got there?"

The fact that she did not care if *he* saw her standing there in a towel was not lost on him as he made his way up the steps. "Just some drawings," he said, lifting the presentation case slightly. "All my NightHawk stuff. Von's helping me with the storyline—you know, the comic book we were working on?"

"Ohhh good! That's great!" Lorelei stepped aside and let the boy through the door. She was beaming like he was a Publishers Clearinghouse representative with a check for a million dollars instead of a kid with a stack of rough drawings. "He's downstairs, honey. You know the way. I've got to finish getting ready for work. You go right down."

"Thanks, Mrs. V," Jason said over his shoulder as he made his way through the small living room. He paused at the basement door. "Nice seeing you."

"You too, Jason," she smiled. She watched him disappear down the stairwell with a twinge of sadness. She had always liked Jason. He had been Von's most steady friend since fifth grade, which was a good thing, seeing as he did not have *a lot* of friends. She wondered, not for the first time, how Von would react, if the friendship would survive—if her suspicions about Jason were true.

The scent had been lingering on the outskirts of his synapses but Von was too focused on the task at hand for it to register. Only after he had completed his eleventh rep (always one more than before) did the familiar smell of his friend jolt him into awareness. Still prone on his back, Von's eyes darted to the foot of the stairwell, where Jason stood watching him, a portfolio dangling loosely from his arm. Von raised himself up to a sitting position on the weight bench and pulled the Walkman headphones off his ears. The muffled blast of AC-DC spilled out from the tiny foam earpieces and filled the room before Von reached to the unit at his waist and dialed it down.

"Hey, man, what's up?" He smiled at his friend, then narrowed his eyes. "How long you been standin' there?"

"Not long," Jason lied. Von was naked except for a jockstrap and an airy pair of gym shorts. Jason pulled his gaze from the tight six-pack of his friend's abdominal muscles and looked around the refurbished basement, hoping Von didn't catch the stare. "Geez," he said, "look at this place. You do this all yourself?"

"All by my lonesome," Von said. He switched the

Walkman off and stood up, his muscular legs straddling each side of the bench. He raised his arms over his head in a wind-mill fashion and worked the pain out of his tortured muscles as he talked. "Wasn't so hard. I got a couple of those Time-Life do-it-yourself books and McGann let me use some of his tools. Amazing what you can do with the right set of tools."

Jason whistled. "Not bad for a lame-ass like yourself. I'm impressed. Holy cow," he said, noticing the iguana tank. "Look at this."

Von beamed. "Pretty cool, huh? Totally climate-con-trolled. The walls are solid oak, but the best part is the inside. Check it out."

Jason knelt down and inspected the carefully landscaped interior. Ignatz lay sprawled across a supporting branch, her reptilian eyes regarding the stranger warily.

"Very cool," Jason said. "I don't know who got bigger over the summer—you or this lizard."

Von sidled up alongside Jason and looked at the reptile. "Yeah, she's close to four feet long with the tail. Way too big for that aquarium I had her in. I had to do something." He looked at the presentation case dangling at Jason's side. "What you got there?"

"NightHawk," Jason said, somewhat taken aback. "The new panels. We were going to work on it tonight. You said to stop by, remember?"

Von grimaced. "Oh, yeah. Hey, I'm sorry, man. I forgot all about it."

"What do you mean you forgot?" Jason asked. "You didn't even work on the draft?"

"Uh, well—no," Von said sheepishly. "But we can work on it now." He pulled his friend over to the study nook in the center of the room, eager to make amends. "Let's see what you got."

Jason pulled the panels of illustration board from the case and laid them out on the area rug. He stepped back as Von looked them over. "I didn't ink them yet," Jason said, as Von inspected the first panel. "I'm afraid I'll screw 'em up. You can't erase India ink. I guess I'll have to practice on some old ones."

"This is good stuff," Von said, genuinely impressed. A pretty decent artist himself, Von had always been a little jealous of his friend's ability, but now he felt nothing but admiration. "You must have worked your ass off on these."

"Yeah, it's a lot of work," Jason said, placated by the praise. "You like the cape?"

"Yeah, I guess it's pretty cool," Von said, gathering up the panels. "Why don't you leave these with me over the weekend and I'll re-work that origin?"

The glow faded from Jason's face. "I thought we were going to work on it now?"

Von shook his head. "Can't get into it now. We got a game tomorrow, Jason. Eisenhower. The opener? Remember?"

Jason looked at him, puzzled. "Yeah, so?"

"So I think we should be ready, that's all," Von replied, unscrewing the collar from one end of the barbell. He added another plate and moved to the other end of the bar as he talked. "You know, if I was you, I'd be more worried about keeping my starting job. Tomacek is right behind you on the depth chart and coming on strong, in case you haven't noticed. Now stop your whinin' and spot me while I do this last set." He eased under the barbell and smiled wickedly at Jason. "Then it's your turn."

Chapter 13

Tom Houghwat was dreaming of his wife, healthy and alive, her face distinct and extraordinary among the sea of thousands in the south end zone. She was no college sophomore, but a woman of forty-five, mature and complete, as he always remembered her. Her blonde hair, whipped across her face by the lash of the swirling winds, was shot with a silver too lustrous, too alive, to be called gray. She smiled at him as he grew closer, swept along in the clattering wave of blue and maize that was the victorious Michigan Wolverine football squad. The cheers rang down upon them as they passed beneath the goal post and neared the tunnel beneath the adoring throng, but he heard only his name as she mouthed it silently. It lingered in the cold air, carried to his ears in a frosty cloud of her sweet exhaled breath. She leaned over the rail, so close now he could almost reach up and touch her gloved hand.

"Daddy?"

There was a muffled jolt, then only her face, much younger now, her ice blue eyes only inches from his own—so beautiful.

"Daddy!"

Another jolt and he was full awake, staring up at Melanie, her eyes—her mother's eyes—wide beneath fine arched brows knit with concern.

"You were dreaming, Daddy—moaning in your sleep again."

He was in the living room, deep in the cushy embrace of his La-Z-Boy recliner. The game plan for Eisenhower was spread out haphazardly across his lap. Cheryl was gone.

Gone.

"Ooh. I'm sorry, honey," he said, blinking back into the harsh reality. "I must have dozed off. Where are my reading . . ."

"Here, Daddy," she said, handing him his glasses. "I took them off. I wanted you to have a nice nap." She reached down and deftly swept the scattered game plan off his lap, shuffling the sheets back into order as she spoke. "Give it a rest, Dad. You guys are going to kick major butt. Why don't you relax and watch a little TV? Isn't *College Countdown* on ESPN?"

"Hmmm . . . what time is it? Eight o'clock? Ah," he sighed, disgusted with himself, "I missed it."

"I taped it for you," Melanie said. She giggled as she waved the black videotape in the air, knowing how he enjoyed watching it.

"You're the best," he said, delighted. And he meant it.

"I know." She bent over and placed a kiss on top of his balding head. "Mom again?"

Tom looked at his daughter, confused.

"Were you dreaming about Mom again?"

"No, no," he lied. "I don't remember."

"You called her name. You were fidgeting, reaching out."

"Hmmm . . ." He looked sad, and old.

"We all miss her, Daddy," she said putting her hand on his shoulder. "I miss her terribly."

"I know, honey." Tom looked at his daughter, the spitting image of Cheryl in her younger years, only taller (she had his bones), and even more beautiful. Her hair, long and blonde, spilled like wheat into the hood of her nylon pullover. She carried an umbrella and a thick, ratty paperback copy of *Peyton Place* under one arm. "Where you off to?"

"The Regent. I'm going to read to Miss Ahern," Melanie replied. She gave her hair a shake, letting it fall out across her shoulders. "Then I think I'll stop by Kerri's. I don't know."

"The Regent? I thought you finished that up?" Melanie had gotten involved in the *Senior Share* reading program over the summer. Two nights a week at the nursing home, reading to the old folks with bad eyes and too much time on their arthritic hands. It looked good on her college apps and her listing in *Who's Who Among American High School Students*, but Tom knew she did it because she liked it.

Melanie smiled. "I did. Well, the program's over, but we never finished the book. We've still got five more chapters to go and I don't want to leave Shirley—Miss Ahern—hanging." She winked at her father, a sly, precious gesture between the two of them, and held the book up for him to see. "She really likes this old potboiler."

Tom grinned. "I bet she does. Be careful you don't give her a heart attack."

"Daddy! You're terrible." Melanie bent and kissed his cheek. "I gotta go. I want to get there before the rain gets too bad. You want me to hit *play?*"

"No, just pop it in the VCR. I want to finish going over this first," he said, plucking the game plan from the end table. He watched her head for the door. "Be careful driving."

"I will, Daddy. Don't worry."

"That's my job, honey," he said watching her close the door behind her. But he never had to worry much with Melanie. She was a good girl.

Melanie Houghwat dialed the wiper blades off as the dirty drizzle that had lingered in the air all evening finally diminished and died altogether. She powered down her window, her nose wrinkling at the musty ambiance of the damp night. Melanie didn't like lying to her father about what she was doing and where she was going but the whole nursing home thing was just so convenient she couldn't help it. It freed her up for all sorts of things and gave her time for herself. She smiled, without a trace of joy, and accelerated, catching the yellow and turning left on 183rd Street. The Regent Extended Care Center appeared on her right moments later, tucked behind a new Burger King and a dying strip mall. She drove past without a second look and hooked another left at Marine Drive. She cruised down the winding slope, past the VFW hall and took a hard right behind the scrub of tree line, following the narrow single lane into the parking lot of the Brookshire Glenn Apartment complex. Melanie motored around to the back and tucked the Escort discreetly between a hulking Ford Navigator and a pick-up truck. Touted as luxury units upon opening in the mid-eighties, the "Brooks" was one of the few complexes in town not to go condo. The somewhat transient nature of its occupants contributed to a slow but steady decline in its upkeep, reducing the once pristine grounds to middle-of-the-road at best.

With a quick look-around, Melanie scampered across the lot to the rear door of the nearest six-flat. Ignoring the row of buttons on the intercom, she twisted hard on the wobbly doorknob (still broken) and stepped into the tiny foyer.

She bounded up the stairs to the third floor, her footfalls muffled by the worn Berber carpeting. She stopped at the door of E5 and gave a quick four knocks, pausing a moment before adding a fifth.

The door opened before the last knock could land. The initial anger on the man's face upon seeing her was diffused by the innocent laughter in the blonde girl's frosty blue eyes.

"I thought I told you never to come here again," he said.

Mike Minot pulled her inside and slammed the door shut behind them.

Chapter 14

Sitting on the leather couch and looking around the room, Melanie couldn't help but smile at the almost prim tidiness of the man's living quarters. Growing up with three brothers (slobs all) might have jaded her thinking, but she thought the sheer orderliness of the place bordered on obsessive. Even the magazines on the glass coffee table before her were fanned out uniformly, as if on display in an upscale reception area.

Melanie examined the titles: *Sports Illustrated, Alton's Pro Football Preview, Maxim, GQ* . . . She was reaching over for the topmost issue of *S.I.* when she caught her reflection staring back at her from the high polish of the smoked glass table.

Melanie closed her eyes, unnerved by the sense of alienation. Visions of a long-ago childhood flashed through her mind's eye. She held them close, finding a momentary comfort in the little girl's face—her face, a face lit by the simple joy of a Saturday morning cartoon or an X-Men comic book. Sitting at the breakfast table, surrounded by her brothers, Mommy and Daddy looking on fondly, laughing as she told them that she was going to play for the Chicago Bears when she grew up.

That was before.

Before the blood. Before the budding breasts and the changes that had forced her to alter her wardrobe and her lifestyle so. The way men—grown men—had begun to look at her. She felt the desire burning in their stares when she passed them on the street, afraid to meet their gaze lest they find her eye contact suggestive or deviant. Their wanton carnality, at first frightening, later disgusted, then amused her.

She knew, deep down she knew, that she was better than they were. A better all-around athlete than most boys her own age, Melanie was shackled only by the restrictions imposed upon her by her gender. Upper body strength, mean muscle mass, fat to muscle ratio—all these intangibles were denied her with the advent of puberty and the blossoming of her womanhood. Well, she thought, save that for the Barbie dolls and the Suzie-homemakers. Melanie saw through her brothers the doors that could be opened by athletic excellence. Estrogen be damned. Stanford, UCLA, USC . . . she could have her pick if she could bring her game up just one notch. And who's to say the Olympics were out of the question? Her potential was unlimited. Of all the things in this world, her father had told her, nothing is sadder than wasted potential. Daddy would be so proud when she walked out on the court wearing the star-spangled uniform of the United States women's volleyball team. Thousands cheering in the stands, millions more watching on—

"All right," Mike Minot said, his light footstep catching her off guard, "listen up. This is serious."

He stood before her holding a large Ziploc bag bulging with all manner of jars and prescription vials.

"I'm all ears," Melanie said, sitting straight up as if in school. She knew the coach was not pleased with her for coming here. She also knew that nobody else would have made it through the front door. Estrogen did have its advantages.

"Okay," Coach Minot said, settling into the chair directly across from her. Melanie noticed that he was careful not to sit next to her. He dumped the contents of the bag on to the table. "This is Sustanon," he said, holding up a large brown jar. "The boys know how and when." He shuffled through the pile and counted out a handful of foil-wrapped sample

79

packets. "These are Primobolan. You tell Jacobson to take it easy on these and keep to his cycle. You can't take these on an empty stomach, although I don't think we have to worry about that with Jake."

Melanie laughed, perhaps a little too loud, at the joke.

Minot seemed not to notice. "These," he said, plucking a small white jar from the pile, "are for you. Deca-Durabolin. Increases mean muscle mass but contains no diuretics. You won't have to worry so much about appearance and loss of body fat." Minot looked at her, hoping she understood exactly what he was saying. "You know, that's what did in the German women's team in Seoul. They all looked like Lou Ferrigno."

Melanie nodded, waiting for him to get to the good stuff.

Minot stood up as if on cue and reached into the pocket of his black Dockers.

"This is pure dynamite," he said, gingerly holding the small plastic phial up to the light. "Something new. Brand name *Equipoxigenin*. Equipoise with a hydrox enzyme converter and digitoxigenin boost. Stimulates your entire metabolism. Increases lean muscle mass faster than anything on the market. Inject directly into the muscle you are working. One milliliter for every cycle. *One milliliter.* Make sure they understand that. This stuff is definitely not for the faint of heart."

Melanie stared at the clear liquid in the tiny vial and saw only the sun-splashed campus of Stanford University. The doors of the admission center were opening wide.

Chapter 15

Mike Minot was whistling as he eased the Corvette through the parking lot of Donovan's Reef, a lowbrow watering hole nestled in the apex of the peninsula framed by the sprawling J&T Railroad yards and the high bank of the Cal-Sag Channel. On the ride over, he had managed to clear his mind of any lingering guilt (worry) he might have felt about selling steroids to Coach Houghwat's teenage daughter. Melanie Houghwat was smarter than any seventeen-year-old girl had a right to be. He wasn't worried about her getting caught with the stuff, and the Durabolin he had sold her was the lowest dosage he could find. On top of that, she proved to be a convenient buffer between him and the boys on the team. Let *her* sell them the junk. She had to quit coming by the apartment, though. That was trouble just waiting to happen. She was so damn pretty . . .

He cut that last thought short upon spotting the Ford Ranger with the bed-cap parked at the far end of the lot. Minot wheeled the 'Vette around and cruised past the vehicle, double-checking the license plate against the number scrawled across the manila envelope resting at his side.

Bingo.

He parked a few rows back and flipped on one of the interior lamps nestled into the dash. Riffling through the contents of the envelope, he extracted the mug shots and looked long and hard into the pitted face of Paul Knoll, scumbag extraordinaire.

Mike pulled the grisly photos of the mutilated animals from the back of the envelope and forced himself to look. His adrenal glands kicked in as if on cue, his anger rising in almost direct proportion to his heartbeat as he shuffled

81

through the glossy, full-color gore. With his frame of mind firmly established, the former Kansas City Chief headhunter cut the ignition. Mike Minot reached behind the sumptuous leather bucket seats for the 42-inch Louisville Slugger he always kept in the tiny trunk although he rarely, if ever, played baseball.

Stepping carefully around the large puddles in the muddy lot, Minot approached Paul Knoll's pick-up truck, keeping one eye on the dingy windows of Donovan's Reef some fifty feet away. His lip curled in disgust as he noted the metal dog crates stacked in the bed under the fiberglass cap and eased into a sly smile when he noticed the large cargo van parked a few spots down.

With one last glance towards the windows of the Reef, Minot circled Paul Knoll's Ford Ranger, noting the Cobra car alarm sticker in the corner of the driver's side window. He stepped around to the front of the truck and wound up, bringing the meat of the bat down across the windshield. The Cobra's high-pitched howl of protest nearly coincided with the splintering of the safety glass as it caved in, but refused to give, beneath the initial blow. Undaunted, Minot dug the timber out of the sagging windshield and struck again. This time the stubborn glass shattered, sending a shower of crystalline pebbles across the hood and into the cab of the shrieking Ranger. Two more quick swings obliterated the flashing headlights and he added a few well-placed blows to the hood before sliding back behind the shadowy cover of the freight van.

The blistering guitar crescendo of Lynyrd Skynyrd's *Free Bird* escaped into the night air as a handful of the Reef patrons spilled out the door and stood on the landing, staring stupidly at the vandalized pick-up.

"What the hell?"

"Damn! Glad it ain't my car."

Three men, bolstered by curiosity and alcohol-fueled indignation, ventured out into the lot, their voices growing louder as they approached.

"Damn, Paul. Now who would do somethin' like that?" asked one man with a pool cue in one hand and a near-empty beer mug in the other.

Paul Knoll could only stare, his dull gray eyes brimming with rage.

"Turn that alarm off," snipped a large fellow in a black Donovan's Reef T-shirt. "Before the cops come."

"The cops probably *did* this!" Knoll moaned. A bigger man than Minot would have guessed from the mug shots, he lashed out and kicked the door of his truck. "Sonofabitchmother . . ." He fumbled for his keys and unlocked the door. As he switched off the blaring alarm, Mike could see the other two men snickering to each other. "Truck's only two years old!" Knoll hissed as he backed out of the cab. He stood with his fists clenched, glowering at the damage. "I'm going to kill someone . . ."

"I got a buddy who's a pretty good body-man," offered the fellow with the cue-stick. "He's got a shop over on—"

"Screw your buddy," Paul Knoll growled. "And screw you too, dumb-ass. You think this just *happened*? Twenty cars in this lot and mine's the only one that gets jacked up?"

"Come on, Jim," the bouncer said to the man with the cue-stick. "To hell with this asshole."

The two other men began to head back to the bar when the bouncer glanced back. "Get that piece of shit out of the lot. If it's sittin' here come morning, we'll have it towed."

"Up yours," Paul Knoll mumbled under his breath. He reached back into the cab, gingerly brushing the shattered glass away as he retrieved his cell phone, some coke, and other valuables from the glove box.

"Woof-woof."

Paul Knoll turned to the noise and was blinded by the pain and the blood that exploded from the epicenter of his shattered nose. Mike Minot's leather-gloved fists struck his head three more times before he hit the ground, landing face-first on the scarred asphalt.

The sound of locusts filled Paul's brain as he tried to pull his head up, choking and hacking on the gravel and blood swimming in his windpipe. With the clearing of his head came the intimate and horrible realization that it was not cinder or stones, but his own teeth lodged in his throat. Nausea welled up in Paul Knoll's gut, the vomit mercifully expelling the blood and teeth from his throat and over his broken jawbone. He rose somehow to his knees, puke and blood dripping from his split lips.

"Get up."

Paul Knoll looked up to see his attacker standing over him, a baseball bat clutched in one gloved fist.

"Who—who ah you?" he asked, the words garbled through blood and shattered bone. Paul Knoll needed to buy some time. He could get out of this—he had been through worse—if he could just buy some time.

Mike Minot smiled. To Paul Knoll, he looked just like the devil.

"I'm a representative from P.E.T.A.," Minot said. "People for the Ethical Treatment of Animals? They've asked me to come and talk to you. They're really pissed off."

Knoll raised his hands in surrender, his eyes darting from the Louisville Slugger to the face of the madman circling him. "I gah mu-nee," he pleaded, indicating his back pocket. "How mush you nee?" Knoll reached around and snatched the compact .22 caliber snubnose from the small of his back.

He brought it around in a smooth arc and was squeezing the trigger just as the bat landed flush against his cheekbone, bathing his entire existence in a shower of stars and crippling pain. Two more blows landed on the prone body of Paul Knoll as he fought to regain consciousness. His right lung was filling with fluid, a result of his fragmented ribcage. He fought for a gulp of air, defeated as the baseball bat whistled into his soft, exposed belly. A gloved hand gripped his hair, jerked him rudely from the advancing darkness. He could feel the devil's hot breath on his face.

"I killed the last man who pulled a gun on me," Minot said matter-of-factly. "You won't be so lucky."

Andy Freeman was sitting in his patrol car in the parking lot of Dunkin' Donuts on Armstead Boulevard, enjoying a large Boston coffee and a cruller, when he got the call over the radio. *Lincoln-seven, we have an eight, possible three, Donovan's Reef. See the man.* His partner, Carmen Ruiz, an eager young rookie, reached for the transmitter to respond. "Hold off on that one," Andy said, reaching over and dialing the volume down. "It's covered."

Carmen Ruiz shot a puzzled look at the senior officer. "You sure, Andy? The call just came over. We're only a mile away."

Andy smiled at her. He liked Carmen. She reminded him of himself when he had first joined the force. She was going to be a good cop someday, but she would have to be brought along slowly. "Trust me," Andy said, wolfing down the last of the cruller. He licked a trace of glaze from his fingers. "It's covered."

PART II

THE RISE

Chapter 16

Von stood on the forty-yard line, bouncing on the balls of his feet in an effort to contain the adrenaline rush coursing through his bloodstream. He looked out over the first bar of his facemask looping just across the bridge of his nose. Ridgewood Stadium was packed and the crowd was whipped into a lather in anticipation of the opening kickoff. This was the first game of his final high school season and his first as a starter in nearly four years.

He had fixed less than two hours ago, timing the injection so that he could ride the crest of the initial rush throughout the game. He rocked his head from side to side, enjoying the snug, secure fit of the Riddell helmet, the feeling of invincibility it imparted to him, and the comforting click of armor against armor as it met his shoulder pads. The uniform had never felt so right. From the tape the trainers had reinforced his ankles with, to the top of his formidable headgear, the equipment was more a unified extension of his body than a jumbled collection of parts. He was a modern day gladiator, trained in the most manly and primal of sport, drawing fire from the beast within himself and feeding off the bloodlust emanating from the hungry crowd.

The referee walked across midfield some ten yards ahead of him, surveying the opposing battalions. He did a quick, silent count of the men on the field and nodded to the RedHawks' kicker, Pete "the foot" Russo. Von toed the yard stripe at his feet, a cloud of lime rising around his ankles as he dug his cleats into the turf like a sprinter settling into the blocks. He eyed the two return-men of the Eisenhower Eagles standing at the ten-yard line, fixing a bead on number twenty-two, Damon Young. The dangerous wide receiver had returned the opening kick-off eighty-seven yards for a touchdown against them last year, opening the doors for an embarrassing blowout. Von had had an open shot at him and had missed the tackle.

It would not happen again.

He was the only member of the starting line-up on this year's kick-off team; a *suicide squad* made up of second- and third-stringers eager for playing time. Coach Minot had placed him there, the flyer on the outside wing, the first line of defense. He had told Von he expected him to do some serious damage.

The long blast of the opening whistle cut through the night air, eliciting a gluttonous roar from the crowd. The din was maddening and exhilarating all at once. Von watched Pete Russo advance on the football propped up like a time bomb on the kicking tee. He crouched, every muscle in his formidable frame buzzing like a live wire.

Von took off at the exact instant the ball left Pete's foot, the sweet thud of shoe leather against pigskin being the last sound he heard. Like a shark knifing though a school of pilot fish in a sea of tranquility, he exploded down the sideline, weaving toward Damon Young, who stood with his eyes raised to the heavens, waiting to catch the prize that would turn him into a human bull's eye. Blurs of Ridgewood red and Eisenhower green dotted his peripheral vision, irrelevant distractions, no more capable of hindering his purpose than the muted crowd or the school band he could no longer hear. His world was at once serene and furious, a silent panorama of Kafkaesque dreamscape that he floated through with sovereign indifference.

The silence was breached by the muffled whisper of the football landing in the basket of Damon Young's sinewy forearms, then shattered by the bone-crunching impact of Von's tackle a split-second later. The football squirted from Damon Young's sure hands like a greased melon. The music of battle exploded in Von's ears as they spilled to the ground, primal and delicious in its violent reality.

Von was up in an instant, glowing with the pure elation and joy that can only come from such perfect contact. He spied the ball teetering on the four yard line and lunged for it, scooping it up with the opportunistic speed of a seasoned thief. His momentum carried him into the end zone, somersaulting blindly ahead of the press of humanity and high-impact plastic that closed in behind him. Von lay beneath the tangle of arms and legs, waiting for the pile to lighten as the referees stripped the Eisenhower return team from his back one by one. The head linesman already had his hands in the air, signaling *touchdown* as Von shrugged the last of them off and rose from the turf, clutching the football in his bloodied hand. His teammates mobbed him, their congratulatory slaps and head-butts raining off his helmet and shoulder pads like confetti in a ticker-tape parade.

Hustling back to the sideline, engulfed by glad-handing teammates and the roar of the Ridgewood faithful, Von saw the Eagles coaches and trainers jogging across the field, their faces knit with apprehension and fear.

Damon Young lay in a crumpled heap at the six yard line, his face twisted in agony, clutching his shattered ribs.

Von stopped and watched. Long moments passed before the referee signaled to the Ridgewood bench for a stretcher. A pall settled over the stadium with the realization that the youngster would not be walking off the field under his own power.

Von felt no remorse. He felt no pity. It was a good hit—a clean hit. A vindicating hit.

The three years he had spent warming the bench were a

distant memory, replaced by a sense of purpose and camaraderie he had not known since he had been a standout player at the Pop Warner level.

They had all been equal then, before he had been denied the growth spurts and natural development enjoyed by his peers. He had watched for years in silent surrender, trapped in the body of a child as his classmates crossed the threshold into young adulthood. That was before—before his father had reached out from the grave and offered his hand, had given him the key. It was his birthright, his legacy, and one day he would share it with the world, just as his father had intended.

But for now it was his, and only his.

Chapter 17

"Thirty-eight to three!" Ryan Amberson accentuated each syllable of the lopsided score, pounding the side of the half-barrel with his huge fist, "Thir-ty-eight-to-freak-in'-three!"

Jason Jankowski raised his cup and surveyed the manicured rolling landscape of the Ridgewood Greens golf course. Moonlight glittered off the murky water of the lagoon that ran though the tiny nine-hole public course and the sky hummed with the soft purple of twilight reserved for the last sweet nights of summer. "Beautiful night to be alive," he said wistfully. He noticed Tim Halloran looking at him kind of funny then added, "Thirty-eight to three! Who would have thunk it? We should be ranked come Monday."

Ward Starret laughed and poured himself a fresh draft, deftly tilting the cavernous cup to counter the thick head of foam belching from the freshly tapped keg. "Would have been thirty-eight to *nothing* if it wasn't for numb-nuts over here," he said, nodding toward Donny Musconi.

Donny, who had been explaining the intricacies of the wishbone offense to Brandi Brewer and a sophomore with the most beautiful blue eyes he had ever seen, turned toward his quarterback. "That was a bad toss, Star-man," he said, trying to make light of his fumble. "You should have kept it." The truth was, it was a perfect pitch and Donny felt terrible about coughing it up and ruining the shutout. It was early in the third quarter and Ridgewood was up on the number four-ranked Eagles, 24–0. Eisenhower had never recovered from the disastrous opening kick-off and was on their heels at the twenty-eight yard line with the RedHawks driving towards mid-field. Donny had just taken the pitch from Ward and was heading to the corner when an Eagle linebacker came un-touched through the number-three hole and blasted him. Ei-senhower could only manage two yards on the subsequent possession and had to settle for a field goal, but that did little to take away the sting.

"Besides," Donny said, turning back to Brandi and the nameless sophomore, "I could have used some blocking." Donny wasn't smiling as he said this. A spectacular purple and yellow bruise covered the top of his hand where the line-backer's facemask had mashed it and he suspected he might have fractured a bone in his thumb.

Jason looked across the green where Dan Jacobson was laughing it up with Frank Lally. "Hey, don't worry about it, Donny," he said. "We're just busting your chops." Jake had responsibility for the three-hole on the 36 Sweep where Donny fumbled, and he didn't want Donny shooting his mouth off about Jake getting whipped on the play.

"Yeah, c'mon, Donny," Ward said, wishing he hadn't said anything at all. "Don't worry about it. It happens. You played a hell of a game."

"Talk about a hell of a game," Owen Daniels said, draining his beer in three long gulps. He belched loudly and looked around. "Anyone seen Von?"

"It's awful nice of you to take me to your party," Haley McBride said. "I've never been to one of these before. I've heard they're notorious." She turned toward Von and arched a perfectly sculpted eyebrow, accentuating the sly smile that danced on her lips. "And to think I'm being escorted by the star of the game." It was a sweet, fleeting expression, gone in an instant, but burned into the far wall of Von's subconscious where it would stay forever, like the pentimento effect of an old masterpiece emerging through layers of new paint. It might have been that exact moment, sitting shotgun in the dimly lit interior of her mother's Dodge Neon, that Von fell in love with her.

It took a moment for him to recover. "Well, I don't know about that," he offered up with the best *aw, shucks* demeanor he could manage. "It's a team game. We all had a hand in it."

Haley smirked. That eyebrow again. Mercy.

"Yeah, right," she said. "If you insist, but all anyone could talk about was you. The guy on the loudspeaker sounded like a broken record." She launched into a dead-on impersonation of Angus McLeod, the RedHawks' stadium announcer, "Brought down by Vo-*nos*-o vich! Ka-*ruuuuuunching* tackle by Vo-*nos*-o vich!"

Von laughed. "Hey, that's pretty good," he said, genuinely impressed. She was so cool. He couldn't believe she was with him. "You'll want to turn up here," he said indicating the side street that ran parallel to the forest preserve. "Park anywhere you can find a spot—but not too close to the woods. If the cops see a bunch of cars, they'll get suspicious."

"Gotcha," she said. "We wouldn't want to raise *suspicion!*" She laughed, and cruised a half-block up, nosing the Neon discreetly into a tiny spot between a minivan and a station wagon in front of a new townhouse development, impressing him even further.

They got out and walked across the street, following the asphalt-jogging path into the mouth of the woods where she took his hand.

"Kinda scary," Haley whispered.

Got that right, Von thought, feeling his hand grow sweaty. He hoped she didn't notice. They came upon the clearing where the cement bridge arced across the lagoon to the golf course. Haley could hear muffled shouts and muted conversation coming from the outcropping of trees up ahead. A chain-link gate, ten feet high and padlocked shut, denied them passage.

Von grinned sheepishly. "It's closed after dusk. We have to climb around. Here, let me show you."

Haley followed closely behind as Von reached up and grabbed the metal pole bolted to the cornerstone. Planting the toe of his gym shoe in a gap of chain-link, he hoisted himself up and swung around the gate, teetering just a moment over the black water of the lagoon before touching down on the broad cement rail on the other side.

"See?" he said, looking at her hopefully through the chain-link. "It's easy."

Haley stood with her hands on her cocked hips, taking in the vision of the handsome young man perched so gracefully on the cement bridge. From this vantage point, standing a few feet below him, he looked liked a clothed version of Michelangelo's David—*the ultimate personification of male beauty,* her art teacher at Luther South had called it. Yes, that's about right, she thought.

Mistaking her admiration for indecision, he reached around the gate and gallantly extended his arm. "C'mon, I'll catch you."

"Well, there's an offer I can't refuse," she said, reaching up and looping the toe of her shoe into the chain-link. She swung around in one athletic, fluid arc, deliberately overextending herself at the last minute so that she could fall into his waiting arms. They stood frozen on the rail, her breasts raking the taut muscles of his chest, their faces—their lips, only inches apart.

They looked long and deep into each other's eyes, lost in the magic of the moment that comes only with the realization of one's first true love. After the briefest uncertainty on his part (she would not make this first crucial move), he kissed her—a soft, exploratory kiss, electric and fascinating, that melted into a dizzying melding of their souls.

When it finally broke, they could only stare, wide-eyed and delighted. Haley spoke first, her voice a husky whisper.

"Wow," she said, lowering her eyes. "What was that?"

"Don't know," Von replied, his voice sounding weak. "But it sure was nice."

Haley smiled at him. "Yeah. Yeah, it was."

Von swallowed hard and cocked his head towards the sounds of the party swelling in the trees behind them. "You still want to go?"

Haley pursed her lips in mock contemplation. "I suppose we should," she said, reaching up and tracing his mouth with her finger. "I can't deny them their guest of honor."

They rounded the bend and were greeted by a chorus of cheers and raised plastic cups. Haley guessed there had to be close to thirty-five to forty of her classmates dotting the green, the majority of them centered around the keg perched atop the closely cropped turf of the eighth hole. A Creed song poured out from the speakers of a massive boom box and a glow-in-the-dark Frisbee sailed over their heads as they approached. Haley smiled, happy for Von and his newfound popularity. Although she had only been at Ridgewood High for one semester, she knew enough of school politics to know Von had been a nobody—a minor player in the cruel and unforgiving hierarchy of the high school microcosm. Ward Starret, the golden boy, handed them each a beer as classmates gathered round, eager to be part of their world. Haley took a sip of beer from the clear plastic cup, feeling at ease for the first time since transferring from Luther South last spring, since the *trouble*.

Maybe things were going to be all right after all.

Chapter 18

"Did you hear about Jake?"

Jason Jankowski plopped his lunch sack down on the table next to Von, who was already well into his second Fluffernutter. Several others at the table, which now included the bookend linebackers, Ryan Amberson and Owen Daniels, looked up from their lunches, eager to hear the buzz on the hulking lineman. Word had spread throughout the school that he was seen storming out of Dean Fowler's office, red-faced and teary eyed! Teary-eyed! All two hundred and seventy pounds of him.

"What about him?" Von asked through a mouthful of peanut butter and Fluff. Von really didn't care at the moment about Dan Jacobson. He was scanning the crowded lunchroom for Haley McBride. He hadn't seen her since second period and was looking forward to sitting with her at lunch.

"Disciplinary probation," Jason announced to the table. "He blew off Saturday's jug. Didn't hand in the essay that Kroc gave him."

Ryan Amberson, an academic All-American, was unfamiliar with the term. "So what? What's that mean? More jugs?"

"Means he's off the team, Ryan," Jason said, settling in across from Von.

Owen Daniels looked like he was about to shit himself. "No way!" he said, leaning over the table to accentuate the words. "No way. You can't kick a guy off the team for not writing a paper."

Jason emptied the contents of his lunch bag onto the table as he spoke. "He didn't hand the paper in *twice*. And he skipped the Saturday jug. I think that's what really screwed him." Jason peeked under the top slice of bread and inspected the guts of his sandwich. Ham and Swiss Lorraine with shredded lettuce. Good old Mom. "It's official," he said taking a bite out of the lovingly crafted sandwich. "Staci Nowicki was in the waiting room in the Dean of Discipline's office. She got caught smoking again. She heard it all. Off the team until further notice."

Owen Daniels shook his head in disbelief. "Staci Nowicki's a ditz."

"That may be true," Jason said. "But Jake's still off the team. You can bank on it."

Ryan Amberson whistled. "Wow. I can't believe Kroc took it this far."

Von took a long swallow of Mountain Dew and belched. "Hey, it isn't Mr. Kroc's fault. Jacobson screwed up. He had plenty of time to write that paper. What was Kroc supposed to do? Let some kid walk all over him? What the hell was Jacobson thinking—because he's on the football team the rules don't apply? C'mon, man. That's not the way it works around here. You guys know that. If anything, it's the other way around. Coach Houghwat doesn't put up with any bullshit."

Ryan Amberson nodded in agreement. "Yeah, what the hell *was* he thinking? I don't think Coach likes him anyway."

"Guy's a psycho," Daniels said. "It's the steroids. They mess up your head. Turn you into a Neanderthal. But still . . ." He trailed off, hoping he hadn't offended Von.

The table fell silent for a moment. Von, who was well aware of the rumors, let it go without a beat. "Screw him. We don't need him. You guys," he said, looking at the two star linebackers, "are afraid that without Jake's big can up front clearing the way, you won't be able to swoop in and grab all the glory. Fuh-geddaboutit!" he said, laughing. "Seriously, though. We'll be all right. Lally and Steponic will plug up the middle, and Carmody will probably step in for Jake. He's small for the interior, so maybe they'll move Mark inside from end to tackle and play Tom outside. Don't worry about it. We'll be—" Von stopped abruptly and looked up.

Kyle Griffith, the mousy leader of the outcast clique known as the *God Squad* was standing a few feet away. He stood with his lunch tray clutched to his narrow chest, staring at Von as if he were scared to death.

The others at the table turned to look, as did everyone in the immediate area, so strange was the expression on the wispy boy's face.

Von looked around to be sure the boy was indeed staring at him. "What's up, Kyle?" he asked, mystified.

The boy continued to stare, his eyes growing wider before speaking. "And the Lord God commanded the man thus, 'From every tree of the garden you may eat; but from the tree of the knowledge of good and evil you must not eat; for the day you eat of it, you must die.' "

The stillness that spread though the vast cafeteria with the horrible silent speed of a mushroom cloud at flashpoint was broken by a nervous giggle from Brandi Brewer at the next table. Kerri Wheeler, fascinated by the whole bizarre spectacle, motioned for her to be quiet. Jason looked from Von to Kyle and back to Von again, before deciding that Von was the one who appeared to be more shaken by the incident.

Several members of the faculty, including Coaches Minot and Mangan, seated at the monitors' table on the dais near the entrance, peered up over the sea of bodies, scrutinizing the situation like riot police stationed at ground zero.

It was Ryan Amberson who mercifully diffused the surreal stare-down with a candor that was somewhat out of character for the straight-laced linebacker. "Keep it moving, bible-thumper," he said, glaring at Kyle with unbridled contempt, "or I'll shove that good-book so far down your throat, you'll be puking Leviticus for a week."

Laughter, one part genuine, and one part relief, roared up from the assemblage. The willowy evangelist was rattled, but determined in his cause.

"The sins of the father shall be visited upon the son," Kyle warned, his voice cracking with solemn desperation.

Von felt something snap in the back of his mind. "I'll kill you . . ." he mumbled, rising from his seat. Both Jason and Owen Daniels moved to restrain him but Von stayed rooted to his seat in a half crouch, gripped by an unnamable pain.

"I said *move it,* prayer-boy!" Ryan growled. "Don't make me get up or I swear—"

Kyle Griffith turned to go, his departure hastened by Cassie Cafferty at his elbow. A recent convert from the Goth crowd, he had saved her from the *Lord of the Flies* and welcomed her as one of his own. Cassie still bore the scars of the desecration of her flesh—ugly wounds from the multiple piercings and the garish tattoos that so delighted the Dark Prince—but her soul was on the mend, praise be to the Lord Jesus Christ. He glanced back at the afflicted one as she led him away, knowing *that* one could not be saved.

Von eased back into his seat. Taken away from the moment, he tried to make light of the whole situation. "Weirdo," he said with a grin, and chimed in with the opening notes of the old *Twilight Zone* TV show. "Doo-do doo-do doo-do . . ."

Jason laughed a little too loudly. "We're gonna be reading about that guy some day in paper," he said. "Cult leader orchestrates mass suicide! Jimmy Jones Kool-Aid and the whole bit."

Ryan Amberson was not laughing. At any moment it

looked like he would either cry or explode. Owen Daniels noticed it first. "Hey, Ryan, chill out. Settle down, dude. He's just a little—"

"You guys remember the Heaven's Gate cult a few years back?" Ryan asked, dipping a French fry into a tiny plastic cup of ketchup.

His query was met by blank stares, before Jason offered, "The spaceship guys in California?"

Ryan nodded. "Yeah, the spaceship guys in California. Big religious cult? Had their own website on the Internet? They followed this Marshall Applewhite guy. Very charming. Very charismatic. He told them Jesus was coming down in a spaceship to take them all back to heaven, and that the Hale-Bopp comet was the green light—had a date set and everything."

"Didn't they all kill themselves?" Von asked, remembering the story.

Ryan stuck a single fry in his mouth. "Yeah, that was the one little hitch. Apparently Jesus didn't want a whole lot of chatter on the trip, so on the night this spaceship was supposed to touch down—"

"They all drank poison or something," Owen piped in. "Died in their beds."

Ryan nodded. "My cousin Terry was in one of those beds."

A collective gasp welled up from everyone at the table. "Wow," Owen said. "You're kidding, right? I'm sorry. Oh man, that sucks. I—"

"He was about seven years older than me," Ryan said. "It's not like we hung out or anything, but he was a real cool guy. Real smart. I idolized him when I was a kid. He went out to California to become a park ranger. A tree cop, he called it, but—"

"You guys enjoy the show?"

Mike Minot was standing behind Von, his hand placed in a fatherly manner on the boy's shoulder.

"Hey, Coach," Owen beamed. "Ryan's cousin was one of the guys on the spaceship that was going to heaven. You know—the guys in California a few years back?"

Minot looked at Ryan for confirmation. "Is that right?"

Ryan nodded.

"Tough break," Minot said. "I've got film on Bremen— their game with Hinsdale Central. We're going to be breaking it down after practice. You guys are welcome to come in and observe if you want. Strictly on a volunteer basis, you understand. ISAC won't let you practice more than two hours a day."

The boys nodded wildly. Breaking down film! Just like the pros. How cool was that?

"Yeah sure, Coach, I'll be there," Ryan said, glad to change the subject. Von and Owen also assured the coach they would participate. Jason shrank back and said nothing. He would be working on his comic strip tonight.

"Good," the coach said. He gave Von a hearty slap on the shoulder before walking away. "Remember, strictly on a volunteer basis."

"That guy's awesome," Owen Daniels gushed. "They break down film all the time in the pros. That's how you have to approach the game. Know your opponent. Recognize their tendencies. Then you—"

"Hi, guys."

Haley McBride was standing at the head of the table, clutching an armful of books to her chest. A can of Diet Coke and a bag of Fritos dangled precipitously from her fingertips.

Von bolted up to help her with the load and Jason slid one

103

seat over. Haley smiled at Jason, acknowledging the courtesy. "What's up?"

"Ryan's cousin was one of the guys on the spaceship that was going to heaven," Owen said. "You know—the guys in California a few years back?"

Ryan stared at the inside linebacker. If he said it again, he was going to smack him right in the head.

"Really?" Haley asked, sitting down next to Von in the seat Jason had vacated. "I'm sorry to hear that," she said, flashing Ryan a quick sad smile that made him hate Von for just a moment. She turned and looked across the crowded cafeteria, at the table where Kyle Griffith and the God Squad sat in quarantine from the sinners and the fornicators. "So what was all that about?"

Von bit his lip. He had hoped Haley might have missed the whole weird incident. "Ahh, it was nothing," Von said, waving it off, eager to change the subject. "Preacher boy was walking around quoting scripture and he said something that rubbed me the wrong way. Something about my father." He narrowed his dark eyes at Haley. "Where you been? I was looking for you."

"I was at a D.A.R.E. meeting," she said, a trace of annoyance in her voice. "I told you that." Oh God, she thought. Please don't let it start again.

"Oh yeah," Von said sheepishly. "Sorry, I'm still a little creeped out from Bible-boy."

Haley relaxed. She knew about Von's father. Knew that he had killed himself when Von was just a boy. "S'all right, babe," she said in a motherly tone. Haley reached over discreetly and patted his thigh. The simple gesture made Von's head swim. She tore open the bag of Fritos and offered them around the table before dipping in to the bag. "You need a ride home from practice?" she asked Von. She felt bad about snapping at him like that and wanted to make amends. "I have to put some time in at the library after school. I can hang around a bit. I don't have to be at work tonight until seven. Your grandfather will be looking for me, I suspect. I usually pop into his room around six, after he's had his supper."

"No, that's all right," Von replied. He looked at Owen and Ryan for confirmation. "We have to break down game film after practice," he sniffed a little too proudly. "We're gonna be late."

Haley stifled a giggle. For one comical moment he reminded her of Barney Fife from the old Andy Griffith show. *Gotta' break down game film. Tough being a lawman!* "Oh," she said, "just like the pros."

Ryan Amberson and Owen Daniels were looking at her as if she were too good to be true. Haley was so relieved by the simple and wonderful notion that Von didn't *have* to see her tonight that she didn't even notice.

Chapter 19

There was a tactile spring in Haley McBride's step as she crossed the expanse of the Ridgewood High parking lot, a bounce intrinsic to the young, happy, and healthy that had been missing for longer than she could remember. The pop of tennis balls echoed from the courts off the baseball diamonds, split by the occasional angry whistle from the athletic fields at the far end of the blacktop. The sky that dominated the flat landscape was a rare and vibrant blue, usually reserved for postcards and the mass-produced oil paintings one would find in the homes of people who knew absolutely nothing about art but knew what they liked. She thought the air smelled of green somehow, pine needles maybe, as if the last true days of summer had exhaled one final robust breath before giving way to the orange scent of the coming fall.

She spotted Mom's blue Dodge Neon, polished to a high shine by her and her father yesterday after the Bears game, a heartbreaking, last-minute loss to the hated Minnesota Vikings. The simple pleasures of life, watching football with Dad, going out for a girls' lunch with Mom, things she used to take for granted, were starting to become fun again.

It was a good move, heading south and getting out of the city. Away from the trouble.

She slowed upon reaching the Neon and walked around it once. It was such a cute little car. The front quarter panels sported those little decals that looked like random splashes of paint, a detail her father frowned upon but she and her mother found delightful. The car would probably (definitely) become hers upon graduation if she kept her grades up. It was nearly three years old and Mom was getting tired of it, as Mom was apt to do. Haley felt as though she already owned it though, having attached the key to her key ring long ago. She popped the door lock and looked around apprehensively, scanning the area for any thing out of the ordinary—any trouble. Old habits die hard.

She did not see the black Grand Prix parked a block down on Lawler Avenue.

The Ridgewood boys' cross-country team, a rolling, gangly storm cloud of skinny arms, long legs, and baggy shorts, rambled around the quarter-mile track that circled the football field. As they plodded into the far corner, she could see the Varsity football squad gathered in a semi-circle at mid-field, down on one knee, helmets off, listening intently as Coach Houghwat preached the gospel of football. She picked Von out of the herd immediately, his face so hand-some, framed in the diagonal of the chain-link fence like a cherished photo in a locket. Von sensed her gaze (or maybe he was thinking of her already) just as she allowed herself to think she might be falling in love with him. He winked at her and waved discreetly with the two fingers cradling his rugged jaw. She smiled and gave her own quick wave before opening the door and pitching her backpack onto the Neon's pas-senger seat. Haley settled in behind the wheel and dialed up the eighties station before the initial warning lights on the dash could fully fade. Susanna Hoffs and the Bangles droned on sweetly about how they hated Mondays—Sunday was their fun day. Haley laughed (she loved that dopey song) and adjusted the rearview mirror, surprised to see something re-sembling a smile had made its way back into her bright green eyes.

Dominic Teresi blew the red on 183rd Street, nearly clipping the back-end of one of those faggoty new VW bugs turning left through the yellow. He laid on the horn, just to let the guy know that he was a dipstick, lest there be any lingering doubt. Dominic deftly merged into the right lane and tucked behind a soccer mom in a Ford Windstar with a *It's hard to be humble when you own a Pekinese,* bumper sticker. The Pekinese lover turned right at Belmont as Dominic saw Haley's blue Neon two blocks up, its rear flasher copping a plea to edge back into the flow of traffic as Homan narrowed from two lanes to one. A Good Samaritan finally slowed and saved her from being squeezed into the oncoming lane. He grinned, recalling all the times he had told her she needed to be more aggressive on the street.

She needed him. Why couldn't she see that?

All that trouble. So unnecessary, so sad. That business with her father—that put the capper on it, but things were going stale long before that. Why couldn't she wake up and see that they were made for each other? And moving way out to the boonies? What was all that about? Did she really think she could hide from her true feelings—from her destiny? It had been a simple matter to find her once school had started. He knew they would head south, out of the city, but not too far from the West Lawn area on Chicago's southwest side where *Daddy* worked—a big shot at the Union Carbide factory on 68th Street. Ridgewood was the third school he had staked out, but he knew, even before he saw the little blue Neon in the parking lot, that she would be there. He had felt it the moment he cruised past, had felt her presence, her love for him.

Dominic gunned the accelerator and cut the wheel to his left as Homan Avenue expanded into multiple lanes at the intersection of 171st Street.

True love would conquer all.

★ ★ ★ ★ ★

She thought at first that it was a just another false alarm. There had been so many in the past. She was ready to laugh it off—to dismiss it as just another old black Grand Prix or Monte Carlo, but the second glance into the rearview mirror only confirmed her worst fears.

Dominic Teresi was charging up through the traffic, making no effort to conceal himself. She couldn't see his face behind the tinted glass—not yet, but she knew the car. Oh, did she know that car. A 1973 Grand Prix, long, black, and sinister, with its tinted windows and rakish styling; the kind of car that had become obsolete when gas prices crested a dollar a gallon back in the late seventies. He had restored it to showroom quality, had poured thousands of dollars into it— to get it just right. It had been his obsession.

Until he met her of course.

Haley could feel the tears welling up in her eyes as the monstrous car grew larger in her rearview mirror. She could hear the roar of its glass-pack mufflers as it snaked its way through traffic, closing the distance between them. Anger overtook her and she bit her lip, cutting the wheel to the right and coasting into the Steak N' Shake at the mouth of the mall. She would not bring this home again. She would confront this, end it here and now. If Dominic Teresi was going to kill her—and she had always feared that he would, he would have to do it right here, in front of witnesses.

The Steak N' Shake was operating at peak capacity, so close to dinnertime, and the lot was near full. Haley brought the Neon to a stop, double-parking between the line of cars snaking into the drive-through and a small fleet of touring motorcycles. She got out with the car still running and stood in the protective nook of the half-open door as the Grand Prix pulled in behind her.

Dominic Teresi emerged from the car with his hands up and exposed, a ludicrous smile on his face. "Whoa, settle down, Haley," he said, waving his open hands. "We need to talk about this, babe. We need to talk about us."

"Get away from me, Dominic!" Haley said, unable to believe her own ears. "It's over. It's over! There is nothing—*nothing* to talk about. There is no *us*. There can never be an *us!*"

"Baby," Dominic said, taking a step toward her. "You know there ain't a man on this earth that will ever love you as much as I do. Why you lookin' so scared? I would cut off my right arm before I would hurt you."

Haley inadvertently raised her hand to her cheek, where he had struck her not twenty months before, effectively and finally ending their doomed alliance. "Don't come any closer," she said reaching one hand into her purse. "You're violating your restraining order. I could have you arrested right now. You could go back to jail."

The anger, the awful blind rage exclusive to the sociopath, flashed in Dominic's dark eyes. "I'll never go back to jail!" he screamed. "Damn it! Can't you see I'm only trying to make things right?" He softened his tone. He would show her that he could talk about this, that they could work it out. "I forgive you for all that. I mean c'mon, baby. You know we were meant to be together. It's the only way it can be."

"There a problem here?"

Haley turned to see a bear of a man in a leather jacket approaching them, a full-face motorcycle helmet dangling from his gloved paw. He was a grandfatherly type, more cuddly than grizzly, but an imposing figure nonetheless. His female companion trailed behind him, short and squat, her leather riding-suit packed tight with the middle-aged spread of her hips.

"No problem, pops," Dominic sneered, his eyes immediately darting back to Haley. "Just two people talkin'.

Why don't you just move on?"

Bob Medsker sighed and switched his helmet from his right hand to his left. He was a little logy and bleary-eyed from covering eight hundred miles in two days, but he knew an asshole when he saw one and he had little doubt he was looking at one of the all-time greats right now. The girl had been crying and he would bet it wasn't because she was so overjoyed to see the kid in the Marilyn Manson T-shirt who was standing between him and his bike.

"Well now, I would, junior, but you're in my way," Bob said, feeling a little of the old hell-raiser in him floating to the surface. He eyeballed the cherry Grand Prix with a sly grin. "Why don't you just hop in that shit-heap of yours and haul your skinny ass out of here?"

Bob's wife, Sandy, moved back two steps, a move that was not lost on Dominic. The rest of the motorcycle club, about a dozen in all, had made their way out of the Steak N' Shake and were looking at the scene with amused anticipation. Dominic swallowed his anger, forcing it back down his throat like bile rising up at a black-tie dinner. He turned to Haley, his voice measured and precise. "Come on, babe. Let's get out of here. We'll go somewhere and talk."

Haley clenched her fists in exasperation. She looked as if she might crumble into a million pieces on the spot. "Just *go*, Dominic. Go away and leave me alone, please . . ."

Medsker pulled a cell phone out of one of the many zippered pockets of his jacket and pulled the antennae up theatrically. He poked at the tiny buttons three times and waited a moment before he spoke. "Hello, officer? Look, you need to get an ambulance down here right away at the corner of . . ." He turned to the group. "Where we at again? Oh yeah, the Steak N' Shake at the corner of 163rd and . . . Green Meadows Parkway. That's right. We got a real sorry-lookin' fella here with multiple contusions and lacerations. He looks busted up pretty bad."

Dominic hopped in his Grand Prix and squealed off with an angry cloud of white smoke pouring from his wide-profile radials. He shot a cowardly middle finger out the window as he cleared the curb and shot out into the street.

The Jackpine Cruiser Motorcycle Club was roaring with laughter. Bob, ever the comedian, stared into his phone and started to giggle. "Cancel that call, operator," he said, flipping it shut.

Even Haley had started to laugh. She laughed until she started to cry again.

"You like that one, honey?" Bob asked Haley. "I got that from an old Clint Eastwood movie! Ha! I always wanted to do that! What was that movie, Sandy? *Magnum Force?*"

Sandy had moved over and put an arm around Haley. "I don't know, Bob. One of the later ones I think." She looked at Haley. She could see the kid was still scared. "You okay, honey?" she asked. "You want us to see you get home all right?"

The neighborhood kids playing in their yards all looked up and ran to the curb when they heard the sound. John McBride was cutting the front lawn when the Jackpine Cruiser Motorcycle Club rolled up and came to a brief stop in front of his house, the motors on their full-dress Harleys and Honda Goldwings idling patiently. He was more than a little surprised when his daughter emerged from the middle of the pack in their little blue Neon and pulled onto the driveway wearing a sheepish grin. Haley beeped the horn and gave a little wave as the Jackpine Cruisers rolled away in a staggered two-abreast formation, wondering how on earth she was going to explain this to her father without mentioning Dominic Teresi.

Chapter 20

"Sixteen yards! That's too much, that's too much!" Donny Musconi was shaking his head, lamenting Bremen's longest gain of the night.

"That's a first down," Owen Daniels barked. "Fifteen more yards and they're in field goal range. We'll lose the shut-out!"

"They ain't gonna try a field goal down thirty-five to nothin' in the fourth quarter, numb-nuts!" Lally laughed. "What—"

"Hey, golden boy, where were you? I thought—"

"Listen."

The huddle fell silent with the one word and a few seconds of calm was restored amidst the pandemonium. Von stood at the head of the RedHawks' "square" huddle, his back to the Bremen offense, in control and taking no back-talk. Having already located Coach Minot standing on the new line of scrimmage at the end of the last play, Von had acknowledged the coach's signal to make the next call his own. He looked at Ryan Amberson, the player responsible for getting the down and distance from Trevor Matthews, Ridgewood's back-up quarterback.

"First and ten on the forty-two," Amberson sighed.

Von's eyes darted to Owen Daniels, fresh from processing the personnel signals from Coach Mangan.

Daniels nodded. "Wide spread."

Von's mind raced. "Wide spread" indicated one back and four wide-outs with no tight end. They were going for six. "Okay," he said, "listen up. Over, red. Monster fade." He looked at his friend Jason, the one man that would be free to blitz if Von dropped into coverage. "Got it?"

Jason breathed hard through his mouthguard, still winded from being taken downfield on a post pattern on the last play. "I got it. I got it."

"Not another inch," Von commanded. "Ready—break!"

The RedHawks' defense stood tentatively on the line of scrimmage seconds before the Bremen Bandits broke from their own huddle. Von watched them approach, already checking tendencies, looking for a clue, anything that might give him an edge. Three wideouts sprinted to the left of the formation, leaving one lone flanker split wide on the right.

"Liz!" he yelled, indicating the stacked left side of the line.

Ryan Amberson floated over into a soft zone, next to Halloran, the right corner.

The tailback, lined up in the slot as the third wideout, was leaning to his right. Von sniffed a crossing pattern—maybe an attempt at a pick.

"Owen, watch flow! Watch lead weak!"

Von advanced to the line, standing in the gap between Lally and Carmody, who was filling in quite aptly for the suspended Dan Jacobson. He looked directly into the blackened eyes of the Bremen quarterback. What he saw was fear. Plain and simple. The kid had hung in through three and-a-half quarters of hell, having been sacked eleven times and hit after the throw too many times to count. The fight was out of him, though; he was just going through the motions and trying to get out of here in one piece. Von almost felt sorry for him.

Almost.

The ball snapped and the silence descended like a curtain. The flurry of activity, a blur for the average player, barely manageable for the really good ones, was for Von, a frame by frame series of snapshots, that he could process almost at his leisure.

The right guard pulled and clogged the middle, amounting to what would have been a triple-team block, had Von not already decided to back off the blitz and drop into coverage. Just as he had envisioned, the tailback came across the middle on a crossing pattern with the weak-side wideout in an attempt to pick apart the zone coverage in the flat.

Von didn't buy it for a moment. He backpedaled and fell into a man-to-man coverage with the tailback, following the quarterback's eyes the whole time. Timing his leap perfectly, he leaped high—*over the receiver's head*—and came down with the ball in a somersault landing more reminiscent of Olga Korbut than Dick Butkus.

He heard the roar from the stands for a brief moment before his cleats dug into the thick green grass and the calm returned. Von reversed field and cut toward the right side-line, his peripheral vision picking up the pursuit already starting to accumulate to his left. He accelerated, faking an offensive lineman out of his jock and picking up a nice block from Tim Halloran that gave him a seam to the open turf of the RedHawks sideline.

The end zone lay some fifty-five yards away, giving Von ample time to scan the stands as he galloped toward glory. He saw Haley McBride, next to Kerri Wheeler, her face lit up with pride, standing and cheering him on. Their eyes met, adding to his elation, just before he felt the searing jolt of pain shoot through his lower leg.

The Bremen wideout had come from clear across the field, having been knocked out of the play and on to his back by a vicious chuck from Daniels at the line. All but forgotten amidst the chaos of the ensuing return, the skinny flanker leaped to his feet and drew a bead on the big free-safety gal-loping unimpeded toward the end zone.

Go low, his father had taught him since he was just a boy. Go low and you can bring 'em down, no matter how big they are . . .

Mike Minot flinched when he heard the sound, a sickening pop like the report of a starter's pistol, and then the ripping noise. It was a sound he'd heard before—louder then, echoing through his headgear as he writhed on the turf at the Oakland Coliseum, his knee ligaments stretched and shredded like an over-stressed rubber band. It was a sound that had ushered in the sleepless nights, the addiction to Vicodin, the long, painful hours of rehab—the end of his playing career.

Knees. Was there ever a more poorly designed joint than the human knee?

Sitting in the hallway at Palos Community Hospital, amongst the madness that permeated an Emergency Room on a Friday night, the coach wrestled with the prospect of a promising season down the toilet and, strangely enough, the distress he felt for the Vonosovich kid. It wasn't often that Mike Minot would risk graying his hair over anyone other than himself, but he knew right off the bat that this kid had the goods. He could have made it to the big show with a little luck, all the way to the NFL.

At least Mike had gotten that far. Now this kid would be lucky to be able to jog through the park on a Sunday—

"Mr. *Mi-not?*"

Mike looked up. A tiny Nescafe colored man in a white lab coat was standing over him. The doctor. Cane and . . . *Cannon* something.

"Yeah?"

"I am Dr. Kaanan. You are the guardian for Sergei Vonosovich?"

"I brought him in," Mike said. "I'm his coach. We're

trying to contact the mother. She's working."

The little man nodded. "Very good. You can sign him out then?"

Mike Minot was silent for a moment. "Sign him out?"

"Yes," Dr. Kaanan said, writing instructions down on the release form. "I write him prescription. Tylenol Three. He will be fine. No running. No *football*." He said the word like it left a sour taste in his mouth. "No football for a week."

Mike stammered. "What about the L.C. ligament? What about the break in the fibula?"

"No break," the doctor said. "Lateral collateral ligament is fine—is a little stretched," he said, holding his thumb and forefinger a quarter-inch apart, "but fine." He handed Mike the Tylenol prescription and the release papers, obviously eager to be done with the whole matter.

"Wait a second," Mike said, clamping his hand down on the little man's shoulder as he turned to go. "Aren't you the same guy that showed me an X-ray not a half-hour ago? That kid's knee is shot. You know it and I know it."

Dr. Kaanan blustered. He wasn't going to get out of it that easy. He motioned for the coach to follow him.

"Is very strange," the doctor said, leading Mike through a set of double doors. They turned down the hallway and into a side room. X-rays hung from clips on wires suspended across the length of the room. "I can only think that somehow there was a mix-up—that the X-ray was . . . mislabeled."

Dr. Kaanan pulled a sheet of the black film from a wire over his head and placed it on the illuminated display frame on the wall. Mike recognized it immediately as the X-ray Kaanan had shown him earlier.

"You see here," the little man said, pulling a pencil from the pocket of his lab coat. Minot followed the pink nub of the pencil's eraser along the glossy film. "Lateral or *fibular* collateral ligament is stretched—torn here at junction with the femur. I say this trauma occurs right before fibula snaps . . . " He paused and traced the inverted pencil along the length of the leg bone. "Here. Is very bad break. Much trauma to leg."

Minot nodded. "No kidding."

Dr. Kaanan pulled another X-ray down and placed it on the wall directly alongside the first. "Here is X-ray we take just five minutes ago, in preparation for temporary cast."

Mike stared and said nothing. The LCL was intact, swollen maybe, and not as tight as it could be, but intact, with no sign of a tear. He moved closer, his eyes crawling over the ghostly skeletal image with disbelief. A hairline fracture, barely perceptible at first glance, drifted superficially across the surface of the fibula in place of the clean break so apparent on the first X-ray.

Kaanan cleared his throat. "We take another X-ray, just to be sure," he said, sliding a third sheet of film on to the backlit plastic. "You see," he said, tapping the pencil on the two fresh X-rays. "We make a mistake."

"No," Minot said in a voice so low that it was almost a whisper. "No you didn't. Look. It's the same leg in all three."

"No," Dr. Kaanan said, hastily pulling the X-rays down from the case. "That's impossible."

Chapter 21

"You know that's a filthy habit you've got there, Larry."

Lawrence Blodgett cracked the window in the teachers' lounge a few inches and pulled his favorite chair up alongside of it. "Yeah, I think you've told me that before," he said, fishing a pack of Camel Lights from his sport coat. "So sue me."

"Better watch what you wish for," Eugene Kroc said to his friend. "It just might happen. Smokers are getting sued all the time."

"Yeah, I know," Larry replied, lighting up. "We're unjustly persecuted." He crouched and blew a stream of smoke out the open window. "I mean, if we want to commit suicide it's our own problem." He fanned the lingering smoke toward the window with his hand as he spoke. "Damn bureaucrats. Just leave us alone and let us die in peace."

"Amen to that," Kroc said, tapping a cup of impossibly black coffee from the large stainless steel urn. He set it down on the table across from Larry, noting with disgust the viscous residue it left on the white Styrofoam walls of the cup. "And then your surviving relatives can sue big tobacco for forcing you to smoke for forty years."

"Ah yes," Larry said, taking another deep drag. " 'Tis truly a great country."

Kroc settled in across from the art teacher, positioning himself away from the offensive cloud of smoke. He took a pull from the coffee cup and set it back down with a grimace. "Oh God, that's awful. When was the last time that urn was cleaned?"

"Hard to say," Larry replied. "Ninety-two or three maybe?"

They sat in comfortable silence for a moment, letting the stress of the day's first six periods dissipate. Kroc had taken an immediate liking to Larry upon meeting him seven years ago. Larry was six years younger than he was, but they were both creative types and that seemed to draw them together. He and Trish had had him over to the house on several occasions, usually accompanied by a different woman each time. Larry came off as the type of guy who liked to play the field, but Kroc suspected that he would jump at the chance to marry if the right woman came along.

"So how is it so far?" Kroc asked, breaking the silence. "Anyone worth getting excited about?"

Larry tipped the long ash of the Camel into a Styrofoam cup, where it landed with a muffled splash in a quarter inch of forgotten Boston coffee. "Eh—got one kid, a freshman who's pretty good. Might even be a genius. He did a charcoal drawing last week that blew me away—way too advanced for a fifteen year-old." He laughed. "I hate him, of course. He's lazy, though. I think he smokes too much pot. I got a few other kids that are pretty talented. Jason Jankowski's got a shot at making a career of it. He's got the passion. Other than that, just the usual assortment of kids hopping in for an easy credit."

Kroc nodded. Jankowski was a good kid. He had three older brothers who had gone through Ridgewood. Big-time jocks, but not a lot upstairs. Jason seemed cut from a different mold. "Yeah, I know Jason," he said, testing the waters. "Hangs around with Sergei—Von, Vonosovich."

Larry looked at the English teacher. He took another drag off the Camel, not bothering to blow the smoke out the window. "So what's up with that?"

"What do you mean?" Kroc asked innocently.

"Come on, Gene. Look at the size of the kid. He must

have packed on forty, fifty pounds over the summer. All muscle. And it's not just that. He's . . . he's—"

"Beautiful?" Kroc asked, finding the word for him.

"Yeah. Yeah, I guess that's the word I would have to use. I mean, he looks like an Adonis. You think he's on steroids? He wouldn't be the only one, you know."

"Jesus, I hope not, Larry," Kroc replied. "I don't think so. I think he's smarter than that. He doesn't appear to have any of the side effects—acne, thinning hair, violent mood swings . . ."

Larry nodded. "Like Dan Jacobson?"

"Yeah," Kroc said. "Like Dan Jacobson." He took another sip of the foul coffee. "I think he's on the junk, but it's hard to tell. He's got the acne—and the 'roid-rages too, as they call them. But as far as the mood swings . . . the kid's always been trouble as far as I can tell. So who can say?"

"Who can say, indeed?"

Both men turned to look, startled, at the door where Mike Minot stood. Neither man had heard him come in.

"You know, gentlemen," Minot nodded to them in greeting, "trouble is such a relative term. It all depends on your point of view." Minot reached for a cup next to the urn and tapped himself a cup of the inky coffee. "Grammatically speaking, I mean. Wouldn't you agree, Eugene?"

"Gene," Kroc said. "Just Gene. Sure. It would all depend on the person's point of view."

Minot laughed. "Or in this case, everyone's point of view. I think we can all agree that Jacobson is trouble waiting to happen."

"Well . . ." Kroc mumbled. He was a little embarrassed to be caught talking about a student in that context. Besides, he didn't know where Minot was going with this, but he had a pretty good idea.

Larry Blodgett considered his cigarette as Minot sat down across from them. It had burned almost down to the filter. He normally would have pitched it by now, but he didn't want Minot to think he was putting it out for his benefit. He took another drag, exhaling the smoke out the open window before dropping the butt into his makeshift ashtray with a muffled *pfffft*.

"No," Minot continued, "the jury's in on this one. Jake's trouble, no doubt about it. But he's young and not very bright. He's got his whole future ahead of him. He can still turn it around, but he needs help."

Larry Blodgett smiled to himself. This guy was pretty good. A real charmer. He had no doubt Kroc would see right through it, but there was an intimidation factor here that could not be ignored. The man was physically imposing, but there was more to it than that. There was something about the guy that made you want him to like you.

"Jake's a football player," Minot continued. "An average football player, sure, but he's got a decent shot of at least a partial scholarship to a junior college. Without that, the kid's working in a factory or pumping gas his whole life." Minot looked at Kroc with eyes as big and brown as a Labrador puppy's. "But he needs to be on the field if he's going to attract any attention from college scouts. Now, I know—"

Kroc raised his hand like a traffic cop. "I know where you're going with this, Coach. I didn't want to put Jacobson on D.P. but I had no choice. He was disrupting my class. I gave him ample time to complete the assigned penalty. He didn't hand it in. I extended the deadline and added a Saturday jug. He skipped detention and—"

Minot shook his head in vigorous agreement. "There's no doubt the kid screwed up and deserves a kick in the tail—none at all. I'm just asking for some time. Give him three more days. He'll do the assignment and the jug. If he doesn't, he'll never wear a RedHawks uniform again. I'll see to it myself."

Kroc ran two bony fingers along his dimpled chin. "I'll agree to that—but it's out of my hands now, Mike. It's a disciplinary issue. Dean Fowler has to rule on it."

Minot hedged, unaware of this snag in procedure. "All right," he said, pushing himself away from the table. "But you agree to the conditions?"

Kroc took another sip of the coffee. It was cold. "Sure," he said. "That's more than fair."

"Thanks, Gene." He nodded to Larry and headed to the door. "Oh, and gentlemen," he said, pausing a moment, "let's be very careful about what we say about steroid abuse among our student athletes. Those are serious allegations."

Mr. Kroc and Mr. Blodgett watched the door click shut behind him.

Larry laughed and shook his head. "What was that you were saying about trouble?"

Chapter 22

Every member of the faculty at Ridgewood High had a nickname bestowed upon them by the students, most of them deriving from some less than flattering physical attribute.

Dean Fowler was known as "The Skull."

Tall and thin (but not nearly as skinny as Mr. Kroc, a.k.a. "The Stork"), James Fowler sported an unusually high hairline, even as a boy. Male pattern baldness swept in with devastating results while he was still in his late twenties, further accentuating his pivotal cheekbones and weak chin. Two dead, black bullet holes rested in the hollows above those cheekbones and his prominent brow, devoid of emotion and impossible to read. More than one student was reduced to tears simply by staring into those cold dark orbs and it was said if you looked into them long enough, you could go insane.

Larry Blodgett had mentioned to Kroc one night after too many Heinekens that he looked just like Edvard Munch's painting, "The Scream."

The Skull pulled Dan Jacobson's file from the top drawer of his desk and casually flipped it open, more for the benefit of the small crowd assembled in his office than his own. He had been through the incident several times, most recently with Coach Minot, and was determined to put an end to it.

Jacobson squirmed in his chair as Dean Fowler scanned his file, his black eyes darting up and down the page before he finally spoke. "What I fail to understand, Mr. Jacobson, is your frame of mind regarding this whole situation." He brought his eyes up from the paper and fixed them directly on Jake. "Did you think for one minute that being a student athlete would make you exempt from procedure? Are you somehow under the impression that we would deviate from our standard agendum because you are on the football team?"

Jacobson could feel Coach Houghwat glaring at him from his seat by the door.

"I guess what I want to know, Mr. Jacobson," Fowler continued, "is, what were you thinking?"

Jacobson bowed his head, unable to look into the cold depths of The Skull's black eyes, unable to answer the simple question, unable to look at Coach Houghwat, Coach Minot, and that skinny sonofabitch, Kroc—the guy that started all of this. He could feel the heat rising in his cheeks as they all stared at him, waiting for him to answer. "I don't know, sir," he said finally, only because he had to say something. He wanted to tell the freak that he didn't do it because he didn't give a damn about Shirley Jackson and her stupid story. He wanted to tell him that if they were out on the street instead of sitting in this smelly little office, that maybe he would beat the crap out of both him and Kroc and make them apologize to *him*. But of course he didn't say any of that. He was in it deep here and Coach Minot had thrown him a rope. Jacobson bit his lip, remembering what Minot had told him to say and how sorry to sound when he said it. "I don't know, sir," he repeated, lifting his gaze from his shoe tops. "I guess I just sort of thought it would go away if I ignored it. But," he said, looking as contrite as he possibly could, "I guess your problems don't go away if you ignore them. They only get worse."

Eugene Kroc couldn't help but roll his eyes but he did manage to stifle the guffaw that was rising in his throat. Maybe the kid should have been pushed toward the drama club.

"Yes," Fowler nodded gravely, "indeed they do. And to

that end, it seems that you have a quite a problem here. Coach Minot has spoken out on your behalf and has come up with a possible solution, which Mr. Kroc has agreed to. Bear in mind, this offer is not being tendered because you are a football player, and it is a one-time deal. You will complete the assigned punishment," Fowler paused here and shuffled through the file, "a two-thousand word essay on Shirley Jackson's short story, *The Lottery*, and hand it in to Mr. Kroc in no less than three days, which would be Monday. You will also serve *four* detentions on consecutive Saturdays, starting this Saturday. If you fail to complete the assignment or serve the jugs, the time frame for the disciplinary probation will be doubled, in effect, rendering you ineligible to play football for the remainder of the season."

The soggy cloak of hubris that Dan Jacobson wore as he lumbered through life fell from his broad shoulders and hit the floor, leaving him naked and exposed for the entire world to see his fear and confusion. What kind of a deal was this? Four jugs? And what about this week's game? He looked around the room stupidly, trying to comprehend. "I don't play *again* on Friday?" he asked. "What if I complete the assignment by Friday?"

Coach Houghwat folded his arms, thick with muscle and white hair, across his chest. "You don't suit up on Friday, Jake," he said flatly. "That's *my* decision." He shot a glance at Mike Minot and added, "And that's the only input I've had in this matter. It's not my style to make deals for my players. I only agreed to this because you're a senior and this is your last chance to show the scouts what you can do. You would have missed six games if Coach Minot didn't stick his neck out for you." He looked at the boy, wondering when it was going to sink in. "This is a good offer, Jake—and the only one on the table. Take it or leave it."

126

Dan Jacobson swallowed the lump rising in his tightening throat. The muscles in his temples throbbed as he willed back the rage and the tears. He could not—*would not*—cry in front of these people. Jacobson raised his bowed head and nodded, finally realizing he had run out of road. "Okay," he croaked, barely able to speak. "Sure."

Mike Minot looked at the big lineman, disgusted and amused by his pain. "Oh, and Jake," he said, leaning forward earnestly, "there's just one more thing."

Jacobson looked at him, surprised. "What's that, Coach?"

"Apologize to Mr. Kroc for disrupting his class."

Chapter 23

The weight stack rose and fell in a furious rhythm, matching the beat of Dan Jacobson's heart before the cadence began to falter on the thirteenth rep. The flat-black plates quivered with uncertainty, suspended in mid-air along their track as he reached the point of momentary muscular failure. He pushed past the pain, ignoring the protest from his body and completed the lift, locking his arms over his chest as muscle tissue throughout his upper body broke down under the unnatural strain. Over the course of the next thirty-six hours, his body's immune system, with its natural propensity to heal, would replenish the damaged tissue. The muscle would be bigger—stronger than it was before—until he could break through the wall and damage it again, starting the whole process anew. Such was the weight lifter's regimen. A systematic demolition and rebuilding process, utilizing the body's intrinsic healing tendencies.

And the steroids, of course.

Frank Lally had turned him on to the junk at the start of their sophomore year, and it didn't take long before the fat dumpy kid from St. Terence was throwing his weight around with a whole new attitude and sense of purpose. Jake had been lifting off and on since seventh grade, never seeing much in the way of progress and frustrated by the lack of quick results promised by the slick ads in the muscle magazines. In his first cycle with Lally-gags, a six week odyssey of stacking testosterone cypoinate, and Sustaton, oral diuretics, and lifting three hours a day, Jake had increased his lean mass by sixteen percent and trimmed his body fat a full three percent. By his junior year, Dan Jacobson was a starting lineman on the varsity squad and on most everyone's top-ten list of people you do not want to mess with. While his mentor, Frank Lally, took a more orchestrated approach to his juicing—cycling and tapering at specific intervals, Jake went hog-wild—megadosing and shotgunning with little regard to the side effects. Whereas the average male naturally produces anywhere from two-and-a-half to eleven milligrams of testosterone daily, Jake was pumping over one hundred milligrams a day into his body, more often than not through direct injection. The acne flare-ups, muscle cramps, and seemingly manic mood swings, were in Jake's opinion, a minor inconvenience compared to the benefits. He was a warrior—a lifetaker and a heartbreaker. He feared no man or beast.

And they were trying to take him down.

Jake rose from the bench and wiped the sweat from his face with a towel. He looked around the empty weightroom, enjoying the solitude. This was his temple, and the Universal Multi-Station upon which he now sat was his altar. In ten minutes, it would be crawling with freshmen geek faggots from Coach Houghwat's seventh period gym class. Turncoat. Kicking him off the football team! And for what? For being late with a paper?

Hell, he tried to do the paper—gave it a shot last night—but who was he kidding? Just thinking about all that writing gave him a headache.

He was going to need some help on this one.

Chapter 24

There is a deceptive emptiness that permeates a locker room after the final bell, a calm not unlike the eerie tranquility that lingers on a battlefield in the wake of a slaughter. Spent electrons hover aimlessly in the stale air, ghostly remnants of the manic energy dispelled in the three-minute clothing swap necessary to make the hasty transition from student to athlete. Von sat on the varnished pine bench below his locker, taking it in; the silence broken only by the occasional muffled blast of a coach's whistle from the gymnasium and the almost hypnotic shimmy of metal rolling into metal coming from the weightroom behind the stage. Being a senior, Von's academic day ended after the sixth period, leaving him two full periods to kill before football practice started at three. Seventh period was normally reserved for the library, a good forty-five minutes to put a dent in his homework before heading to the weightroom or the running track for period eight. The day's unusually soft workload found him in the locker room a period early however, with a full hour-and-a-half of free time on his hands.

He decided to have an all-out workout instead of the usual light lifting he would normally squeeze in before practice. This would allow him to skip tonight's workout altogether and maybe see Haley for a while after supper. Von reached up and pulled the fingerless leather workout gloves from the top shelf of his locker with a frown. Haley hadn't been herself for the last couple of days. She seemed moody and distant.

A car started up outside. Von's ears perked up, zoning in on the motor's hum, separating it from the cacophony of sounds he could pick up from hundreds of yards away. It wasn't Haley's car. Sounded more like Halloran's Chevy.

Von didn't consider it strange to be able to do such things. He merely considered his acute hearing another side effect— another benefit, from the elixir, just like his keen eyesight. Von didn't quite know exactly when he stopped needing his glasses. Sometime last June, maybe a few weeks after he had crafted his first batch of the elixir, he had put them on and found his vision distorted and swimmy. A trip to the eye-doctor confirmed his suspicions. Von's vision had gone from a steadily declining 20/40 to 20/10 since his last check-up. The optometrist was baffled and ordered more tests but Von blew off the subsequent appointments. He pitched the dorky glasses along with his acne medication and all the other stuff he didn't need anymore: cold medicine, antibiotics, aspirin— overpriced, synthetic derivatives, all rendered obsolete with the development of his father's elixir.

Von took a moment as he undressed and looked down at his body. He had added another half-inch to his chest in the two weeks since school had started and there were times—he would swear to it, that he could feel his body actually *changing* from the inside out. He had been wrestling of late with the thought of going public with it—of sharing it with the world. He knew of course, that his father had grander plans for the elixir. He didn't spend years developing the stuff so his son could look good in a locker room. Hell, the stuff could probably cure cancer. He was no genius, but he had read enough of his father's journals to know its main function was the optimization of cellular development and transmuta-tion. Still, his father hadn't left the journal to the world. He had left it to Von. Deep down Von knew he must have had a reason for that and until he knew what that reason was, the secret would stay his.

Von rummaged through his gym bag and pulled the med-kit from the zippered compartment tucked into its side. It had been three days since his last boost. He really wasn't due for another shot until Friday—before the game. Von zipped the kit open and contemplated the vial of green liquid Velcroed securely into the corner. An hour-and-a-half on the Universal set with the goo pumping through his veins was too good to pass up.

He was getting ready to jab the needle through the corked cap of the vial when he realized that something was amiss. His ears perked up—actually twitched in the direction or the weightroom, searching for the sudden discrepancy in his surroundings. The sounds from the weightroom had stopped—replaced by footsteps—one pair.

Von panicked for a moment before fumbling the works and pitching them into his locker and slamming it shut. He had been so lost in his own thoughts that he had failed to hear the steel-latticed door of the cage open and close, had failed to hear the steps of the intruder until they were at the foot of the stairs.

Von was stepping into his gym shorts when Dan Jacobson lumbered around the corner, flushed from his workout and soaked in sweat. Von tried his best to look casual, and nodded in acknowledgment, realizing too late that his shooting gear lay exposed through the ventilation screen of the locker door.

Jake grinned, his numb intellect telling him he had somehow just gained the upper hand in this encounter. "Hey," he said, "I thought that might be you. Coming in to hit the weights before practice, huh?"

Von stood up, hedging toward his locker to shield the contents from the grinning oaf. "Yeah."

"Coach had a frosh class in there but they're in the gym now running laps."

Von, having regained a bit of his composure, nodded warily, "Uh-huh." Not only did he not trust Jake, he flat out disliked him, and had for a long time.

There was an incident—just three years ago, although it seemed more like thirty—that had left an ugly scar on the rind of Von's soul. A brief but shameful venture into cowardice that lasted only seconds but had haunted him from that day forward. Both boys had been freshmen, three weeks into the new school year, in Mr. Blodgett's Art 101.

Mr. B had been handing back that term's first test, a rather involved analysis and breakdown of the triangle composition popular in early Renaissance painting, worth a whopping thirty points toward their final grade. Two tests had been handed in unsigned and when all were returned, Von and Jake were left empty-handed. Mr. Blodgett had called them both up to his desk to identify their respective papers.

Without the slightest hesitation, Dan Jacobson had reached down and plucked Von's test, meticulous and wearing a score of ninety-two percent (minus five points for no signature) from the desk.

"This one's mine," he had said.

Von could only stare in shock and disbelief at the remaining paper staring up at him, a garbled collection of gibberish and frustration, sporting the ugly score of thirty-six percent.

"Is that your test, Von?" Mr. Blodgett had asked him, knowing full well that it wasn't.

Von had felt Jake's icy stare. "Yeah, I guess so," he had answered, unable to meet the teacher's eyes. Von had walked back to his seat in a daze, unable to look at the paper in his trembling hand. It was an abominable thing, scrawled in the clumsy hand of a brutish lout, made even uglier by the huge red "F" emblazoned across the top. As he settled into his seat, he had caught Jacobson looking at him from across the room, a smug, stupid smile on his face.

The same smile he was wearing now.

Jake moved closer, boldly stepping into the narrow aisle where Von stood pressed against his locker. "Guess you heard what happened, huh?" he asked. His gaze drifted over Von's shoulder and zeroed in on the locker.

"Yeah," Von said. "That's too bad. We'll have to get by without you for one more game."

Jake snorted, feeling his way along. "Yeah! One more game—that's *if* I write Kroc's paper in the next three days. And that's a big *if*. If I don't, I can forget about the rest of the season."

Von whistled, acting as if he cared. "That's rough," he said pulling a thin T-shirt over his sculpted torso. "You better get crackin'. That's gonna be tough."

Jake moved in closer still, thinking his bulk still held some sway. "Yeah, that's kinda what I wanted to talk to you about. Being a team and all—we always help each other out." He was looking right into the locker now, staring at Von's shooting gear. "You know, anyway we can." He smiled triumphantly. "I figured maybe you could help me with it—help me write it. You're real good with that kinda stuff."

Von sensed what was coming but he didn't know if the big oaf would actually have to nerve to ask him. He said nothing for a moment, weighing his options. Jake had seen the hypo, had seen the vial. Jake obviously thought he had him by the short ones. Von remembered, with startling clarity, the shame he had felt that day in art class three years ago. He knew this would be his only shot at redemption.

"Sorry, Jake," he said coldly. "Not a chance."

Jake laughed. "What'd you say?"

Von moved closer to the bigger man. They were inches apart, separated only by the tension in the air. "I said *no*. No way. Write the paper yourself."

Jake nodded towards Von's locker. "You help me write that paper or I spill the beans. I'll tell everyone you're on the juice—and they'll believe me, too. No one gets that big that fast. You'll never play football in this state again."

Von opened his locker, calling upon the only bluff card he had left in his deck. "This isn't juice, you moron," he said pulling the hypo and the vial from the locker and flashing it in front of Jake's face. "It's *insulin*. I'm a diabetic!" Von lowered his head. "I didn't want anyone to know. It might keep me off the team."

Jake grinned. "Yeah, right. Well, who cares? Like you said—either way you're off the team. Unless you write that paper for me."

"You might want to think about that, Brainiac," Von said in a low measured voice. "Let's say it's insulin. You turn me in. How's that going to make you look? The guy that fingered the poor sick kid? And don't think for a second that I wouldn't let everyone know it was you. Let's say it *is* steroids. You drop a dime on me and it will have a ripple effect." He paused here and lowered his voice. "I'll see to that. I get tested, *everyone* gets tested. Again: I'll make sure everyone knows it was you."

The grin faded from Jake's face as Von turned and methodically placed his shooting gear back in the locker beneath his street clothes. "You do what you gotta' do, Jake," he said, slamming the door and padlocking it shut. "But you can bank on this: there's no way in hell that I'm helping you with that paper."

Chapter 25

The anger that had fueled the initial stages of his workout had given way to frustration by the time Von had moved on to the leg-curl station. Distracted by the shouts and whistles radiating from the gymnasium, Von lay on his stomach, dissecting the earlier encounter with Jake like a scout breaking down film on an upcoming opponent.

Had he bought it?

Von didn't think so. Still, he might have spooked him enough to keep Jake's mouth shut. Jake was easily confused and besides, he'd be cutting his own throat if he went off on a tangent, babbling about steroid abuse in the RedHawks' locker room.

But then again, what would Jake have to lose if he never got back on the team?

Von pulled himself off the bench and sat upright, weighing his options. He thought of striking a deal—of writing the paper for him. It didn't have to be a masterpiece. Hell, he'd have to dumb it down anyway, just so Kroc would think Jake actually wrote it. That would cement the deal. He could probably knock that out in two-three hours . . .

Jake's fat grinning face—three years younger, leering at him from across the room. Jake fanning himself with Von's test, while Von fought back tears, staring with disbelief and shock at the red F scrawled across the abomination he held in his hand . . .

"No," Von whispered in the silence of the empty weightroom. "No way."

Von got up and walked from the cage, his workout unfinished as his business with Jake, but strangely satisfied with both. Hoots and hollers from the gymnasium fell on his ears as he descended the wooden stairs, followed by the shrill blast of a whistle and Coach Minot's hearty laughter.

Driven by curiosity, Von veered left at the foot of the staircase and picked his way across the backstage clutter of props and pulleys. A red sphere whistled past his field of vision as he parted the curtain and stepped on to the stage. Coach Minot stood at the edge of the rostrum, a red dodge ball wedged under each beefy arm between his biceps and lats. He stood perfectly still, his forearms dangling at an odd but relaxed angle off the large rubber balls. From Von's vantage point, directly behind him, the coach looked like the world's most well-developed scarecrow.

Minot sensed his presence and turned, his handsome face breaking into a genuine smile.

"Hey, killer," the coach said, the silver whistle still clenched between his white teeth. "Wanna play? I got a bunch of rag-arms out here."

Von looked out on the hardwood floor of the gymnasium. The class looked to be frosh-soph, but he could see a few juniors he knew bunched together under the basketball net on the south wall. With the exception of Shane Daley, a wing on the RedHawks hockey team, it was a pretty sorry looking group physically—all skinny arms and legs swimming in ratty oversized red Ridgewood gym suits. As if to underscore the athletic futility, Lester Lesko, Ridgewood High's official computer geek, stood on the periphery, trying to blend in inconspicuously with his junior classmates.

The group returned his stare, their eyes wide with wonder, horrified at the prospect that he might actually play.

Von held an impartial view on the game of dodge ball. He had always been agile enough to last until the final rounds but he had never once come out on top. He had never had that great an arm—not bad, but nothing like some of these kids. Hell, Jeff Brija, fat as he was, he could take your head clean off with one of those things if you weren't careful.

But of course that was *before*.

Being a senior, Von didn't have to take gym. He hadn't played since last year and really had no idea how hard he could throw that nasty rubber ball now.

But wouldn't it be fun to find out?

"Yeah, sure, Coach," Von said. "I'll play."

"Excellent. Now we got a game." Minot gave a blast on his whistle. "Freshmen—north wall. Sophomores—south wall." The coach tossed a ball to each opposing side. "Juniors—you too, Daley, over there with the freshmen. Von, you're with the sophomores."

A collective groan rose up from the group trotting to the south wall as Von jumped from the stage and joined the pack of underclassmen spreading out beneath the RedHawks scoreboard. Thom Jorelle, a face Von recognized from Mr. Blodgett's art class, tossed the ball his way.

"Here you go, Von," he said with forced familiarity. "Let's get at 'em."

Von caught the ball on one bounce and nodded his thanks to Jorelle. The kid looked like he was about to wet his pants. The hero-worship thing got old after a while, Von thought, quickly turning away (but hey, it beat being a nobody). He bounced the springy ball off the hardwood floor and palmed it with one hand, relishing the elastic texture of its thick pebbled surface. Oh yeah, he was going to do some damage with this.

Two shrill peals from Minot's whistle cut through the air and the teams scrambled into position. Von advanced to the half-court line, weapon in hand and arm cocked. Shane Daley, the opposition's designated stud, stepped from the pack and hovered over the free-throw circle, keeping a respectable distance.

The two eyed one another warily for a moment before Daley, rumored to possess the nastiest slap-shot in the city, suddenly cut loose with a quick, half-cocked release that almost caught Von off-guard.

Realizing he wouldn't have time to throw, Von simply dropped his ball, freeing up both hands for his defense. He caught the missile at eye level before his own ball hit the hardwood floor. With his hands stinging slightly from the impact, he brought the ball down from his face and watched Daley trot off to the side, shaking his head. Their only threat was gone.

Von knelt down and scooped his own ball up from the floor, palming it effortlessly in his powerful hand.

Now he had two.

Had there been another viable gun on his team, Von would have handed one off and set up a deadly double-throw. Given the sorry state of his teammates however, he prowled along the half-court boundary, a ball in each hand, both barrels loaded. His victims scattered, the larger specimens pushing their smaller brethren into the front-line like human shields.

Von wound up, making no pretense of his intentions and let the first ball fly. It whistled through the air like a comet, parting the sea of terrified underclassmen before striking the retractable wooden bleachers with a sickening whack of rubbery thunder.

There was no scramble to pick up the loose ball bouncing on the gymnasium hardwood, only the reverent silence wrought by dread. Even Coach Minot needed a moment to recover, before he laughed and barked, "Somebody better pick that up or you'll all be running laps until the end of the semester."

The ball rolled precariously closer to the half-court line where Von stood, poised to throw again should some brave soul attempt to make a move on it. Antonio Garcia, a wiry forward on the freshman soccer team, broke from the pack, zigzagging to half-court like a crazed water bug.

Von drew a bead and released.

Garcia dove to the hardwood and scooped up the dead ball coming out of a nifty somersault, the wind from the errant missile still fresh in his right ear. Von's throw, unimpeded by Garcia's head, struck Dana Perillo square in his skinny chest, knocking the little freshman off his feet. Garcia, playing it safe, scrambled to the opposite end of the court and threw a line-shot that took one of Von's teammates out at the knees.

It had taken a good ten minutes to vanquish the elusive soccer star, but when the dust had cleared, the lone survivors on the hardwood court were none other than Von and the diminutive computer genius, Lester Lesko. Lester's raw fear, combined with his all but translucent frame, had made him nearly impossible to hit in a crowd. Over and over, the big defensive back threw, unable to nail the wispy bookworm, but wearing him down, growing closer with every shot. Smelling blood, Von's teammates began to chant as Von prowled the half-court line, both balls in hand.

"Delete the geek! Delete the geek! Delete the geek!"

Lester skittered along the wall of retracted bleachers, his legs growing weak with fear. Now the freshmen and juniors— Lester's own teammates, joined in, the taunts getting uglier by the moment.

"Yoo-hoooo . . . Lester, you little pusssyyy!"

Von tensed and threw a decoy shot, knowing that Lester was far too elusive to be taken down with a single projectile. Sensing where the little flea might jump, he released the second ball a split second later, cursing aloud as it sailed a hair over Lester's head as the boy dove for cover. The ball crashed into the drapery of hinged planking, rattling the bleachers right down to the steel bolts that held them to the wall.

Lester lay cowering on the gym floor, his eyes darting madly, following the path of the cursed red balls as they rolled back to half-court, back to his tormentor. The early bell, obnoxious and blaring, cut through the sweat and hate-soaked air of the gym, falling on Lester's saucer-like ears like notes from Gideon's Trumpet. Tears, born of shame and fear, but now sprung from joy, welled up full in Lester's eyes. He raised his head triumphantly, unable to suppress the grin on his face.

He'd made it.

The ear-splitting peal of Coach Minot's whistle rang out as Lester got to his knees. It was not the long "hit the showers" whistle he had been praying for, but a short staccato series of angry, halting blasts that at once filled him with dread.

"Yo!" the dark man bellowed above the groans and mumbling of the retreating barbarians. "No one's going anywhere. This ain't over till it's over!"

The groans erupted into cheers upon hearing Nero's words.

"We have five minutes," Minot continued. "We can finish this in *two*. The problem is," he explained, tossing two more of the hated rubber balls onto the gym floor, "we have a serious shortage of *balls* out on the floor." He looked at Lester, making no attempt to hide his contempt for the miserable physical specimen. "I think we're two short!"

Von marched, amid the laughter and the cheers, to center court, where he stopped the errant roll of the two additional balls with his foot. He stood there in the spotlight that he had always yearned for, the spotlight he had come to love so quickly. With theatrical indolence, Von laid one ball down so that he had three lined up and waiting at his feet. He prowled the half-court line, aping Lester's nervous pacing like a cheetah toying with a zebra in tall grass. The chant, like music, filled his ears.

"Von! Von! Von! Von . . ."

He threw low, as hard as he could, missing Lester's knees by scant inches. He darted back and scooped up two more balls and launched them in rapid succession with a much deadlier intent. The first ball flew past Lester's nose as he turned to run and slapped the bleachers with a deafening splat. The second missile found its target, hitting Lester square in the side of his face. Lester's thick, black-framed glasses flew high in the air as the boy crumpled backwards and fell to the hardwood.

Minot's whistle, long and long overdue, rang in Lester's ears as he rolled on the floor. He could still hear the cheering.

"Okay, that's it! Game, point, match! Hit the showers!" The coach grinned at his star DB, standing limply at the half-court line. "Nice job, killer," he winked.

So why did he feel so shitty?

Chapter 26

The first raindrops were still more than an hour away when Dan Jacobson pulled his substantial bulk off the aluminum planking and made his way down the bleacher seats to the exit gate of Ridgewood Field.

He had seen enough.

It wasn't just the score—28–0 at the half—that made the game so unbearable as much as the ridiculous ease with which the RedHawks had built the early lead. They had run the ball seemingly at will, piling up over close to two-hundred yards rushing in the first half alone and controlling the clock for a staggering twenty-one minutes, thirty-six seconds. To make matters worse, most of the yardage had come off the left side of the line where Jake had been anchored for the last two years. Houghwat had plugged Tom Carmody in at left guard and Steponic had moved over to Jake's tackle spot—where he looked way too comfortable. Jake had been hoping they would tank without him in the line-up. He really did. Serve 'em right. Instead, the rushing game had been so dominating that Starret had thrown only one pass the entire first half—a little dink screen in the flat that Matt McGee had broken for a thirty-yard gain after being sprung by a crunching block from *Vo-nos-o-vich*. Vonosovich.

It was the name—that name constantly blaring from the loudspeaker—more than anything else that had driven Jake from the stadium.

Jake hated Sergei Vonosovich more than he hated anyone—and Jake hated a lot of people. That rat was on the juice. He would bet his life on that. No one got that big that fast. He wasn't fooling anyone with that *diabetes* crap either.

143

Jake's aunt had diabetes and that freaky green juice Vonosovich had in that vial didn't look like any insulin he'd ever seen. Nah, he was on the junk and whatever he was shooting was doing the job. As much as it pained Jake to admit it, the skinny little dweeb had packed on some major beef over the summer, and it wasn't just gym muscle either. He was the fastest guy on the team—faster than Musconi and faster than Curtis DuPree, who took State last year in the 220. If Vonosovich had any decency at all he would have shared the stuff with the rest of them—would have been a team player. Not that Jake felt any camaraderie with those turncoats right now. They seemed to be doing just fine without him.

Jake quickened his pace toward the stadium gates. He had to get back on that field and fast, or he would never see his starting job again—even when (if) he did hand Kroc's paper in. As Jake passed the refreshment stand, he saw Jonathan Howell, wearing his prissy band uniform, emerge from one of the Port-a-Johns along the fence.

Howell nodded at the bigger man, obviously unnerved by the unexpected encounter.

"Hi, Jake," he said, standing in the threshold of the fiber-glass enclosure. He held the door halfway closed, giving the brute plenty of room to pass. "Good game, huh?"

Jacobson stopped in his tracks and turned around. "What did you say?"

Howell swallowed. Why didn't he just nod at the big lummox and leave it at that? "Nothing. I just said *good game*."

Jacobson advanced on him, the pent-up rage and frustration of the slow-witted burning in his dim eyes. "What would you know about it, puss?" he asked. "You ever play football?"

Howell, fearing for his life, backed further into the stall. "No—uh, yeah. I watch a lot. I—"

Jake's open hand thudded into Jonathan Howell's narrow chest, landing squarely on the scripted *R* of his pressed white band tunic. The impact knocked Jonathan back onto the toilet seat in a crumpled heap.

"Stick to what you know, faggot." Jake smiled and slammed the door of the Port-a-John shut. "And you know jack!" A roar came up from the crowd in the stands. Sounded like another Ridgewood touchdown. He looked around for good measure. No one in sight. Jake tipped the Port-a-John on its side, letting it crash to the pavement with a thud and splash of chemicals and human waste. He could hear Jonathan Howell's horrified and unbelieving screams of protest as he calmly walked away.

Good game, huh?

He showed him.

He would show them all.

PART III

THE FALL

Chapter 27

Being the male of the species, Von instinctively reached for the remote control, despite the fact he had never operated a DVD player in his life. Haley settled in next to him, a freshly popped bowl of Orville Redenbacher sat on the coffee table in front of them, flanked by Haley's Diet Coke and the Mountain Dew she had bought specially for Von.

"This is a nice little set-up you have down here," Von said absently as he studied the monolithic slab of plastic in his hand. He thumbed a button and the picture tube suddenly buzzed with electric snow and white noise.

"You changed the video feed, Einstein," Haley said, pulling out from under the crook of his arm. "The little wheel lets you choose the options. Here," she said reaching for the remote, "let me show you."

Von playfully held the remote control high out of Haley's reach. "Man always controls the remote," he said. He fumbled through several screens after getting the picture back on line, landing on the options menu through sheer luck. "Let's see, subtitles—no, widescreen format—yes, director's cut—*big* yes." He leaned forward and grabbed a handful of popcorn, his eyes fixed on the studio credits unfolding on the 46-inch screen. "Oh man, this is gonna be so cool. *T-2* is my favorite movie of all time. It's the role Arnold was born to play."

Haley smiled. It did her good to see him so happy. "I thought *Goodfellas* was your favorite movie of all time."

"Favorite *DeNiro* movie," he said, correcting her. "*Terminator 2* is my favorite *Ah-nold* movie."

Haley laughed at his Schwarzenegger impersonation as he explained further.

"You can't take a DeNiro movie and an Ah-nold movie and compare them," Von said. "They exist for totally different reasons. DeNiro is simply the greatest actor that ever lived—period. Ah-nold is the greatest bodybuilder that ever lived but he'll never win an Oscar. What makes him great is he doesn't take himself too seriously. You can tell by watching him onscreen that he's having fun, sort of taking you along for the ride."

Haley looked at him, so pleased he wasn't just another dumb jock. "Thank you for that insightful analysis, Mr. Ebert. Maybe you can get your own TV show someday."

"Maybe when I retire from the NFL," he said through a mouthful of popcorn. "That wouldn't be a bad gig."

Haley looked at him. "The NFL? I thought you were going to be a writer."

"Who says I can't do both?" he asked. "Look at Peter Gent. He played for the Cowboys and then wrote a couple of books. One of them—*North Dallas Forty*—was made into a movie. One of the better football movies—not that there's a lot of them—and a pretty good book."

Haley shrugged. "I don't know. I guess. You just never mentioned it before."

"Well, it's not like it's some impossible dream," Von said. "I figure I'll play five, six years, make a few million," he pulled her close and gave her a squeeze, "set you up in a mansion with a butler and a maid . . . some tennis lessons—and then retire. Then I could spend all my time writing."

"Hmmmm . . ." Haley said, snuggling in close under the crook of his arm, "I guess that sounds like a pretty good plan." On the television screen, a naked Arnold Schwarzenegger materialized from a sphere of blue static electricity. "I like the mansion and butler part."

"Yeah, I kinda thought you would," Von replied, staring

at the television. "Now check this out. It's kind of subtle. Arnold is scanning all the bikes parked in front of this bar. See, he passes up the Honda . . . the Yamaha . . . and zooms in on the Harley Fat Boy. That's because—"

The heavy fall of footsteps down the bare wooden stairs cut Von short. Haley instinctively skittered out of his embrace, putting a good foot between the two of them as her father's voice rang out from the landing behind them.

"Well there he is," John McBride said, smiling at the two of them, "the pride and joy of Ridgewood High."

Haley and Von both turned to look.

John McBride stood at the foot of the stairs, clutching the incredibly thick Sunday edition of the *Chicago Tribune*. He was dressed for a night out, crisp Haggar slacks with a serious pleat and a mock turtleneck beneath a tan sport coat. Von thought he looked like a writer fresh off a dust jacket photo shoot.

"Hi, Daddy," Haley said. "You look very handsome."

John McBride smiled at his daughter. "Thank you, dear."

Von nodded. "Hello, Mr. McBride. Big night out?"

"Dinner and show at the Martinique," he said, thumbing through the hefty stack of newspaper. "I'm not much for going out on a Sunday night. I'd much rather be on the couch with my feet up and *The Simpsons* on the box. However, Haley's mother has this ticket package . . . ah—here we are." He plucked a section from the center of the newspaper and set the bulk of it on the end table. "Five star final—late sports edition."

Von's eyes lit up. Could it be in the paper already? The reporter last night had told him Tuesday at the earliest.

John McBride opened the section up and began to read:

"VONOSOVICH HAS REDHAWKS FLYING HIGH.

151

Former powerhouse back on top after years of mediocrity. By Lonnie Bell Staff Reporter.

"After only five weeks, Ridgewood High has emerged as the team to beat in the state's ultra-competitive 6A division. The big red machine has rolled to a perfect 5–0 record. The only blemish on their imperial defense being a chip shot field goal early on in their season opener against third-ranked Eisenhower. After demolishing Eisenhower 38–3, the RedHawks have not allowed a single point, beating Bremen 42–0 and Reavis 37–0. The Blue Island Whalers fell 33–0, their vaunted offense failing to produce a single first down until late in the third quarter when many of the RedHawks starters were on the bench. Last night at hostile Andrews field in Oak Forest, the big red machine demolished the Bulldogs 28–0 in a romp that wasn't nearly as close as the score indicated.

"The gaudy offensive numbers may look impressive but anyone who has seen them in action knows the RedHawks dominance begins and ends with defense. New defensive coordinator Mike Minot, who spent several years as a safety with the Kansas City Chiefs, has installed a new defensive scheme, dubbed 'the Monster,' that has left division rivals reeling and opposing coaches scratching their heads.

"Disguised as a 4–3, the RedHawks defense is actually a variation on a standard 3–4 with the weakside linebacker lined up at the end position in a rush-crouch. Two linebackers, Ryan Amberson and Owen Daniels, returning seniors with all-state honors, are stacked over the tight end, shifting the four-man front into an 'under' alignment, overloading the weak side of the offense."

Haley, amused by her father's renewed passion for the high school game, but weary of the technical jargon, rolled her eyes. "Dad . . ."

John McBride held his hand up to silence her. "Hold on, honey. Here comes the good part."

Monsterman

"The middle linebacker assumes the strong safety role, leaving the strong safety or 'Monsterman' free to roam and wreak havoc. And wreak havoc he does. The Monsterman is the key to the scheme. He must be athletic enough to cover the flat from sideline to sideline, fast enough to cover a wideout or rush the passer, and big enough to come up and stuff the run."

John McBride paused a moment and raised his voice an octave before reading on.

"Sergei Vonosovich, a 6'2", 210 pound senior fills the bill and more. Vonosovich is averaging twenty-two tackles a game and has four picks, two of which he has returned for touchdowns. He has terrorized opposing quarterbacks, racking up eleven sacks in five games. In last week's 33–0 drubbing of Blue Island, Vonosovich knocked all three Whaler quarterbacks out of the game, forcing Coach Corey McGrath to finish the game with emergency QB Todd Prazak, a tight end.

"A perennial back-up for three years, Vonosovich has emerged from nowhere to become the dominant player in Illinois Class 6A. Vonosovich owes his late success to a rigorous off-season conditioning program and Minot's unique scheme.

" 'I had a late growth spurt,' explained Vonosovich. 'I grew four inches over the summer and packed on about fifty pounds. In addition to my workout routine, I worked construction six days a week over the summer. By the time two-a-days rolled around in August, I was ready to break into the starting line-up. I was just lucky Coach Minot gave me a shot.'

" 'The kid is a coach's dream,' Minot said. 'He arrives early, stays late, and is a born leader. He raises the level of play of everyone on the field.'

"Indeed. On the other side of the ball, RedHawks head Coach Tom Houghwat has plugged Vonosovich in at both tight end and

153

H-back. Behind a revamped offensive line, the RedHawks are averaging over 300 yards a game on the ground. Running back Curtis DuPree says most of his 842 rushing yards have come courtesy of Vonosovich. 'I just follow Von around the corner or through the gaps,' DuPree says. 'It's almost as though people can't wait to get out of his way.'

"About the only people not scrambling to get out of Vonosovich's way are the college scouts lining up to talk to him when the RedHawks season ends. This reporter is guessing they will have to wait until late December, when the 6A title game wraps up in Champaign-Urbana."

Haley's father lowered the paper and looked at Von. "Anyone contact you yet, Von? College scouts, I mean?"

"I've gotten a few letters," Von said. "Coach Houghwat doesn't want the recruiters coming around until after the season. Says it's too distracting."

"That's good," John McBride nodded. "He's right. Those guys will come by and offer you the world. You have to be careful. Make sure your education comes first."

Von nodded. "Yes sir."

"You know," he said, trying his best not to sound condescending, "if you ever need . . . well, advice, someone to talk to or anything, you can come to me." John McBride knew Von's father was dead. He had made it a point to do a little checking up on his daughter's suitors.

Haley groaned, "Geez, Dad."

Von nodded again. "Thank you, sir, I will."

"You kids have a good time. We'll be home before ten." Haley's father smiled and turned to go up the stairs.

"Mr. McBride?" Von asked.

"Yeah, Von?"

"I was wondering, if you didn't need that newspaper . . ."

He flipped the sports section to Von. "I've got five more copies upstairs. Just leave me one to show the guys at work."

They watched him ascend the stairwell and waited until the door closed behind him.

"He really likes you," Haley said turning to Von.

"Yeah," Von replied, looking at the photo of himself splashed across the front page of the *Tribune*'s Prep Watch page. "I'm glad. I'm sure he's pretty cautious about who's holding your hand after that last . . . well, that last guy."

Haley lowered her head. Deep inside she still carried the shame of putting her family though hell because of her relationship with Dominic Teresi. The crying, the sleepless nights, the phone calls, the fist-fight—her father and Teresi rolling around in the street . . .

Von saw that he had upset her and hated himself for it. "Oh, babe, I'm sorry. I didn't mean anything by it. Geez, I'm such a jerk." He put a hand on her shoulder. "Forget about it. It wasn't your fault. How were you supposed to know the guy was a psycho?"

Haley could not meet his eyes. There was so much she had not told him—so much she would not tell anyone. She had enjoyed the adoration Dominic had lavished upon her. She had ignored the warning signs as it grew into obsession. Of course it was her fault.

"We all make mistakes, Haley," Von said, as if he had read her mind. His powerful hand slid beneath her chin, soft as a whisper and raised her head, bringing her eyes in line with his. "It's over now, babe. It's in the past. Teresi's in jail and when he gets out, he won't know where to find you. It's time to move on. Forget about—" He stopped. Something in her eyes . . . "What is it?"

The sobs came before the words, forcing them out of her throat in a croak. "He's back."

Von looked at her stunned. "What? When?"

"He's back," she said. "About a month ago. He was following me. After school. I didn't know what to do. I was so scared. I pulled over in the Steak N' Shake parking lot by the mall. He started talking all his crazy talk again—how much he loves me—how we were meant to be together forever . . ." She started to sob again, uncontrollably. "Oh God, he's crazy!"

Von held her by her shoulders, squaring her up, forcing her to regain her composure while he struggled with his own. "What happened? Did he . . . touch you?"

"No," Haley stammered. "This guy—a biker—scared him away. But he's not really gone. He never is. I see him sometimes. Driving past the school. In my rearview mirror. Out of the corner of my eye. Sometimes I don't know if he's there or not. Oh God, I think *I* might be going crazy!"

"Have you told anyone? Your father? The police?"

"No," Haley said, shaking her head from side to side. "I didn't want to tell my parents. They're so happy now. And the police—they can't do anything until . . . until it's too late!"

Von brushed her hair back out of her teary eyes. He spoke clearly, his words measured and concise. "Good. Now you listen to me, Haley. You don't have to worry about Dominic Teresi anymore, do you understand? Look at me. If he ever comes near you again I will put him in the hospital. And I swear, by all that's holy in this universe, if he ever lays a hand on you, I will *kill* him. Look at me. Do you believe me?"

Haley looked into his dark watery eyes. Yes, he was speaking the truth, and she loved him for it. "Yes, I believe you."

He brought her in close and she melted into his embrace, finding solace in the contours of his hard body. She surrendered to the easy and natural cohesion of their forms melded together like two halves that had become whole, loving the smell of his hair and the familiar musky scent of his after-shave.

The universe had become very small for Haley and Von, the basement reduced to a warm dark womb, lit only by the glow from a television neither was watching. They lay like that for a long time, speaking without the burden of words, their love confirmed each passing moment by the thrum of their unified heartbeats and the steady hum of contentedness that had become bliss.

The gentle nuzzling and soft, slow, kisses had caught fire by the time Arnold Schwarzenegger's Terminator had completed the last stage of its pre-ordained mission. Their coupling was a duet for the ages intermingled with kisses both sweet and soft and long and lusty.

Clothing lay in a heap at the base of the couch, the only reminder of the furious blur of disrobement that had taken place scant seconds before. Haley halted Von's frenzied efforts to climb out of his jeans, slowing the pace like a seasoned trainer breaking in a young colt. He stepped out of the jeans and looked down at her on the couch—Haley McBride, the most beautiful girl in school and the love of his life, clad only in a pair of white cotton panties.

He took charge, abandoning all thought, guided only by animal instinct and the pursuit of their mutual pleasure.

His body felt as if it were on fire. She could feel individual muscle groupings in his torso quiver and throb beneath her fingers, reminding her of small animals trapped in a gunny-sack. A whisper, a scream. A howl. The wind? Red eyes, pin-point lasers in the darkness. The sudden stab of pain in her shoulder brought her back and Haley woke as if from a dream, a desperate gasp for air escaping from her lips.

Von rolled off and looked at her, his glazed eyes wild and

scared. "I'm sorry. Oh, Haley, oh . . . I'm sorry . . ."

Von ran his finger tentatively along her trapezius, across the oily sheath of blood coating her shoulder and upper back. She felt it at the same moment he did; a puncture wound, small, but deep, and perfectly round.

Von held his finger up, the blood—too much of it, black in the dim light of the basement. He reached over and clicked on the lamp on the side table. Haley gasped upon seeing his face in the harsh and sudden reality of the artificial light. Blood—her blood—trickled from the side of his mouth and stained his white teeth.

"I think I may have bitten you."

Chapter 28

Dominic Teresi had nearly nodded off—had nearly fallen asleep on his watch—when the side door of his girlfriend's house swung open and the jock walked out and ambled down Haley's driveway toward the street. How long had he been in there? Three—almost four hours?

Dominic bolted up in his seat, galvanized by the rage brought on by her betrayal.

The whore. After all he had done for her.

Dominic reached for the Israeli Night Vision goggles on the seat next to him and quickly scanned the McBride house, searching for any sign of the cheating bitch in the windows. The motion-sensor light above the side door switched off just as the glass-block windows sheathing the upstairs bathroom came to life with a hazy yellow glow.

A pathetic moan of despair welled up from the tortured depths of Dominic Teresi's twisted soul. Oh good God in heaven. How could she *do* this to him? He must have brainwashed her or something. Haley never knew what was good for her. She could never see that he was the only one in the world for her.

Dominic trained the glasses on the jock. He watched him make his way down the street to the end of the block and turn at the corner. That's okay. Dominic was in no hurry. He knew where loverboy lived. He was a good three miles from home and he was hoofing it tonight. Dominic thought it was unusual Haley didn't give him a ride home and the notion that they might have had a fight filled him with a malevolent joy.

The light in the upstairs bathroom continued to burn, the

glass-block and vented windows denying Dominic a clear view of his beloved. She could be in there for a while. Haley loved to take long showers. Sometimes Dominic would sit slouched in his car for as long as an hour, watching her blurry silhouette move about behind the translucent portal, tending to her body, shaving her legs, painting her nails—all the things they do . . .

Dominic switched on the ignition and the Grand Prix fired to life, its tenderly stroked motor and glass-pack mufflers just a little too loud for the quiet streets of the new subdivision. He motored away from the curb and leisurely cruised past Haley's house, careful not to open the secondary throttle plates on the Holley four-barrel carburetor until he turned the corner and headed east to the bridge.

There was no telling what she had told him, how much he knew about the two of them, so Dominic took the long route over the Cal-Sag channel back to the other side of town.

Ridgewood was essentially two small villages existing as one, each side seeming to tolerate the other like an incompatible couple staying together for the sake of convenience. The old Ridgewood, incorporated in 1916, was bounded by 159th Street to the north and 183rd Street at the south end. Until 1972 its western boundary ended at the Calumet-Saginaw channel, a dirty, snaking, freight pipeline that stretched from Calumet City clear north into Michigan. The flat prairies and farmland west of the channel were scooped up by developers in the housing boom of the early seventies. After a lot of smoky back-room deals, Ridgewood had annexed the unincorporated land and built the new high school with a state loan and a federal grant. The new Ridgewood, with its strip malls and high-rent, cul-de-sac subdivisions, was a sharp contrast to the one hundred year-old houses and quaint main street business district that lay on the east side of the bridge.

Where *he* lived.

Dominic knew the street, knew the exact house. He knew the route he would take home and he knew the stretch of woods separating the channel from the residential district was where he would take him down.

Von paused a moment at the top of the Cicero Avenue bridge, caught unaware by the sudden wave of vertigo. He stared into the black waters of the Cal-Sag channel below, gripping the flat metal of the handrail to steady himself. His head was pounding from the onslaught of outside stimuli; the cars, too many of them, speeding across the bridge behind him; the scent of small game, rabbits, squirrels, raccoons, opossums, skirting through the woods to the east; the maddening, and delicious, and nauseating smells wafting downwind from Karen's La Cucina Italian restaurant to the west . . .

He looked down at the brackish puddle of water in which he was standing and realized with horror and disgust that it was his own saliva.

A puddle of it.

The vomit rose up violently, spraying his pant leg and shoes before he could lurch to the rail and deposit the next wave into the murky depths of the Cal-Sag. The churning in his stomach did not pass with the voiding of his evening meal, but intensified, the fluttering and convulsions gripping his chest now as he dropped to his knees and gasped for air.

He had bitten Haley. They had made love and he had bitten her—*had broken her skin.* He had no recollection of the incident and had been scouring his brain like a drunk on the wrong end of a lost weekend, trying to fill the gaps in his memory. He wished he could forget the way she had looked at him when he had switched on the light, the initial revulsion and shock he had seen in her eyes. It had passed quickly, but it was there. She had accepted his awkward apology but had refused his offer to tend to the small puncture wound. Just go, she had said, barely able to meet his eyes. Call me tomorrow.

Just go.

Von forced himself to his feet, aware of the spectacle he must present to the passing cars and mindful of the heavy police traffic along Cicero Avenue. He stumbled forward, aided by the pitch of the bridge, eager to make it into the safety of the woods. He could lie down in the grass, in the cool grass and look at the stars, look at the moon . . .

The black Grand Prix pulled into the access road skirting Castle Woods Forest Preserve and cut its lights as it rounded the first corner. Dominic Teresi peered through the windshield, almost laughing with glee when he spotted the figure up ahead stumbling along the curb. It looked nothing like the imposing stud he had spied on the practice field at Ridgewood high, the big football hero who had stolen his girlfriend.

No, he was drunk—or better yet, sick. This was going to easier than he had thought.

And more fun.

Dominic idled along slowly, staying a good three hundred feet behind his target, biding his time. When he saw Sergei Vonosovich drop to his knees, for the first time, he hit the gas pedal hard.

Von had heard the low rumble of the glass-pack mufflers shortly after turning into Castle Woods. He knew, as any animal would know, that he was being stalked, and instinctively sought out the shelter of his den. There was a narrow

162

footpath some thirty yards ahead, barely discernible through the overgrowth of fall foliage, that wound through the peninsula of the woods' southern border all the way to the to railroad tracks that ran behind his back yard. Known only to mountain-bikers and the local kids, it was a convenient and well-worn shortcut into old Ridgewood that shaved a good fifteen minutes off the pedestrian walkway that ran along Cicero Avenue.

And now it just might save his life.

The last major convulsion preceding the metamorphosis hit him just as he spotted the giant willow that guarded the mouth of the path. Von screamed, unable to believe the pain as his spine stretched, nearly doubling its length by the time he hit the ground. His tailbone broke through the skin of his lower back and pitched him on his stomach, its bony tip extending and dancing along the hard surface of the street like a live wire. Von heard the roar of the Grand Prix's 455 motor bearing down on him before it was drowned out by the unearthly howling that seemed to be coming from all directions. It was not until the car was almost upon him that he realized the sound was coming from his own throat.

Von jumped at the last possible instant, the hood of the car clipping his hind leg and sending him tumbling across the roof. Dominic Teresi hit the brakes, sending the Grand Prix into a wild skid. Dominic stared in white knuckled disbelief at the spider web network of cracks emanating from the point of impact on his windshield. He blinked twice, not quite trusting his eyes as much as he did just minutes ago.

"Damn! That's five hundred easy!" he said, sizing up the damage to his car. A smile broke across his face when he noticed the blood splashed across the top of the windshield, black like chocolate syrup in the light of the full moon. "But worth every penny." He laughed and reached down under his front seat for the police-issue nightstick that always rested there.

Time to finish the job.

Dominic switched off the ignition and stepped around to the back of the car.

The football hero was nowhere to be found.

Dominic tightened his grip on the nightstick and walked around the car in a wide circle. The only sound was the slow tick of the Grand Prix's motor cooling off and the distant hum of traffic off of Cicero Avenue.

Even the crickets had stopped chirping.

"Come out, come out, wherever you are . . ." Dominic laughed. But it was a sick laugh, weak and born of fear. "Get back out here boy, and take it like—" He stopped suddenly. There was a shoe, one single shoe, lying in the street, some ten feet behind his car. "Knocked him clear out of his shoes," Dominic giggled. He walked over and picked it up, inspecting it in the moonlight. The giggling stopped.

When Dominic and his brother were just kids they had placed an M-80 firecracker in an old gym shoe they had found in the trash. The explosion had blown the front out of the shoe, leaving only tattered canvas and smoking rubber.

This was a fairly new Nike running shoe and it looked a lot worse. The heavily padded toe lay dangling from the reinforced instep, shredded, as if from knives, from the *inside out*. Dominic tossed the shoe down, unnerved by what could have possibly done such a thing. He ran back to the Grand Prix and popped open the trunk, pulling his flashlight and a large Bowie knife from the toolbox. There was a small puddle of blood, starting at the skidmark where he had found the shoe, trailing off into the grass. Dominic knew that he had better find this kid and fast. He had done three months in county and he had sworn he would never go back. He would kill him before he would allow that to happen.

Dominic followed the blood all the way to the mouth of the footpath. He picked his way along carefully, the trail of blood growing more scant as he made his way deeper into the woods. He was standing in a thicket, strobing the flashlight across the forest floor where the path seemed to end altogether, when he heard it.

A baneful howl, long and horrible and unlike anything he had ever heard. He dropped the flashlight and fell to his knees, gripped by an instant and debilitating fear.

It was not a dog. Dogs did not sound like that.

Coyotes. There were plenty of coyotes in the area. They were overrunning the state. Hell, they had even caught one in downtown Chicago last year—right on Division Street. That's what it had to—

The awful wail rose up again. It pierced the night air like a saber ripping through a nylon curtain. It was closer now.

Dominic scrambled for the flashlight. It lay helter-skelter on the forest floor, its powerful high beam shining high into the trees like a distress signal. He quickly turned it off and huddled into a ball, making himself small and inconspicuous in the darkness. He sat there pressed against a tree, trembling like a child under the covers, hiding from the bogeyman. He almost cried out when the next howl welled up, angry and earsplitting—so loud that it seemed to rattle the trees all around him.

Oh sweet Jesus Mary Mother of Christ.

It was right on top of him.

A twig snapped—off to his left.

A tiny mewling sound escaped his throat. Jumping to his feet, Dominic scooped up the flashlight and ran blindly to his immediate right.

Branches and thistle lashed, wicked and thorny, across his

face as he ran, propelled by sheer momentum and blind fear. Dominic's foot caught the underside of an exposed tree root, pitching him high into the air. He did not even realize he had been screaming until he hit the ground, limp and disorientated by the dark silence all around him.

The trees broke directly in front of him and the nightmare became flesh. It stood before him perfectly still, magnificent and horrible all at once, illuminated by the light of the full moon. Dominic knelt on the forest floor and simply stared at the creature, so awestruck he could neither move nor speak.

It stood well over seven feet tall, but it looked even larger to Dominic from his vantage point on the leafy ground. Although it stood erect, the creature's anatomy suggested it would be more adept at moving about on all fours like a great ape. The beast's legs were squat and powerful, covered by a shiny coat of short hair that grew more profuse along the hindquarters. A small trickle of blood ran from the wound on its bony calf, matting and staining the thick hair a dark black. The thighs were heavy with muscle, like the flanks of a bull mastiff, tapering gracefully at the hip where they met the trunk. Most of the creature's great length came from its torso. It was the most humanoid aspect of the creature's anatomy, particularly around the chest and shoulders. The breastplate, dark and shiny, bore only a subtle coat of hair and so it was all the way down the impossibly long column of abdominal muscles until the hair again grew coarse and dark around its pubic region. A sartorial mane of luxurious fur cloaked the beast's upper back, turning long and bushy along the underside of the front legs—or as they seemed when it stood erect like this, its arms.

One of those arms reached out now as if in slow motion, each movement deliberate and concise. The claw, a horrible marriage between a human hand and an eagle's talon, finally came to rest beneath Dominic Teresi's chin. A long leathery finger traced its way along the tender flesh of his exposed throat. It was at that moment that Dominic lost control of his bowels.

The beast snorted and its great head cantilevered forward, extending from the neck and shoulders like an entity unto itself, riding a rail of muscle along a track of bone. Wet puffs of steam belched from its leathery black nose, twitching only inches from Dominic's face. Dominic looked up the length of the wolf's snout into its red eyes and saw something between amusement and disgust flashing behind the cold indifference of instinct and hunger. The ears, long, pointy, and nearly translucent in the light of the moon, cocked back suddenly along the top of its great shaggy head.

Suddenly the werewolf scooped him up off of the ground, the horrifically sharp claws rending the flesh from Dominic's arms as it shook him like a rag doll. A blast of air, smelling of canine and rotten meat, hit Dominic in the face. Tumultuous, deafening growling filled his head, so loud he thought he must surely be inside the creature by now. When it finally stopped a few short seconds later, Dominic blinked through the tears and snot covering his face just in time to see the thing open its jaws wider than he would have ever thought possible.

He closed his eyes as the horrible pressure crushed his trapezius and the teeth tore through skin and bone, deep into the muscle of his chest and back. The thing pulled its great head back, leaving a horrifying void of forest air where a good portion of Dominic's upper body used to be.

It champed the quivering tissue back in its jaws where it disappeared down its gullet with a long wet swallow. As the numbing properties of shock finally began to settle in, Dominic could see bloody little shreds of himself clinging to the werewolf's teeth, pulsating and glistening in the monster's black drool.

The pressure was lifted from the shattered bones of his right arm as the creature released its grip. He felt himself being lowered back to the ground, dimly aware of the cool breeze flowing through the gaping cavity in his torso. He saw the creature cock its great hairy arm back, like a baseball player digging in for a juicy pitch.

The stars pinwheeled above him and then the forest floor below. The tops of the trees flashed into view and then again, the moon and stars above. Dominic's last thought as his head sailed high into the night sky was of the great wolf walking beneath this moon and what a wild and wonderful thing that was.

Chapter 29

Lorelei Vonosovich stood in her kitchen window watching the sun break over the expanse of trees that marked the easternmost boundary of Castle Woods. Anxiety had kept sleep at bay more than the pot of coffee she had brewed at four A.M., shortly after waking up on the couch and scurrying down to Von's room, only to find it still empty, as it was when she had arrived home at midnight. She had nearly called the McBride house but thought better of it. She had yet to meet Haley's parents and a harried phone call at two in the morning was not the best way to make a first impression.

Instead, she had called the hospitals. St. Francis, Palos Community, and South Central. Nothing, thank God. Good thing for him, because she was going to kill him when he got home.

He had probably run into Donny Musconi or one of those other wild kids from the football team. Von was a good kid— she had been lucky so far, but boys will be boys. They liked their beer and their roughhousing. He was probably crashed out over at Jason's house or . . .

Bullshit.

He would have called. He would have left a message on the machine. Von knew he had a ten o'clock curfew on school nights. Something was wrong. Something was horribly wrong.

He had been in a car wreck.

He had been arrested.

He was fulfilling the Vonosovich family . . .

She cut the last thought off and reached for the phone. Screw first impressions. It was nearly five-thirty. The

McBrides should be out of bed, and if not, too bad. She would at least find out what time he had left last night.

Lorelei was punching up the number when she looked out the window. The phone fell from her hands, and crashed to the floor, taking her "Mom" coffee mug with it for good measure. She stared, not wanting to believe it could happen all over again.

That was her son walking out of the woods. Von was shirtless and near naked save for the tattered remains of the blue jeans cinched around his waist. He was covered in a slick sheen of morning dew, as if he had slept on the grass and had just woke up. As he crossed the tracks of the J&T Rock Island Line, she could see his shoes—or what was left of them—dangling from his right hand. Von scampered over the tracks, his bare feet raw and tender on the coarse stone of the rail-bed. Their eyes met as he crested the last rail and she saw not guilt, but confusion and bewilderment.

Lorelei met him at the door, still refusing to consider the unthinkable. "Where were you?" she asked sternly, looking him up and down. He was disheveled and she could see a spectacular purple and yellow bruise on his left calf through the torn fabric of his Levi's.

No blood. Thank God.

Von stood on the back porch, every muscle in his body groaning with the familiar pain he would feel after an intense workout—only amplified by ten. He looked his mother in the eye.

He did not have to lie to her. "I got hit by a car," he said, and then he broke into tears.

"Oh God! Oh thank God," Lorelei gasped. She felt a guilty relief wash over her with the words. Of course! What a perfectly sane and logical explanation! She rushed to him and squeezed him tight, her own tears flowing now. They were the tears a woman would cry upon hearing her son's leukemia was in remission, tears reserved for good news outside the operating room after an extensive and risky surgery. Well-earned and bittersweet, she let them fall without shame or pretense.

"Oh goodness!" she said breaking the clinch and stepping back from him. "Are you all right, Sergei?" She looked him up and down. "Any broken bones? We have to get you to hospital for X-rays! We have to call the police!"

Von shook his head. He wiped his face with the back of his dirty hand, ashamed of the tears. "No, Ma. I'm fine, really. Just a little busted up. I just want to get cleaned up. I want to lie down. I just want to lie down for a while."

Lorelei looked at her son. "Are you sure, honey? You're sure you're okay?" She was so tired. She had been up all night. "I think we should get some X-rays—and call the police."

Von looked at her, his eyes pleading. "I'm all right, Mom. I know my body. There's nothing broken. I walked two miles home. I'm fine. I . . ." He looked around and reached for the door handle. "Let's just get inside—and forget the police."

She followed him inside. "We have to fill out a report, Von."

"It wouldn't do any good. I didn't even see the car. It clipped me from behind—as I was walking down Cicero—by the hill. It must have jumped the curb or something—knocked me into the retaining ditch." He looked so tired. "Please, Ma. I just want to go to bed."

Lorelei pursed her lips. So what was wrong with that? She had had enough of the police and their questions to last two lifetimes. "Okay," she said. "I'll draw you a hot bath with some Epsom salts. You can soak in it. I'll call school—tell them you won't be in today." She put her hand on his head, feeling for bumps. "You sure? I mean . . ."

He forced a weak smile. "I'm okay, Mom—no concussion—really. How about that bath?"

Lorelei nodded. "Okay," she said, running her fingers through his hair. She felt as if she might cry again and kissed him on the cheek. She noticed the tattered Nikes still dangling from his right hand. She saw the shredded toes and quickly looked away.

"Throw those out," she said turning her back on him and heading down the hall to the bathroom. "Throw them in the cans out back, not here in the kitchen."

Lorelei Vonosovich sat at her kitchen table and lit another Salem with the butt of the last one still smoldering in the ashtray. She watched the steam from Von's bath waft down the hall and mix with the cigarette smoke, trying to think of nothing at all. She would let him lie down for a while, see how he felt upon waking, and take him in to see Dr. Harlan if he didn't seem quite right.

Didn't seem quite right.

"I swerved to avoid a deer on Route 83, hon. Ended up in a ditch . . ."

Sound familiar?

She shuddered and mashed the Salem out, not bothering to shoo the smoke away.

Von was fast asleep on clean, crisp sheets by the time his mother had given up on conventional sleep, opting for the immediate tranquility found only through modern medicine. Lorelei doubled up on her Prozac dosage, chased it down with ten milligrams of Valium for good measure and brewed herself a mug of Sleepy Time herbal tea. She had finally drifted off to sleep on the couch, her mind growing as numb as her body, just as Oprah was wrapping up another enlightening episode of change-your-life TV.

The dream came at the point of her deepest sleep, seamlessly blending her last waking thoughts with memories long buried beneath years of denial and chemical camouflage.

"You gotta be strong, girl!" Oprah told her, reaching over and taking Lorelei's hand in both of hers. "Now you been through a lot, but you got to be strong for that little boy!"

Lorelei looked down, startled by the cold, clammy touch. She stifled a gasp. Oprah's palms were covered with shiny, green scales like a reptile, but the backs of her hands were matted in thick brown fur, meticulously brushed and coifed by her make-up people. Now how come she had never noticed that before? Poor thing. And all that money . . .

"I know, Oprah," Lorelei answered. "I try. I really do. But it's so hard. At first I thought it was another woman. The late nights at the lab, the mood swings . . . sometimes it was like he was a million miles away, even as he sat across from us at the supper table . . ."

Oprah nodded compassionately. She had long, pointy ears like a lynx. "Bring it in real tight, Carl," she said, motioning to one of the cameraman. "I want the folks at home to see the tears when she starts to blubber." Oprah turned again to Lorelei. "Go ahead, honey. So you had no idea?"

"Well . . ." Lorelei replied. "That's not entirely true . . ."

A collective gasp rose up from the studio audience. Oprah silenced them with a wave of her hairy hand.

"I'd heard the legends growing up as a little girl," Lorelei continued. "Whispered talk among the adults . . . rumors. There are not a lot of secrets amongst our own kind—the gypsies, I mean. It was said that Alexei was descended directly from the king's bloodline. I can't say I was surprised." Lorelei felt the first tears well up and choked them back.

Oprah winked at Carl the cameraman. "Go on, honey," she said, patting Lorelei's hand. Lorelei noticed for the first time that she was strapped into an electric chair. "Tell me about these late nights at the lab. He was trying to find a cure?"

"Not a cure, exactly," Lorelei answered. "More of a refinement I think. Alexei was a brilliant man. He was simply trying to use the tools available to him through modern science to . . ."

"*TO PLAY GOD?*" Jerry Springer burst through the stage door followed by Steve the cop and a small camera crew. "Isn't that what your husband—this *King of the Gypsies*—was really doing, Lorelei? Playing fast and loose with the laws of nature? Juggling chromosomes and amino acids like some Machiavellian court jester in the palace of—"

"Jerry!" Oprah bolted up out her chair. "You get out of my studio! This isn't one of your damn freak shows! This is *change your life*—"

"Shut up, Oprah," Jerry said. "Steve . . ."

Steve the cop dragged Oprah, kicking and screaming, from the studio as Jerry calmly sat in her vacated chair across from Lorelei. The crowd, smattered now with several large werewolves, started its frenzied chant. "Jerry, Jerry, Jerry . . ."

"So," Jerry prodded, "this husband of yours—this *man of science*—he started soliciting prostitutes shortly after he began tinkering with the elixir?"

"No," Lorelei stammered, surprised by how quickly Jerry had turned the tables. "No, it wasn't him . . . he wasn't himself. His behavior started to degenerate—along with his physical appearance. After awhile, he was nothing at all like the man I married. Alexei was a good man, a noble man. He—"

"Well," Jerry said, standing up. He walked around Lorelei's electric chair and carefully inspected the fittings. "It's almost time for my sanctimonious wrap-up, but we do have someone waiting backstage that we'd like you to meet." Jerry strapped the ball gag into her mouth and lowered the apparatus on to her head. "Let's bring her out, shall we?"

The audience hooted and hollered. Lorelei turned her head as far as she could, straining to see who Jerry was springing on her.

A rotting female corpse dressed in streetwalker garb shambled in to a chair a few feet away from Lorelei. Her throat was torn and ragged.

"This is Helen Ramirez," Jerry said. "A prostitute from Chicago Heights. Police suspect that your husband, *King of the Gypsies*, killed her after soliciting her on the night of May 3rd, 1986. Helen . . ."

"Hi, Jerry," the Helen corpse pulled back the shards of flesh clinging to her teeth in a ghastly semblance of a smile. The thing turned to Lorelei. "Yeah, this high-class tramp! Maybe if she could have kept her old man happy at home, he wouldna' been out cruisin' an' slicin' up us workin' girls!" Worms crawled around the perimeters of her eye sockets and black ooze belched from the gaping wound in her throat as she spoke.

Lorelei squeezed her eyes shut and squirmed against her restraints, unable to look upon the atrocity.

"Look at me!" the thing croaked. "Look at what your husband, Professor Freaky, did to me!" The Helen thing's head tilted backwards as if on a hinge and thousands of maggots poured like white lava from the corroded stump of her neck.

"Ohh . . ." Jerry groaned, "I don't know if I'll ever eat rice again!" The audience roared.

Helen turned in her chair, swinging herself around so that

her dangling head could talk directly to Lorelei. "How am I supposed to work? How am I gonna support my family?" Helen asked. "You think anyone is gonna pay for this? You know, I got a kid at home the same age as your son—the same age as your little *monster!*"

Lorelei woke with a scream caught in her throat, her eyes red and puffy from crying. There was no comfort to be drawn from familiar surroundings of her living room, only a suffocating sense of dread. She shuffled to the bathroom and took stock of her medicine cabinet. Lorelei settled on the Valium and shook two more Roche 10's into the palm of her hand. She wondered, just for a moment, how many it would take to kill her.

Chapter 30

Melanie Houghwat sat behind the wheel of her Escort GT and stared pensively up at the light burning in the third story window. Nightfall had come less than an hour ago but the moon, while not quite as big as last night's full moon, loomed large and luminous in the October sky over Mike Minot's apartment building. He had told her never to come here again. She could tell from the way that he looked at her that he didn't really mean it.

Oh sure. He was an old guy—well, not *too* old. What, twenty-five, twenty-six? Eight, nine years older than she was, tops. That might seem like a lot now, but it was all a matter of perspective. If she was thirty, he would be like, thirty-eight. What was the big deal? Brandi Brewer's dad was almost ten years older than her mom and no one said anything about that. And look at Michael Douglas and Catherine Zeta-Jones. Besides, she was so much more mature than the boys her own age, and Coach Minot was a four-star hunk. All the girls thought so.

And he liked her too. She knew that. She knew of course, he would never make a move on her. That might be up to her and it would come some time down the road. Maybe as soon as next year when she came back to visit the hometown, on spring break from Stanford or USC. Melanie smiled at that last thought, letting the scenario play over in her mind. She would be an adult then. Eighteen years old. A legal adult.

But first she had to get there. A free ride to college was in the cards but she wanted a sure hand. A top school on the west coast. Nothing else would do. If she kept playing like she did last night (spearheading a big-time tourney win over

Bogan where the RedHawks swept all four games) she could have her pick. Melanie's play had been the story of this season and the press clippings were starting to pile up. Still, she needed to be sure. She needed a trump card.

The Equipoxigenin.

She had been using it on and off (more often on) since September, but last night was the first time that she had actually *injected* it as was prescribed. The effects were amazing and immediate. She had felt as if she had landed on a planet with a lower gravitational pull than our own. Sort of like Superman free and clear from the red sun of Krypton. The cardiovascular benefits were even greater than the substantial boost in strength and speed. She had literally covered the entire court last night (much to the ire of some of her supposed teammates) and was ready for more when the whistle blew on the final match.

Frank Lally and Dan Jacobson had never seen the stuff. Let those barbarians gorge themselves on the Sustanon and the Durabolin. Giving the Equipoxigenin to them would be like feeding caviar to swine. Melanie had done a little research on her own. The stuff was the most sought-after boost on the street and it was nearly impossible to find. Strictly a black-market item. Melanie didn't know where Coach Minot got it (probably his old NFL connections) and she didn't care. She just knew that she wanted more.

Mike Minot nearly groaned aloud when he looked through the peephole and saw the statuesque figure of Melanie Houghwat standing outside his door. He cursed himself for his stupidity and opened the door, making no effort to conceal his displeasure.

"Hey," she said.

"What are you doing here, Melanie?"

"I was on my way to my game. The guys are looking for—"

Mike Minot peered down the hallway. Footsteps? He yanked her across the doorsill and shut the door behind them. "I thought I told you not to come here anymore—and yet, here you are . . ."

Melanie blustered, surprised and hurt by his acerbity. "I'm sorry. It's just that the guys need more—they want more Equipoxigenin. I was driving right past so I—"

"So you just thought you would pop on up and get some, huh?" He softened his tone. The kid looked great. She was wearing a hooded nylon pullover that barely covered the brief volleyball shorts (but just barely) showcasing her long athletic legs. "That's not how it works, Melanie."

"I know," she said. "Anyway, now that I'm here, the guys need more of the Ex."

Mike Minot rubbed the five o'clock shadow spreading across his chin. He had to make a tough call on this one. "No," he said.

Melanie stammered. "What do you mean, no?"

Minot reiterated. "No. No means no. No more Equipoxigenin. Those guys are going through it way too fast. I told you to tell them it was strictly a game-day thing. They must be using it for workouts too. No, no more." He felt better immediately. The junk was too much for high school kids. Someone was going to blow his heart up using the stuff like this. He would get rid of it at the college- and pro-level.

Melanie looked as though she might cry. "But Mark only uses it on game day . . . how about just for him?" Mark Steponic had had a crush on her since seventh grade. He would cover for her if the coach asked. But he wouldn't. Coach never spoke of the steroids to anyone but Melanie. That was the arrangement.

"No, Mel. Sorry. Besides," he lied, "I can't get the stuff anymore."

Melanie frowned. Men were such lousy liars. "Mmm, okay. Well, their tough luck. Can I use your bathroom?" she asked, bouncing on the balls of her feet to emphasize her haste. "I really have to go. My game's at Richards and that's a half-hour from here."

Mike stepped back, allowing her across the threshold. Had he flushed the toilet? "Eh, yeah. Sure." He watched his boss's seventeen-year-old daughter saunter through his living room with her long legs and disappear into his bathroom. He decided then and there that it was time to find another buffer between himself and the gym rats at Ridgewood High.

To her surprise, Melanie really did have to use the bathroom. She finished quickly but did not flush, instead turning the faucet on in the sink full blast. With the running water providing some auditory cover, she went about her snooping. She checked the vanity under the sink first. A quick perusal, she didn't think he would stash them there. Oh, but she hoped he didn't hide the stuff in his bedroom (like a woman would). The medicine cabinet. Shaving cream, razors, gauze, medical tape, a few prescription vials—she checked those briskly. Nothing. On to the linen closet.

If she could only get her hands on some more—one more—one more hit before tonight's match with Richards. Then that would be it. She knew the stuff was dangerous. She knew she was playing with—

Melanie saw the gray metal box tucked high up on the top shelf, sandwiched between the thick folded bath towels, and her heart jumped. That was it. She knew it before she pulled it down and opened it. Melanie popped the tiny latch and stared at the pharmacopoeia nestled inside: Hybolin, Dufine,

Jebolan, Roboral . . . *bingo!*

Melanie rifled though the clutter and extracted one of the seven phials of Equipoxigenin from the tin. She would take just one. No need to be greedy but she had to work fast. It took a little less than an hour for the stuff to work its way through your system. If she fixed now she would be peaking before the second game. Melanie pulled the works from the pocket of her nylon pullover (thank goodness she hadn't left it in the car) and was screwing on a fresh needle when the knock came at the door.

"Yo!" Coach Minot's voice boomed through the pressed wood. "You all right in there?"

Melanie stepped back and sat down on the closed toilet seat cover. "Um, yes. Another minute, here please?" she called out over the running water. "I'm . . . I'm having a female issue here!" That would hold him. Men were scared to death of anything having to do with menstruation.

A pause, then, "Oh . . . okay—sorry . . ."

Mike Minot backed away from the door, thanking the powers that be that he was a man. Now why did she have to do that here? In his bathroom? He folded his powerful arms across his chest and toed back into the living room. He did not sit but continued to pace. Good lord, but she was taking an awfully long time in there. He was contemplating another knock on the door when he heard the thud.

Minot was at the door in a heartbeat. "Melanie!" He pounded on the door. "Melanie, are you all right? Open the door!"

No sound at all after that sickening thump—like a melon falling on hardwood—just the drone of the running water.

Mike Minot laid his shoulder into the door, splintering the lock clean off the jamb. He burst into his bathroom and froze, unable to comprehend how his life could change so quickly.

Melanie Houghwat lay dead on the cold ceramic tile. She stared up at him, her eyes lifeless but unforgiving. Her head was bleeding where it had struck the sharp edge of his sink. A hypodermic needle lay off to the side, a few feet away from the spent phial of Equipoxigenin.

Mike Minot groaned aloud and then braced himself for the task that lay ahead. There was work to be done.

Wet work.

Chapter 31

Von stood at his grandfather's bedside, watching the sheet rise and fall with the even rhythm of his breathing. He hated to wake him at a time like this. The old man looked so content. Maybe he was dreaming again—dreaming of the days when he was . . . complete. Von slid one of the boxy visitor's chairs silently across the floor and was about to settle in, when Drajac Vonosovich spoke.

"You are a man now."

Von looked up, startled. Save for the twitching in his nostrils, the old man still looked to be asleep. Drajac opened his eyes and looked at his grandson, looked at him as if it were years, instead of days, since his last visit.

"You are a man now," Drajac said, "and the beast within you no longer sleeps."

Von blinked but said nothing. He rose up from his half-crouch and craned his neck around the curtain that split the semi-private room in half. His grandfather's roommate, a former fireman, lay sleeping, skeletal and semi-comatose, reduced to a mummified shell by the rot of cancer and its subsequent cures. An intermittent beep from the banks of machines monitoring his vitals was the only indication he was alive at all. Satisfied they were truly alone, Von pulled the chair closer to Drajac's bed. He leaned forward and asked the question.

"How did you know?"

Drajac tried to smile but it looked more like a frown. His leathery hand snaked out from under the bed sheet and reached unsteadily for Von's. Von clasped his grandfather's hand in his, surprised by the strength of the old man's grip.

They had the same hands, large and broad and flat. Like his grandfather, Von's index fingers were longer than his middle fingers. He had never thought much of that, until now.

"Yes," Drajac croaked. "Your father's hands, too." He sighed loudly and swallowed hard. The old man eased his only functioning hand from Von's grip and motioned to the side table. "Some water, please, boy."

"Sure, Papa," Von said. He stood and hefted the brown plastic pitcher from the mobile tray, noting it was recently filled, cold, and packed full with fresh ice. That had to be Haley's doing. Von filled a cup and placed an elbow straw in it—those weren't standard issue. Haley again? Drajac sucked greedily at the straw before motioning to Von that he had had enough.

"Sit," Drajac said. He pushed with his good arm, propping himself up against his pillows into a reclining position. He looked at Von, a sly smile twinkling in the corners of his dark eyes. "It was the girl, no? Your friend? The girl who takes such good care of me?"

Von knew what he was asking. He nodded.

"Good," Drajac said. "That is good. She is a fine girl, pure of heart. It makes a difference, you know."

Von pursed his lips, a little exasperated. "Papa, I—"

"Sit," Drajac repeated, "and I will tell you all that I know." The old man paused, his dark eyes shining. "Where to start? The beginning, heh? Yes, I suppose . . ."

Drajac sighed and collected his thoughts. He would not let his muddled brain interfere with the telling of this tale. "You want to know about last night, your first night beneath the stars, your first night as one of nature's children under the moon. You want to know of your father and the dark gift he passed on to you." Drajac's eyes sparkled.

"Story starts long before that, Sergei." He raised the

plastic cup to his lips, taking a long, loud, pull from the straw. "It starts at the dawn of man. In the beginning, all God's creatures lived in harmony in the Garden, just as Bible tell you. There is much, however, that Bible fail to tell you. Garden holds many of God's secrets, Sergei—secrets that God did not want to share. The Serpent that you read of in your Bible class—you think this beast, this fallen *archangel* was happy to crawl around on its belly?"

Von shrugged impatiently. "Papa, what does this have to do with—"

Drajac's face twisted into a scowl. "You listen, Sergei! I am only going to tell this once. You make of it what you will. You want to hear?"

Von nodded. He was sorry that he upset the old man. "Go ahead, Papa. No, I don't suppose the snake was happy crawling around on its belly."

Drajac nodded. "No—but the Serpent was wise, Sergei. Before the Fall, it had sat at the Right Hand of God. It knew of all the secrets of the Garden. It knew of the Tree of Life and the wondrous fruit that it bear. The fruit that the Serpent most desire lay on a branch high out the Viper's reach, as it could only crawl about on the ground.

"As you know, the Serpent approached the woman, knowing of her vanity. It tell her: 'There is a sweet fruit high in your Father's tree. If you eat this fruit you can take the shape of any of the creatures in the Garden.' Of course, the woman was not happy with all she had in this Paradise. As women are, she wanted more. She climbed to the top of the tree, Sergei, and plucked the fruits from the high branch.

"When she climb down, the Serpent trapped her in its coils, squeezing her until the fruit spill to the Garden floor. It ate the fruit, Sergei, and the woman awoke to see the Snake was now a magnificent Dragon, walking on the legs of a lion and even to fly on great wings like the eagle.

"The Dragon took the woman as God had only intended for the man to do. The beast soiled her to show its contempt for God and the beings God make in His own image. When the Dragon is done with the woman, it trample through Garden, breathing fire and crushing the gentler beasts of God's creation beneath its terrible claws. When God return to Garden with the man, He saw what the woman had done. Brandishing a sword of pure divinity, God chase the Dragon from the Garden to the very edge of the earth and slice the new limbs from its body. The Beast fell off the earth into a Flaming Sea of Bile, where it resides to this day, feeding off the withered husks of the Souls of the Damned, growing strong for the Final Day of Reckoning."

Drajac paused and motioned to his empty cup. "Is good story, no?"

Von nodded and poured him a fresh cup of ice water. "It's a good story, Papa." He winked at his grandfather. "It sounds kind of familiar. I suppose there is more?"

The old man nodded. "Is more. . . . When God return to the Garden, He find the woman cowering behind the man, filled with shame and afraid to face their Creator. God smelled the fruit upon them both, for she had offered it to the man and he ate it. As you know, God expelled them from the Garden to lands east where they had to labor under the hot sun and work the soil for their daily bread. Unbeknownst to God, however, the woman took with her the rinds of the fruit from the Tree of Life, which God had forbade her to eat. She hid this trickery from her husband but shared it with her first-born, Cain, who she loved above all her children.

"Cain was eating of the fruit one day and turn himself into an eagle, the greatest of God's winged creatures. Cain flew high into midheaven where he was discovered by the Creator.

In His anger, God raised a great storm and drove Cain from the skies back down to the soil of the earth. Fearing for his life and unwilling to part with his mother's precious gift, Cain fled from his home and traveled further east to the land of Nod. In Nod, he found a wife and she bore him a son and they named him Henoch, and Henoch grew to be tall and strong like his father. Cain loved his son and passed on to him the secret of the fruit, telling him he must shield the rind from the face of God, lest he incur the Creator's wrath. One night Henoch took the form of a tiger and killed a man, a senator in the city of Nod, who had spoken ill of one of Henoch's wives. Henoch become an outcast like his father, a fugitive and wanderer of the earth. Henoch's travels took him north, through the deserts, into the dark forests of the lands that lay west of the Black Sea. When the moon rise, Henoch would take the form of a wolf, the greatest of the beasts in those woods. One night while hunting, Henoch came upon a great she-wolf with blue eyes and they couple. From this union a son was born in human form and they named him Irad.

"When Irad is born, there remain not even a sliver of the fruit smuggled from the Garden so long ago by the mother of all children. The seed flowed only in the loins of Irad, mixed with the blood of his mother, the great she-wolf."

Drajac stopped and looked at his grandson. "We are all sons of Irad."

He motioned for the water. Von handed it to him without a word.

"This story told among our kind for thousands of years," Drajac said. "No one ever write it down—is not our way. You make of it what you will."

Von opened his mouth to speak but said nothing.

Drajac raised a bushy eyebrow. "Questions. Many questions, no?"

"Why last night?" Von asked. "Why all of a sudden?"

Drajac sighed. "Is different with all. First time wolf come is normally time of need. The moon was full last night. This is when the call is the strongest, when the moon is full and high. You will learn to control."

"I don't remember . . . much," Von said, hanging his head. He recalled with a shudder the meat he had picked from his teeth upon waking up in the woods that morning, naked and wet. He saw the terrified face of Dominic Teresi.

"Is like dreams." Drajac nodded. "Bits and pieces. You will remember more as you master the wolf. The man must control the wolf, Sergei."

Von finally found the courage to ask the question. "Will I . . . kill?"

"Kill?" Drajac chuckled, then turned deadly serious. "It is the nature of the wolf to hunt, boy. The wolf kills only to eat and to protect itself and the pack. Wolf does not kill its own kind. Nature of the beast inside is nature of the man outside." The old man looked at the boy. "You have something to tell me?"

Von shook his head. "No, Papa. I was just . . . worried."

Drajac nodded. "There have been . . . incidents, of course. Is not like old days when the forests were vast and plentiful." He sighed and looked out the window. "City is no place for wolf. I tried to tell your father . . ."

Von's eyes brightened. "Tell me about my father."

Drajac sighed. All at once he seemed very tired.

"When we first come to this country, the Great War is brewing in Europe, I am still young man. My Elani and I, we live in outlands of Minnesota, Little Falls is name of town. I work as a lumberjack for Mando Paper Company. Work is hard and winters very cold, but there is forest all around us and we are happy. In 1949 we are blessed with your father.

He grows up as an American boy but he also know and embrace his Vorgo heritage. Alexei do very well in school, so well he attends to the University of Illinois on scholarship. We are very proud." Drajac stopped here and took another drink although he was not thirsty. "Your Nana—she does live to see him become a man, but she dies of the cancer in 1969, only fifty-five years old. After University, your father takes job with Talbot-Hyde and moves here to Chicago where he meet a beautiful girl." The old man attempted to smile here but the soiled relationship he shared with his daughter-in-law would not allow it. "Your mother, Lorelei. She is second-generation like your father, descended from the Moldavian clan where is now Romania. They become husband and wife and you are born shortly after, Sergei. Your father, he seem very happy, but . . ."

Von pressed. "Go on, Papa . . ."

Drajac frowned. "Your father, he always need to know the how and the why. In his veins flow the blood of Irad and he embraced this, but he is not a man to take the good with the . . . with the bad. He is not content to let the wolf walk alongside the man. He wants the wolf to walk *behind* the man.

"One night Alexei say to me when your mother is carrying you, 'Papa, do you know we share twenty-three of twenty-four chromosomes with the chimpanzee?' I say, 'Alexei, you are wolf, why do you talk of monkey?' He say to me, 'Don't you see Papa, it is all in the grouping. That is the key!' From then I know that he is headed to trouble. When you are born, Sergei, your father become obsessed with finding this *key* he speaks of. It is for you he wants this thing that only God knows of." Drajac opened his mouth to speak further, then appeared to think better of it.

Von fought back the lump rising in his throat.

"Is not your fault, Sergei," Drajac continued. "Your father love you more than anything in the world. Soon he is again reading from the old books. One day he tell me, 'Papa, it has been right under our noses the whole time, but it is too small to see.' Now he is spending all his time at the laboratory—at work. This causes some . . ." The old man stopped here, looking for the right word. "Problems . . . at home with your mother and father. Now I start to worry. Your father does not look good, but it is just not lack of sleep or too much work. He is . . . different."

Von leaned in closer. "Different how, Papa?"

"He start to lose his hair. His skin . . . he . . ." Drajac stopped. Von was startled to see tears welling up in his grandfather's eyes. He had never seen him cry before.

"I am tired now, Sergei," he said, turning his head as though ashamed of the tears he shed before the boy. "We will talk again." Drajac looked out the window. The sun was starting to dip below the trees behind the strip mall on 183rd Street. "Remember this: the moon will call to the beast inside, but you are the master of the wolf. In time, you will learn when to call it forth and when to keep it at bay. Is only natural." The old man narrowed his eyes at his grandson. "Sergei?"

Von rose up out of the boxy chair. "Yes, Papa?"

"You will let nature take its course. You will not interfere?"

Von tried to smile. He thought he might be sick. "No, Papa. I won't . . . interfere."

Drajac nodded. All at once he seemed very old and drained. "Is good boy. Go now, Sergei. You must be alone and in the woods come nightfall."

Von bent and kissed the old man's leathery forehead. It was slick with perspiration. "Good night, Papa."

★ ★ ★ ★ ★

Haley was waiting for him around the corner. Von had caught her scent immediately upon stepping from his grandfather's room. He could have avoided her by ducking out the wing door, but that would have been too obvious. Von rounded the corner and tried to act surprised upon seeing her by the nurse's station, chatting it up with the wing supervisor, a powerfully built redhead in her late thirties with a conspicuous metal stud planted in the center of her tongue.

"Oh, there's the big football star," the redhead—her name was Val—said.

Haley looked puzzled. "Hey, you. What are you doing here? I thought you were sick."

Von looked at her and fell in love all over again. "Hey yourself." He could feel the big redhead's eyes crawling over him. "Hi, Val," he nodded to her and turned his attention to Haley. "Feeling better. How you doin'?"

Haley smiled. "Okay." And she meant it. Suddenly, being descended from an ancient line of Romanian werewolves didn't seem so bad. "I was just about to pop in on your grandfather," she said. "How's he feeling?"

"Okay," Von said. "He's tired. I think I might have overstayed my visit."

Haley smiled. "I'll check in on him later. I gotta get back to C wing. See ya, Val." She looked at Von. "Goin' my way?"

"Always," Von replied, falling in step with her.

They walked in silence for a short while before pausing before the oversize doorway of the darkened rec room.

"I missed you in school today," Haley said. "It was weird. I thought you were mad at me."

Von stammered. "Look, Haley, about last night . . . I—"

"Hey," she said. Her smile was loose and dreamy, as if she had stepped back into the moment. "Don't worry about it. It was magic. Like a dream. A wonderful dream. Until . . ."

"Until I *bit* you?" Von asked flatly.

"Uh, yeah," Haley said, lowering her eyes. "Well . . . I won't tell if you won't. You know," she said, reaching up and touching his cheek, "passion is instinctual . . . primal. The animal in you takes over."

Von winced.

Haley ran her finger along his lower lip. She felt a charge standing there with him in the shadowy recess of the doorway, the musky scent of his skin, his teeth so white . . .

"I get off in an hour," she said. "You want to hang out? I can give you a lift home."

Von looked over her head at the purpling sky behind them. "No," he said, more of a proclamation than an answer. "It's getting dark. I have to go now."

"Yeah, so what's the rush?" Haley asked. "You turn into a pumpkin at the stroke of midnight?"

Von kissed her forehead and turned to go. "Something like that."

Chapter 32

Tom Houghwat woke with the quick panic of a man snapping out of a catnap on a commuter train, afraid he had slept past his stop. Blinking through the drowsy brume of a troubled sleep, his eyes darted to the clock on the mantle: 11:42.

Damn! Now why didn't Melanie wake him up? The room was dark save for the glow from the TV, where Jay Leno was working a little too hard with a B-list sit-com actor whose face Tom recognized but couldn't name to save his life. "Jesus, I miss Carson," Tom mumbled, switching the TV off with the remote. He hoisted himself out of the La-Z-Boy, relying more on his arms than his back at this stage in his life. Silently cursing the ravages of his advancing years, the big man lumbered to the window to draw the blinds.

Tom's heart skipped a beat.

Melanie's car was not in the driveway.

If this were one of the boys, he would have been angry. God knows he had spent enough nights waiting up for them long past curfew. This was Melanie though, and this was different. He had never had to worry about late nights with Melanie, thank God.

The coach craned his neck and peered down the street. She did not park on the street. Of course, she never did. He glanced at the telephone on the end table next to his La-Z-Boy. The answering machine displayed a blinking red "0." No one had called.

"Mel?" Tom took the steps up the foyer stairwell two at a time, knowing full well he would find his daughter's bedroom vacant before swinging the door open and switching on the light. "Damn it," he whispered, checking his watch. "Damn it."

Tom turned and headed back down the stairs, his mind working much faster than his feet. Car trouble, a flat tire, a bad alternator . . . a horrible accident. Was she angry with him for missing her game tonight? No, of course not. Melanie knew that he spent Monday nights alone in the AD office breaking down game film. No assistant coaches, no Athletic Director, just Tom, the game film, and a yellow legal pad (this was still his team, no matter what Mike Minot thought). Still, he could have wrapped up a little early tonight and headed over to Richards and caught the last game . . .

Beat yourself up later, he thought. Stay calm and try to think where your seventeen-year-old daughter could be at 11:45 on a school night.

Ah! The nursing home. Melanie had probably stopped by the nursing home after her game to check up on—what was her name? Mrs. Ahern. That would be just like Melanie. She stopped by to check up on the old gal and found her in a bad state. Melanie was so distraught she did not think to call home. The old woman was about to cash in her chips and Melanie would not leave her bedside . . . Tom Houghwat felt a glimmer of shame for embracing such a morbid thought but he could not help himself. It sure beat the hell out of any of the alternatives.

He fished the phone book out of the end-table drawer and found the number for the Regent Extended Care Center written in Melanie's flowing script. (How is it that men could never write in a hand like that?) The coach paused a minute before dialing, for reasons he dared not imagine, and then punched the number in.

"Hello, Regent Extended Care . . ."

"Uh, yes—uh, Mrs. Ahern's room, please. Shirley Ahern.

I believe she is in your D wing."

"One moment, sir. I'll transfer you to that station."

"Thank you."

A nurse picked up after two rings. "D wing."

"Hello, uh, I'm calling to check on Mrs. Shirley Ahern. I'm not sure of the room number."

"Shirley *Ahern?* Are you a family member, sir?"

Tom fumbled. "Uh, no. My daughter, Melanie—she's in your Senior Share reading program. She goes there to read to the folks. I think she may have stopped by to see Mrs. Ahern. The two of them are quite close. I was wondering if everything was . . . all right."

There was a very long pause on the other end.

"Can you hold on for one minute, sir?"

Tom sighed. "Sure."

After almost two minutes, another voice broke through the low hum. "Hello?"

Tom, a bit blustery now, "Yes, *hello.* I'm calling about Shirley Ahern. My daughter, Melanie, was there tonight to read to—"

"I'm sorry sir, but Mrs. Ahern is no longer with us."

"What?" Tom asked. "Well, what wing is she in then? Could you transfer me?"

"You don't understand, sir. Mrs. Ahern passed away. Some time ago. Early September."

A flinty pellet of bile rose up from the pit of Tom Houghwat's stomach, expanding like a balloon in his windpipe as it sucked the air out his lungs. He choked it back down with a hard swallow, staring at the telephone as though it were some animal that had just lit upon his hand.

"Sir . . . ?"

"Yes, thank you," Tom said blankly, re-cradling the phone. The muscles in his face contorted, sculpting a mask unlike any he had ever worn before.

The betrayal.

Tom settled back into his La-Z-Boy, rage and sorrow waging a war in his broken heart, and waited for a daughter who would never come home.

Chapter 33

Von woke Tuesday morning in his own bed, fragments of the night's nocturnal odyssey filtering back into his cognitive thinking like the sweet whispers of a mid-morning dream. He'd hopped a 252 cross-town upon leaving the nursing home and had taken it to the end of the line, a deserted terminal on the north perimeter of the Creekside Wetlands Preserve. Von had walked deep into the woods, following his nose until he had come upon the creek, a token ribbon of shallow run-off, gouged into the leafy floor of the preserve like a craggy open wound.

Stepping onto a broad flat rock overlooking the creek, he had disrobed. He was a son of Irad, a direct descendant of the purest lineage, at home in his domain. Twilight had settled in deceptively, a watery blending of long shadows so subtle that full dark had taken him by surprise. All at once the air around him had changed and the night welcomed those creatures, man and beast alike, that called it home. He had stood there naked and motionless, taking in the loamy smell of the forest floor, the fleeting scents of the subordinate wildlife scurrying to shelter.

The moon was still on the rise when he had felt the first stirrings under his skin, a tick, a murmur, visible in the superficial veins in his hands.

And then the heat.

It was an internal heat, generated from the friction of molecules in turmoil, colliding and vibrating like those of a steak in a microwave oven. It roared through his body like a fever, climbing to an unbearable level in a matter of lost moments, bringing him to his knees.

Did he scream? He could not remember. He had hung on

for as long as he could, staying conscious until the R complex, the most ancient center of the brain, responsible for aggressive behavior, territoriality, and social hierarchy, had swelled to twice its normal size. The brain's limbic system had survived mostly intact, thanks to the rapid shrinking and transmutation of his neocortex inside the shifting bone structure of his skull.

He could remember little after that. He awoke (as he had willed himself to do upon stepping off the 252 cross-town) well before sunrise, on the same rock upon which he had disrobed hours before, his clothes still hanging neatly on a tree limb over his head. The sight of blood on his hands had alarmed him until he had rolled over and seen the eviscerated carcass of the doe laying some thirty yards upstream. The animal's eyes stared up at the fading twilight, wide eyes etched with the terror of the last thing she had seen before dying.

He had shuddered for just a moment but had felt no remorse. It was, after all, only natural. He was a son of Irad, a direct descendant of the greatest hunters this world had ever known, and the doe was merely another link in the food chain. Flashes of the takedown popped and fizzed in his head, violent, beautiful remnants, clinging to the transmuted synapses in his memory banks.

As the wolf inside became less of a stranger, the lapses of memory would become more infrequent; the worlds of the wolf and the man would mesh seamlessly, like the transposition of native tongues in dreams of the multilingual.

You will remember more as you master the wolf. The man must control the wolf, Sergei . . .

He had gained some control last night, bringing the beast in well before dawn had broken, enabling him to find his way home and slip back into his house undetected. That was good. Like the gradual domestication of a stray, he would tame the wolf, with each successive visit, he would gain its trust, make it his own.

He could handle this.

Dominic Teresi's head sailing high into the night sky . . .

He would have to.

Von showered and dressed quickly, skipping his usual hurried breakfast of corn flakes and bananas (after all, he had eaten only a few short hours ago). He slipped out of the house quietly, being careful not to wake his mother. Von didn't want to have to answer any questions about his whereabouts last night. Although he was sure he had made it home before she had, he knew his mother had her radar up and would be looking for any sign of trouble. A sudden thought struck him as he crossed the intersection at Homan and Pearl and turned up the hill.

How much does she really know about all of this?

The thought opened up a cauterized seam in his mind. Scattershot bursts of repressed memories ran through his head like movie trailers on a cheap eight-millimeter loop: padding across the kitchen floor in his footie pajamas, his mother sitting at the kitchen table, the early morning sunlight bouncing hard off the tear-stained mascara around her hollow eyes; the men in suit coats and ties (FBI?) at the door, rummaging through the house, carting his father's books and supplies from his modest home office . . .

Mom knew. She had helped cover for him.

He made a mental note to ask Papa more about the accident at the lab that had taken his father's life the next time he visited him at the Regent. Papa had been pretty sharp lately. Maybe if he caught him on a good night . . .

Von stopped in mid-step, his eyes darting to the white metal newspaper box on the corner of Homan and Lake. The

Tribune morning edition stared back at him, the blurb running across the top of the front page looking surreal, like something from a bad dream.

Sports Exclusive: Steroid Scandal Rocks #1 Ridgewood High. Lineman comes clean, implicates star Vonosovich and others.

Von dug in his the pocket of his jeans. Change: pennies, dimes, nickels, spilled to the sidewalk at his feet. He bent and fished among the coins, plucking a solid quarter, two dimes, and a nickel from the spillage. With his heart pounding, Von poured the coins into the narrow slot in the top of the box, nickel and two dimes first. He forced himself to wait until the heavy quarter fell before pulling on the handle. The whole box rocked but did not open. Von cursed aloud and jammed repeatedly at the coin return button. He stared, incredulous at the metal bandit that had besmirched his name and had stolen his money.

Von brought his foot up high and hard into the clear plastic framing the display copy. The ersatz glass splintered but did not break, a spider web of cracks radiating from the contact point in the center. Von's fist smashed into the epicenter and the high-impact plastic shattered crystalline onto the sidewalk. Clearing a few stubborn shards away from the corners, Von reached in and fished a copy from the top of the pile. He was riffling through the multi-sectioned tabloid when he heard the chirp of rubber coming to a hard stop behind him.

Oh great, he thought, turning to look. Probably the cops.

Mike Minot sat curbside in his red Corvette, a copy of the *Tribune* rested on the tan leather bucket seat beside him. They stared at each other for a moment, Von trying to read his eyes before the coach finally spoke.

"Get in."

* * * * *

"First thing you got to tell me," Minot said staring straight ahead as he accelerated up Lake Street, "what you're on and what's your dosage. We have to get some masking agents into you ASAP. Golden Seal, that's okay for your standard drug tests, but we're talkin' big-time here. If the guys from ISAC come up here—and I think they will—they're going to test for *everything*. They don't fool around. Very thorough—even at this level."

He snatched the newspaper from the console and shook it angrily.

"This is bad. Jacobson really screwed you guys—screwed us all. He named names, said the coaching staff—namely *me*—knew all about it, but looked the other way. Of course, we're going to say it's a case of sour grapes. Jacobson lost his role because of a disciplinary problem and refused to take the necessary steps to get that role back. Still, there's going to be an investigation. Mark my words."

Von, skimming the article, looked up as the 'Vette cruised to a stop at a four-way intersection. Lawler and LeClaire. Coach was really taking a roundabout way to school. Minot waited as an old Buick rolled through the intersection. "Let me have it," Minot said, stepping on the gas. "The juice, the frequency, the dosage—everything. Are you stacking? Do you cycle? Please tell me that you cycle. I need to know, kid. We can beat this, but you got to be straight with me. I still need to talk to Lally and Step—"

"I'm not on steroids, Coach."

Minot turned to him, the agitation clear on his face. "Look, Von, this is no time to play Boy Scout. Everybody juices. It's how you get an edge. You just have to play it smart, not overdo it and most important—don't get caught. Now play it smart and tell me what you're on."

Von looked at his coach, a man he had come to idolize, a gym rat badass who had made it all the way to the Promised Land. All the way to the NFL.

"I'm not lying to you, Coach," he said, looking into his mentor's eyes. "I'm not on steroids. I swear on my father."

Chapter 34

"You know," Jason said, staring intently at his friend across the two desks, "there's a good chance you won't be tested at all. It's like Coach said, Jake's a career troublemaker and crybaby. Who's going to listen to him?"

"Well, *somebody* listened to him," Von seethed. "Or didn't you see the goddamn *Tribune* this morning?" Man, Jason was really starting to get on his nerves.

Jason lowered the sketchpad and looked around. Mr. Blodgett, who had been helping Mary Trembecki find the focal point of Yolanda Witherspoon's face, glanced up and gave them a pass. Probably figured they had enough to worry about.

"Hey, take it easy, bud," Jason replied. "I was just trying to give you some perspective on this. Move your head a little to the left."

Von said nothing but did as he was told. They had been working on these portraits for three weeks—taking turns drawing their partners and he had been lucky enough to get paired up with Jason, Ridgewood's own version of Rembrandt. If it turned out really well, Jason would give it to him and he would give it to Haley.

"Sorry, man," Von offered. "This thing has got me wound up. I feel like a damn sideshow attraction."

"Yeah," Jason nodded, squinting hard at his friend's nose. "I know. Everybody's talking about it. Coach say anything to you yet?"

"Coach Minot picked me up on the way in," Von said in a hushed tone. "Wanted to know what I was on. Told me to come clean and all that. Said he could—" Von stopped him-

203

self. "Said he wanted me to tell the truth. All that crap. You know. He dropped me off two blocks down—so we wouldn't be *seen* together. Can you believe it?"

Jason nodded. His tongue was tucked in the corner of his mouth, the pink tip peeking out. "Uh-huh."

"I saw Mangan in the hallway second period," Von continued. "He told me not to worry—to keep my chin up. He looked like he was ready to throw in the towel. I haven't seen Coach Houghwat yet."

Jason lowered his pencil and held the sketchbook out at arm's length. "And you won't, either," he said, frowning at his drawing. "Coach isn't in today. Neither is Melanie, come to think of it."

Von was somewhat relieved to hear that. The last thing he needed right now was Coach Houghwat's old-school routine. Von had a sneaking suspicion that Coach Houghwat thought he was on the juice—hell, *everyone* thought he was on the juice. If they only knew . . .

"Really?" Von asked. "That's odd—the both of them being out, I mean."

Various scenarios raced through Von's head; car accident, death in the family, could be any number of things, he supposed. "Hmm, hope everything's all right at the Houghwat place." Von liked and respected Coach Houghwat and Melanie had always been nice to him, even when he was a nobody. Besides, Melanie had lost her mother not long ago, and Von knew a little bit about that particular brand of pain.

Jason, struggling with the image on his drawing tablet, grunted. "Uh-huh. And guess who else is out today?"

"Jake?" Von asked.

"Bingo," Jason replied. "I guess he's going to lay low for a while . . . for his safety. Can you see the irony in that? The guy terrorizes the school for four years and then—damn!"

"What?" Von peered across the two desks butted head to head. It appeared that Rembrandt was having an off day.

"I don't know," Jason said. His brow was knit in frustration. He looked at the image on his tablet and back at Von. "I—"

"What?" Von pressed.

Jason frowned, disgusted with himself. "I'm sorry, man. I think I screwed this up from the get-go. Either that or your eyes are moving away from the center of your face to the sides of your head."

Chapter 35

The doorbell roused Tom Houghwat from his afternoon nap, the insistent chiming cutting through the haze like a dull knife. He lifted himself off the recliner and padded to the door. Who could be bothering him at a time like this? Maybe it was the police with some news . . . some good news.

Tom opened the door. A lone figure stood on the stoop in a red hooded cloak, almost engulfed in a thick swirling fog.

"Hi, Daddy," Melanie giggled, lifting her head and pulling the hood back. The cloak fell from her shoulders, exposing her awful nakedness. Her body was gray and blue and bloated; the body of a corpse pulled from the water. Pockmarks and bites marred her skin where the fish and the turtles had begun to feed. A lone blue eye dangled from the empty black sockets.

Tom Houghwat screamed over the laughter and the howls coming from the thing on his door-stoop. It was the scream that propelled him from the bizarre stylizations of the dream world into the cold stark reality of full consciousness. A doleful moan welled up from the core of his being as the fog of the dream lifted and the real nightmare began anew.

His daughter had been missing for three days now.

The police had little to go on. Melanie had simply left the house on Monday night and had never returned. It was painful for Tom to have to tell them of her deceit, her fabricated story about the Senior Share Reading Program at the Regent. The last time Melanie had showed up at the Regent to read was August 2, the last day she was required to read in order to fulfill the obligation of the program. It was quite obvious that Melanie had a clandestine itinerary for her

Monday and Thursday nights and it had nothing to do with reading *Peyton Place* to the deceased Shirley Ahern. They wouldn't say it in so many words, but Tom could see the police were embracing the prospect that Melanie had run off, that she had a lover, and that Tom would hear from her as soon as she was good and ready. Disturbing as that was, Tom hoped that they were right. Deep in his gut though, he knew better.

No matter what Melanie had done, no matter what she was doing on those nights that she should not have, she would never put him through *this*. Never. She simply loved him too much.

No. Melanie had met with foul play. He was sure of it. As horrible as that thought was, Tom knew it to be true. Melanie did not run off to Las Vegas with a lover to get married. She was not casting aside her strict regimen and sowing some wild oats, or off having an abortion, or a baby, or any of the other speculations. Melanie was in trouble and with each passing day, the worst case scenarios loomed larger in his mind. He could only pray, to the God that had forsaken him before, that his daughter was still alive.

Tom pulled himself, fully clothed and soaked with perspiration, off the rumpled bed and looked at his haggard face in the mirror. He glanced at his watch; coming up on four-thirty. He must have drifted off around three. He had slept little since Monday night. Scattered catnaps here and there, more a result of succumbing to mental exhaustion than actually sleeping. Tom found no solace in sleep, as some victims of depression are apt to do in times of stress. The nightmares were becoming more frequent but the worst part was waking up with the fresh realization that she was really gone and having it start all over again. He shuffled downstairs and entertained thoughts of taking a shower and heading downtown. Stop in and see Detective Flannery. He'd known Flannery for ten years and although he wasn't working on Melanie's case, Tom knew that if they had anything, Flannery would tell him. Yes. That was a good idea. He'd eat something, shower, and go downtown.

Go outside.

Tom had barely ventured outside the house since Tuesday morning. After calling in sick at the school (and wasn't that a nice surprise, splashed across the front page of the *Tribune*, that greeted him on his doorstep?), Tom had spent Tuesday afternoon driving around looking for Melanie's car. The police could do nothing until she was missing for twenty-four hours. Funny, but Tom had always thought that that was TV nonsense.

Tom padded into the kitchen and checked the messages on the phone: Mrs. Anderson from school, telling him to take all the time he needed, our prayers are with you. Coach Minot has everything covered. His son, Bryce, asking if there was any news—he could fly in from Frisco Friday night, take a few days off if needed. Tom would call him and tell him to stay put. Bryce had just landed a big money position, fresh out of college, with MicroCom. Tom did not want him to take time off (*because Melanie is never coming back*) and jeopardize his career. For what? So he could sit around and watch his father go crazy?

A twisted growl rose up from the pit of Tom's stomach, reminding him that he had eaten next to nothing in the last couple of days. He nosed through the refrigerator, finding nothing that appealed to him, but eager to quell the rumbling in his gut. He pulled the ham (before it went bad) and some fixins' and fashioned himself a pretty good-sized sandwich between two slices of light rye. Tom placed the sandwich, a jar of Vlasic dills, and a half-empty bag of chips on a TV tray, along with the cordless phone (should the police call) and a liter of root beer.

He shuffled into the living room and eased into his recliner to watch the evening news while he ate. The sandwich was going down much easier than he would have imagined and he was actually considering making another one (God, but he was hungry) when the perky anchorwoman on Action7 news suddenly turned very somber leading into her teaser for the next story after the commercial break.

"Coming up next on Action7. A tragic ending in the puzzling case of a missing teenager."

The liter of root beer fell from Tom's fist onto the floor.

On the television, a wide-angle shot of men in yellow windbreakers, emerging from the woods. Two of the men are hefting a large body-bag while a third lags behind, cradling a smaller bag.

"Police in south suburban Ridgewood uncover the grisly remains of a teenager missing for days! The story when we return."

The pain raced up Tom's left arm and hit him square in his chest like a lead blocker turning a corner with a full head of steam. A half-chewed glob of ham and rye lodged in his windpipe, further cutting off his air as he clutched at his constricting chest with his right hand. Tom reached for the phone and toppled to the floor, taking the snack tray with him in an explosion of potato chips and pickle juice. He fumbled with the tiny buttons on the phone, his meaty fingers stabbing two and three at a time.

I'm having a heart attack. Try to stay calm. Hang up and redial. Slowly. It's only three numbers. Three numbers . . .

Tom Houghwat hacked the blockage out from his windpipe (one down) and held the phone steady in his trembling hand. With excruciating slowness, he dialed 9 . . . 1 . . . 1 . . .

A voice answered after three rings. "South Suburban Emergency . . ."

Tom gasped. Please, please let me be able to speak . . .

The voice on the line, "Yes, hello. Stay on the line. We are tracing this call . . ."

"I'm having a heart—"

Tom's world went black. Somewhere off in the distance he heard a woman's voice.

"Police in south suburban Ridgewood have unearthed the remains of Dominic Teresi from the Castle Woods Forest Preserve. Teresi, a nineteen-year-old auto mechanic from Chicago's West Lawn neighborhood, was last seen by friends Sunday afternoon. Although Teresi's car was found nearby in the parking lot, Police were reluctant to make a positive I.D. until the man's head was discovered just a few short hours ago . . ."

Chapter 36

Von had seen the suit in Dean Fowler's office earlier when he was on his way to Psych 202, so it came as no surprise when Staci Nowicki knocked on the open door of Mr. French's Spanish 301 class and handed Mr. French the crisply folded blue-slip.

A blue-slip was never a good thing. They came off the five-and-a-half by four-and-a-half inch tablet in Dean Fowler's office and were only used to pull students from class for disciplinary or extreme measures. Von was already closing his book as Mr. French opened the slip and called his name.

"Señor Vonosovich," he said, initialing the slip and handing it back to Staci, "the Dean would like to see you."

Von gathered his books and walked to front of the class, feeling the eyes of his classmates on his back. A low, goosey murmur buzzed through the classroom, confirming the rumors that had been circulating since Tuesday.

"Señor Vonosovich," Mr. French said when Von was almost to the door.

Von turned.

"Good luck."

"Gracias," Von replied, forcing a smile. Mr. French wasn't a bad guy, kind of a dork, but not a bad guy.

Staci Nowicki put even more sway in her hips than usual as she led Von down the empty corridor. She turned to speak, hoping to catch him looking at her rear end. He wasn't.

"It really hit the fan, huh?" she asked, looking up at him. "The Skull's got this guy in his office. He looks like he's from the freakin' FBI or something. Coach Minot's in there with them. Are you scared? I would be. Have you heard anything about Melanie? I guess Coach Houghwat is doing okay—in the hospital, I mean. I didn't mean he's doing okay with Melanie. Hold on," she said, taking a breath and pausing in front of another classroom door. "Just one more stop," she said with a goofy smile. "We have to get Mark."

Staci knocked on the door and entered. Von moved off to the side, away from the prying eyes and craning necks of Miss Tipping's Drafting class. Staci emerged with Mark Steponic in tow. Staci was still talking. Mark Steponic, the hulking lineman, looked like he was ready to soil his pants. "Hey, Von," he croaked. "I guess this is it, huh? God damn, Jake. Man, I still can't believe it."

They fell into line behind Staci and hooked a right into the main corridor toward the administration office. "Don't worry about it," Von said. "It's going to be all right. I mean, what can they do?"

Mark frowned and said nothing. They both knew what they could do.

"Lally's already in there," Staci said. "They pulled him out of lunch. You guys are the only ones for today, but there may be more. I can hear them talking. The door's closed but I can hear them through the vent in the floor by Mrs. Anderson's plants. You know she's got seven cats? I mean—eek! Right? She's pretty cool though—for an old lady, I mean. I think she's just lonely. You know her husband died. She talks to me a lot. I'm in there so much it's almost like I work there. Maybe I can work there after we graduate." She giggled. "You know—just do what I do now, only get paid for it. The Skull—everyone thinks he's a real a-hole but once you get—"

"Staci?" Mark asked suddenly.

Staci looked at him, her wide eyes as big as saucers. "Yes, Marcus?"

"Shut up. Just shut up."

Staci Nowicki looked as if she might cry. She opened her mouth to defend herself, but something in the big lineman's face made her think better of it.

Mrs. Anderson looked up from her desk in the Administration Office as they approached and managed one of her patented smiles. "Principal McGowan and Dean Fowler are waiting for you." She motioned with a ruffled sleeve past the Dean's door. "In the conference room at the end of the hall."

The two boys elbowed past the blessedly silent Staci Nowicki and walked single-file down the narrow, carpeted hallway. The door at the end of the corridor was open but Von knocked once before entering.

Dean Fowler's voice, monotone and impossible to read as always, answered. "Come in, gentlemen. Close the door behind you."

Dean Fowler, Coach Minot, and Coach Mangan were seated in plush brown leather chairs on one side of the massive parquet table. Frank Lally sat directly across from them, next to two empty chairs. Principal McGowan stood at the far head of the table, talking to a compact, angular man in a three-piece suit. The man had a ruddy complexion and a lionesque mass of wavy salt-and-pepper hair piled high atop his triangular head. To Von he looked like a shark wearing a wig.

Principal McGowan turned and motioned for them to sit. "Sit down, boys," he said, in his booming voice. Von tried to recall if he had ever heard him speak before without the benefit of a microphone. Principal McGowan sightings were rare, usually reserved for assemblies and pep rallies. "This is Mr. Skafish from the Illinois State Athletic Commission. He'd like to talk to you about the recent, and rather ugly, allegations leveled by your former teammate. I think if we all cooperate, we can wipe this slate clean and restore the honor of the Ridgewood High Athletic Department."

Principal McGowan retreated and hefted his bulk into the chair closest to the door. The shark nodded to them and took the seat at the head of the table. "Mr. Steponic," he mumbled, shuffling through a sheaf of papers, "and Mr. Vonosovich." He looked up at Von and back to the paperwork in his hands. "Congratulations on a fine season, Sergei. Your exploits have not gone unnoticed down in Bloomingdale." He smiled, but continued to stare at Von as if he were a mutant lab animal. Von caught a glimpse of his personnel record, complete with digital I.D. photos, in the shark's ream of paperwork. He had been comparing the photos to the face he saw before him now.

"A fine season for you all," he continued. "Quite a drastic improvement from last year." He looked around the room, fixing his gaze now on Coach Mangan and Coach Minot. "A turn-around like this is bound to raise some eyebrows, and let me assure you, it has. ISAC has received several letters and phone calls regarding the sudden dominance of your program, even before your Mr. Jacobson told his tale to the newspapers. We suspect most of these tips and accusations come from opposing coaches and disgruntled parents of children in other programs. However, because of the sheer volume of complaints and the recent publicity generated by the *Tribune* story, we have no choice but to look into these allegations.

"I have spoken at length with Principal McGowan about the possible ramifications and penalties your entire athletic program may incur if evidence is found that performance-enhancing drugs contributed in anyway to the stellar record of the RedHawks varsity football team. A state championship is well within reach and I know all parties concerned would like to achieve that goal without the ugly and shameful specter of steroid abuse tainting it in anyway. Taking all this into consideration, Principal McGowan has assured me that you fellows would agree, in order to clear your good names, and the good standing of the RedHawks athletic program, to be tested for anabolic steroids and other performance-enhancing drugs."

Mark Steponic swallowed loudly.

The shark continued. "If by chance any member of the program should test positive, ISAC has agreed, because of the cooperation extended to us in our investigation by the Ridgewood athletic program, to let your record stand, upon the immediate expulsion of that individual from the football program. The team will remain eligible for the playoffs and the State crown. Refusal to undergo testing will result in a full-scale investigation of the entire athletic program."

The shark looked up from his sheaf of paperwork. "Do you understand the consequences if you refuse to be tested?"

Von understood perfectly. They were putting the old squeeze play on the school.

The boys mumbled their acknowledgment.

"Very good," the shark nodded. He reached down into his metal briefcase on the floor and came up with three specimen bottles. The brown plastic vessels had temperature indicator strips running down their sides and tamper-proof seals dangling from the caps. "Let's get started."

Chapter 37

Jason spotted his friend walking into the cafeteria almost midway through lunch and waved him over to the table he was sharing with Haley McBride. Von offered up an apathetic wave and drifted into the spotty line along the counter that fronted the cafeteria's kitchen.

"What's he doing?" Jason asked. "He never eats that food. Said he'd starve first."

Haley forced a smile. The buzz had already filtered throughout the entire school. "Maybe he forgot his lunch."

Jason peered over her shoulder as Von made his way toward them. "No, he's got his usual brown sack: three Fluffernutters, two bananas, chips, Ho-Hos, and an apple. The guy's a real connoisseur."

Haley did smile now. She and Jason had a running joke about Von's unwavering lunch menu. The only item that varied was the snack bag, and that was always Doritos, Fritos, or Lay's barbecue potato chips. "And two cans of Mountain Dew to top it all off," she giggled. She really liked Jason. She was glad that Von had such a good friend.

"What's so funny?" Von asked, setting the cafeteria tray down and settling in next to Haley. "You guys talking about me again?"

"Always," Haley answered. She leaned over and gave him a peck on the cheek. Haley was never one for public displays of affection but she felt he could use a little TLC right about now. "We were talking about—oh gross!" she exclaimed, noticing the contents of his tray. "Is that the goo-plate special?"

"It almost looks like meat loaf," Jason chimed in. "Except for being green and all."

Von looked down at the heaping triple serving as if he were surprised to see it. "Yeah, I think it *is* meatloaf. I don't know. It smelled so good, I just had to have it. That ever happen to you?" he asked no one in particular.

Jason raised an eyebrow at Haley. "I'll take your word for it, big fella."

"Go ahead," Von replied, stabbing a forkful of the brackish ground beef into his mouth, "make fun. But you know what? It's pretty good." He swallowed, then added, "A little overdone maybe."

Haley blanched. He was really shoveling it in. Apparently being tested for steroids had not affected his appetite. She glanced at Jason, imploring him to ask the question.

"So what happened?" Jason blurted.

"What happened?" Von asked between chews. "You mean the ISAC guy?" He took a long swallow of Mountain Dew and smiled at Jason. "No big deal. The guy came down, asked us some questions. He had to—after the *Tribune* story broke. Asked us to take a urine—" He looked at Haley. "A steroid test." Von's eyes darted around the cafeteria but he spoke directly to Jason in a low conspiratorial tone. "You know, we may have to get by for a while without Lally and Steps."

"Von, aren't you nervous?" Jason asked.

Von lowered the fork and glared at his friend. "Now, why the hell would I be nervous, Jay?"

Jason shifted in his seat. "Um, you know, man—the test. The steroid test."

Von ceremoniously dabbed at his mouth with a paper napkin. "The steroid test. Yes, well I guess I would be pretty nervous—*if I was on goddamn steroids!*"

Haley let out an audible gasp, stunned by the venom in his voice. The lunchroom all around them fell silent.

"I mean, what the hell!" Von continued, looking at Jason

but speaking to everyone within earshot. "Why don't you just say it? You think I'm on the junk. You're jealous! You're jealous because I worked my ass off to get here," he spit, thumping his chest with his finger. "I'm *starting*. My name's in the paper. The scouts are at every game—checking *me* out. I get letters every day! And you?" Von scowled at his friend. "You're splitting your playing time with a *junior!* You're the one who should be nervous, pal."

Jason replied in a low, measured tone, refusing to play the scene out for the wide-eyed mopes sitting around them. "Did it ever occur to you that maybe football isn't the most important thing in my life? It's just a *game,* man. I've got other interests—and you used to, too. When was the last time you *wrote* anything? I bet you can't remember."

Von smirked and rolled his eyes. "Football is going to give me a free ride to college. What are you going to do?"

"I'm going to art school," Jason replied with a trace of smug pride. "Mr. Blodgett said I've got the goods for a career. He's helping me get a portfolio together and he thinks *NightHawk* can—"

"Ooooh, art school!" Von snorted in a high falsetto voice. "How absolutely fagocious! Do you really think you're going to get anywhere with that fruity comic—"

"Von!" Haley gasped. "Stop it! Stop it right now! Listen to yourself! My God, what is wrong with you?"

"What's wrong with me?" Von mocked. "Gosh, I don't know. Let's see. My girlfriend and my supposed best friend both think I'm on steroids and talk about me behind my back like I'm some kind of mutant. How's that for starters?"

"No one thinks you're on steroids, Von," Haley lied. "We're just concerned about you, that's all. Isn't that right, Jason?"

Jason glared straight ahead and said nothing. Haley could

see that Von's crack about the *NightHawk* comic had really stung him.

Von looked at Jason. The little fruit looked like he was about to cry. He turned on Haley. "Concerned, huh? Gosh, two days ago the only thing you seemed concerned about was your dead *boyfriend*. Maybe you still want to screw him, hmm? Maybe we should go down to the morgue and see if we can't put him back together."

Haley's jaw dropped in disbelief. When the news had broken about Dominic Teresi, the first emotion she had felt was relief. The relief was followed by shame that she would find such comfort in it, and a blurry but lingering sense of guilt. Ridiculous, of course. She had called Von in tears, unsure of how to deal with the emotions roiling inside her and she was taken aback by his indifference to the whole matter.

The guy had it coming, Haley, he had told her. Would you rather it had been him or you?

He said it like she had a choice in the matter. She looked at him now, the mad glint in his eye.

Maybe she did.

"Screw you," she said, holding back her tears.

"Screw me? Screw *me?* You already did, remember?" he leered, raising his voice so all could hear. He stood to go. "Call me when you want some more, baby."

Haley blinked back tears as she watched the boy she thought she loved storm out of the cafeteria.

Jason put a conciliatory arm around her shoulder. She fell into the embrace and let the tears flow. "He's on steroids, isn't he?" she sobbed.

Jason said nothing for a moment. He pondered the physical changes in his friend's face—the personality regression, the mood swings.

"I hope so," he said.

Chapter 38

Von was almost laughing with delight as he scanned the note his mother had left on the kitchen table: *Von—had to go in early. Heres a twenty for a pizza leave me some change! Love you!*

Thank God. The last thing he needed right now was a thousand questions about his day and how was Haley and yaketty-yak before he could steal away and cop the fix that his body had been screaming for since Tuesday. Von snatched the ratty twenty-dollar bill and wadded it into his pocket, noting with distaste his mother's minor punctuation errors and childish handwriting. Why was it so hard for some people to grasp even the most rudimentary aspects of the English language? It must have been hell for his father to put up with such ignorance. A twinge of shame followed that thought but was gone before he hit the third stair on his way down to the refuge of his basement.

Von bounded through his workout/study area and leaped on top of his bed, tearing at the acoustic ceiling tiles with little regard for the sanctity of his hiding place. He fumbled for the works kit lodged in the rafters and pulled it down. It had been three days since the story broke and he had forced himself to stay away, afraid of what might turn up in his bloodstream. Well, it was over now and he could go back to fixing. (Every day? Yes, sometimes twice.) Whenever he felt the need—tests be damned, they could all go to hell. Von spilled the contents of the med-kit onto his bed. He stabbed the hypo through the corked vial, grinning as he drew back the plunger and filled the barrel. He doubled the dosage. Hell, he deserved it after being deprived for so long.

The rush hit him like a blind-side tackle. A low, lusty

moan filled his ears, followed by an almost childish giggle as the elixir surged through his bloodstream with the systematic resolve of wildfire through virgin timber.

When it had finally subsided, Von lay back on his bed, his veins visibly pulsating beneath the surface of his skin. After catching his breath he propped himself up on his elbows and—

His hand darted back to the base of his spine, his mind refusing to believe the information his fingertips were relaying. The boy sprang from his bed and turned his back to the mirror.

A cylindrical nub of horny flesh protruded from his spine, just above his buttocks, almost three inches long and nearly as thick. He fingered it gingerly and shuddered aloud as it twitched in response to his touch. He pulled his hand away, craning his neck to get a better look.

It was a tail. *Bat shit,* he was growing a tail.

Back in the refuge of his bedroom, Von slipped into a pair of gym shorts, forgoing his habit of walking around naked when his mother was not home (no need to be reminded of unpleasant little grotesqueries). He stepped up on his bed and pulled his father's journal out from beneath the fiberglass insulation, frowning at the minor damage he had done to the drop ceiling in his mad dash for the elixir. Von blew the pink dust off the bound manuscript, aware that he could not remember the last time he had read from it. Things were happening so quickly now; school, Haley, football, the college scouts at the games, finding out you are descended from an ancient line of werewolves . . .

He had been meaning to peruse the journal since the story had broken on Tuesday, on the off chance he might find some obscure reference to indicators in the blood should he be tested for steroids.

Given this most recent turn of events, however, steroid markers were the farthest things from his mind.

Von sat on the edge of his bed and flipped through the journal, starting his search from the back end. He had only skimmed these passages before. Muddled and cryptic, they were the ramblings of his father in his last days, oftentimes lapsing into his native Romanian, hard to decipher, and disturbing when clear enough to comprehend. He flipped back to one page that he had bookmarked, a complex, hand-drawn table of coded gene combinations, footnoted and cross-referenced almost beyond comprehension. It was here that Von first took note of the marked change in his father's handwriting.

The chart itself was a model of efficiency, meticulously rendered with a steady and deliberate hand. The mark-ups had obviously come later. Slapdash and furious, they were written in the hurried script that dominated the latter pages of the manuscript.

In one corner of the chart his father had circled the gene code FGFR3 in a hand so heavy, its impression could be seen on the following three pages. Von followed the crescent line stabbing the angry circle to the footnote at the bottom of the page:

Fibroblast growth factor receptor-3 gene, present in parental gametes-splice with p53 suppresser gene?—see Transcription and Frameshift mutations . . .

Frameshift mutations.

Von flipped ahead and saw the phrase at the top of the page in large bold letters like a chapter heading. Immediately below it:

I can no longer deny that the cycle has progressed much faster than anticipated and has in fact advanced past the target apex. Where to go once one has reached the top? Back down of course— in a spiral Darwin no doubt would have loved. That the genetic re- mapping would continue to cycle after reaching the desired coding was unthinkable only months ago. Indeed, in my excitement upon having recreated the nectar of the Father's Fruit, I was left blind to a progression so natural, a child could have seen it looming on the horizon.

Scrawled over this sentence in that disturbing, disjointed hand: *A child burdened by a birthright corrupted by a shortsight-edness equal to my own.*

Von swallowed hard, realizing for the first time his father was talking about him. He continued to read the original text beneath the sporadic and indecipherable rambling:

That the regression has been set in motion is undeniable and would appear to be unstoppable. My only hope is to stack the deck and pray for a wildcard.

The playing card analogy is not coincidental. Indeed, it was not until I had overheard a lunchroom conversation amongst some co- workers that I had even contemplated such a catastrophic turn of events. Two lab techs, upon returning from a weekend junket to Las Vegas, were discussing the strategies involved in stud poker. It is all a matter of chance. If you are holding a relatively solid hand—a Jack-high straight flush, for instance, what are the chances you would be able to improve that hand by discarding and drawing an- other? How about two cards? Three? The number of harmful changes far outweigh the number of beneficial changes that can occur and the risk increases with each successive alteration.

Given that DNA is an extremely complex molecule, there are a number of ways it can be altered—but which method carries the least risk?

Possible alternatives: Multiple base-pair substitutions? Unfortunately, these also are more likely to be harmful because when the base sequence is altered, it disrupts the normal reading and copying of its entire length—not just at that site. We know Point Mutations often cause no effect (not all DNA codes for protein synthesis) but we may be able to induce a minor protein change without the usual lethal consequences normally incurred with this method.

Von closed the journal and laid it down on the bed beside him. The horrific protrusion at the base of his spine rubbed harshly against his gym shorts.

This was a wildcard he had not counted on, but he had stuck with this hand too long to fold now. The stakes were too high. Von reached for the med-kit and held the vial of elixir up to the light. He contemplated the lovely emerald fluid that had blessed him with such good fortune.

It was time to up the ante.

Chapter 39

Haley McBride did not regret her decision to forgo the big game against Bogan and stay home and veg in front of the television. It had been a long time since she had treated herself to such a select night of self-indulgence—not since the trouble with Dominic—but now, as then, she figured she deserved some pampering. A big paper tub of Movietime Popcorn lay on the floor near her feet, barren, save for a few unpopped kernels, alongside an empty box of Black Crow licorice and a nearly depleted liter of Cherry 7-Up.

She had begged off several phone calls from "the girls" trying to pull her out of the house. The thing with her and Von had already become prime grist for the rumor mill and she simply didn't have the stomach to deal with any more nonsense tonight. Losing herself in a movie was a temporary distraction at best but it kept the tears at bay, and that was good enough for her.

She had already watched John Carpenter's *The Thing* (Kurt Russell was so cute), and was struggling to stay awake to the end of *Re-Animator* when the doorbell rang. Now who could be calling at such a late hour and why didn't her parents hear the bell upstairs? She blinked the fog from her eyes, surprised to find herself in the living room after dozing off down in the rec room (on the same couch where she and Von had made love). Just as well, her father was going to have a fit if this woke him up.

She shuffled to the door and peered out the peephole, seeing only the moon, full and bright, hanging low over the Bennets' house, across the street. It was the biggest moon she had ever seen, breathtaking, actually, and she could not resist the urge to step out on the porch and see it in all its glory. She opened the door and Von was standing there in his football uniform backlit by that amazing moon—her moon—brighter and bigger than it was only a moment ago. He cut quite a heroic figure, framed against her moon like that; his torso accentuated by the big shoulder pads, his helmet cradled in one muscled arm, his eyeblack lending a sinister resolve to his gaze and a sharp contrast to the white of his teeth—those long teeth.

"Hey, baby," Von said, reaching up and gently stroking her cheek with two fingers. "I missed you tonight. You should have seen me. I was great."

"I'm sorry," she replied, forgetting for the moment that she was mad at him, that she would never speak to him again, that they were through.

Von stepped closer and pulled her knit top down away from her shoulder (now when did she slip into that?), exposing the crescent shaped scar on her trapezius. He ran his finger over it, raising the goose flesh his initial touch always elicited. "That's healing up nicely," he grinned. "I knew it would. It was a nice clean bite. Come on, let's go for a drive."

He stepped aside and she saw a white 1956 Thunderbird sitting curbside, just like the one Suzanne Somers drove in *American Graffiti*, right down to the porthole window. She had never told him that that was her favorite car—her *dream* car—but Von knew. Von knew everything about her.

"It's beautiful," she said.

"You're beautiful," Von replied. He was wearing a red tuxedo. "Come on," he smiled, flashing those sharp, white, teeth. "We're going to be late."

He took her hand and led her down the porch, the train of her wedding gown trailing out behind her.

Haley climbed into the passenger side, not bothering to duck her head, as the hardtop was now a convertible. They drove through the night in the open air, floating toward the moon that always lay directly just ahead. She turned to look at Von and noticed that he now had the head of a wolf. The Von-wolf returned her gaze, his canine lips pulling back in a sardonic grin.

"My totem animal," he explained. His pink tongue moved rhythmically in and out with each panting breath. He was excited. "What's yours?"

"Why, I don't know," she blustered. "Do I have one?"

"We all have one," he growled. Von-wolf reached over and pulled her visor down for her with a long hairy paw. "Here, take a look."

Haley stared, fascinated at the reflection in the ornate vanity mirror. Fur, silver and gray, sprouted profusely from her wet black nose, covering her face. Feline eyes blinked back playfully, then rolled up in her triangular head and fixed on the ultra-long ears twitching in the convertible's slipstream.

"Hmm," she said matter-of-factly. "I'm a cat."

"A lynx, I think," Von-wolf said. "Methinks you are a lynx!"

Haley giggled. Von could always make her laugh. She took his paw in hers and purred contentedly.

They pulled into the drive-in parking lot and she recognized it immediately. It was *Arnold's*, the teen hangout on that old TV show, *Happy Days*. The whole gang, it seemed, was here for their wedding. Kerri Wheeler ran up to the car pulling Ralph Malph by the hand.

"Ooh, I'm so excited for you, honey," Kerri squealed. "Come on, we don't have much time. Let me help you get ready. Oh, your fur is just a mess!"

The jab about her unkempt fur did not slip by Haley, nor did the sidelong glance that Kerri had shot toward Von. The Bitch. Haley had always known that Kerri had the hots for her wolf. She would have to keep an eye on that. She stepped out of the car, carefully pulling her dress up over her ankles. She didn't want to sully such a beautiful gown. Mike Minot roared up on Fonzie's motorcycle, the front tire just missing her little cat feet.

"Hey!" Haley gasped, "Watch where you're—"

Something like hate flashed in his dark eyes and Haley knew to say no more.

"That's a good little girl," the coach sneered at her, leaning the bike over on its side-stand. "Just keep that pie-hole shut and you'll be okay." He winked at her. "You know what I mean."

"Coach!" Von-wolf howled, ignoring Haley and rushing over to his mentor. He bulled his way past Potsy and Chachi, eager to get a front row seat in the king's court. "Outta the way, numb-nuts," Von growled, knocking Richie Cunningham to the ground with a brutal swipe of his hairy paw.

"Cut!" Richie yelled, pulling himself to his feet. He was no longer Richie, but Ron Howard, the balding director. "Cut! This isn't in the script! This isn't how it's supposed to be. Look, it's right here on page forty-six. Haley McBride is supposed to find true happiness in the arms of the football hero and—"

"Melanie!" Minot yelled, jumping up off the bike. "I thought I told you to stay in the goddamn car!"

Mr. Howard stopped short, silenced by the surprised stares of everyone on the set. Haley turned and followed his gaze.

The rotted corpse of Melanie Houghwat was heading to-

wards them, trudging slowly across the lot with numb deliberation. Pools of brackish water and slime puddled in the
wake of her heavy, laborious footsteps. Seaweed and river-
scum dotted the corrupt, pitted flesh of her naked body. One
eye rolled tentatively in its collapsing socket toward Haley
and a glimmer of life (hope?) flashed through the dead orb.
The corpse stretched its cheesy yellow arms out, pleading,
reaching out for Haley.

Haley woke with a muffled scream in her throat. She was
on the couch in the rec room in her own house. On the television, John Goodman and the cast members of *Saturday Night
Live* were waving a near tearful goodbye to the viewers at
home. She switched on the end-table lamp and turned off the
TV. She thought of Melanie Houghwat and the way she had
looked at her (pleaded with her) in the dream.

She had been driving home from the Regent and had seen
Melanie's car in the lot of the Brookshire Glenn apartment
complex the night she disappeared.

Somewhere off in the distance, a sad and terrible howl
shook the quiet from the night.

Coach Minot lived in the Brooks.

Chapter 40

Friday night's 37–0 drubbing over archrival Hubbard did little to lift the curtain of gloom that had fallen over Ridgewood High since Melanie Houghwat's disappearance and her father's subsequent heart attack. The buzz filtering through the school had the season in the tank anyway, once the results of the steroid tests came back. Everyone, from the strength-and-conditioning coach, on down to the little blue-haired ladies that worked in the cafeteria, was sure that Sergei Vonosovich was on the juice and the day of reckoning was close at hand.

Eugene Kroc thought differently.

Kroc found himself re-evaluating the suspicions he had fostered about Von when the boy had arrived at Ridgewood three years ago. The Order had arranged Kroc's assignment at the south suburban school, so rich with students of middle and eastern European descent, and in such close proximity to the last documented attacks.

And it was starting again, wasn't it?

Von's work had been on a sharp decline since late September. The downward spiral was evident in his test grades, but it was the boy's writing that had troubled Kroc more than anything else. The few essays and creative writing exercises he had handed in were lackluster and uninspired, but there was more to it than that.

Kroc was familiar with Von's work. He had recognized the boy's obvious talent in freshman year and had monitored his development with a nurturing and attentive eye. Kroc had actually looked forward to reading the boy's prose the way an avid fan will wait for his favorite author's latest novel to hit the stands. The writing was indicative of a sly and remarkable understanding of the human condition for one so young, with none of the heavy-handed metaphor Kroc found prevalent in even the most talented beginners.

His recent work was less than the slapdash or hurried scribbling of a talented student who no longer felt the urge to excel. It was, in fact, void of any understanding of basic composition or narrative: a "C" level effort from a "D" student.

It was like another person had written it.

And wasn't that indicative of the *change?*

Kroc's antennae were up and twitching as he watched his students filter in to homeroom with the first bell. Dan Jacobson was due back in school today and the staff was on alert. The fallout from the scandal was far from over and the last thing that the gangly teacher needed this morning was a fistfight between two weightroom Neanderthals.

It pained him to think of Von in such terms.

Dan Jacobson lumbered into his room with the first wave, the earliest and quietest entrance of his high school career. He seemed smaller somehow, stripped of the swagger and meaty bravado that had always radiated from him like a foul odor. Jacobson slipped into his chair like an altar boy late for morning service, his eyes lowered and his head hung low. Kroc could see Von and Frank Lally lingering in the hall, thick as thieves, crowing no doubt, about the traitor that had brought them such grief.

Kroc swallowed and walked to the door in anticipation of the last bell. He held the door open with a sweeping gesture and motioned to the two stragglers.

"Last call, boys," he said, trying to inject a note of levity into his voice. Inside he felt as though he might puke.

"Saddest words in the English language," Lally snorted. He slapped Von on the back. "Come on. Let's belly up to the bar."

Von squeezed past Kroc just as the bell rang, without so much as a smile or a nod.

"All right," Kroc began, keeping an eye on the two as they made their way to their seats. Jacobson busied himself with his textbook and avoided eye contact. "On Friday we were discussing the emphatic voice in conjunction with crafting more effective sentences. Would anyone care to give an example of two similar sentences using a passive versus an active voice?"

Kroc looked tentatively around the room. This was usually the point where he could count on Von or Melanie Houghwat to offer something to the class. He glanced at Von and only caught his dead stare, a sight only slightly less disturbing than Melanie's empty chair. "Mr. Vonosovich?" Kroc implored. "I know this is a subject very dear to your heart. Any thoughts?"

Von shrugged indifferently. "No," he mumbled, and turned his attention to his mechanical pencil.

"Okay," Kroc said. "Anyone else? Going once . . . going twice . . . ? Very well, then. It's a Monday morning. I'll get the ball rolling." Kroc turned to the chalkboard and rattled a sentence noisily across its surface in a cloud of white dust.

A final examination was failed by the starting halfback.

Kroc turned and addressed his fold. "Okay, anyone care to turn this limp noodle into something with a little more structure?"

Kerri Wheeler raised her hand. Kroc braced himself. "Ms. Wheeler . . ."

Kerri grimaced, as if the concentration were hurting her brain. "Mmmm . . . 'The starting halfback failed the final examination . . . ?' "

"Yes!" Kroc said a little too loudly. "Yes. Excellent, Kerri. By placing the emphasis on the subject—*the halfback*—Ms.

Wheeler eliminates the awkward structure shift of the original sentence." Kroc scooped up the chalk and turned again to the board. "Let's try another—"

"What the hell are you doing?"

The chalk fell from Kroc's spidery fingers, so ominous and threatening was the voice behind his back.

He turned and saw Von rise from his chair.

Kroc's eyes widened. A shameful twinge of relief shot through him when he realized the boy was not talking to him. "Vonosovich! Sit down. Get back to your seat."

Von ignored him and advanced up the aisle, stopping three rows from the front. A hush fell over the room that was equal parts terror and excitement. Von placed his big knuckles on Jonathan Howell's desk and leaned over the boy as if he were not there. Howell shrank back in his seat in an effort to completely disappear. Von had leaned his bulk into the next aisle and was staring directly at Jason Jankowski.

"I said, 'What the hell are you doing?' "

Jason returned the gaze but could not speak. The color drained from his face before returning in a blush of crimson. "Nothing," he somehow managed. "Nothing. What are you talking about?"

"Sit down, Von," Haley McBride seethed. She sat two seats away from Jason in the next aisle. "He didn't do anything! Just sit down!"

"He passed you a note," Von said. "I saw him."

"Mr. Vonosovich," Kroc said in a steady, measured tone, "if you do not return to your seat immediately, I will jug you for the next two months and you will never play another down of football for this school. I promise you that."

Von glared at Jason but relented.

"I'm sorry, Mr. Kroc," he said. Something in his voice made Kroc believe he actually meant it. He slid his hands off

Jonathan Howell's desk, straightened his posture and walked slowly back to his seat.

"All right," Kroc said, placing the chalk back on the ledge. "Let's all take a moment here. I know we are all very concerned about Melanie and Coach Houghwat, and tensions are very—"

Kroc stopped and stared at Von. A thin trickle of blood was running out of his left nostril, a bright crimson worm that paused on the bow of his lip before drizzling down to the corner of his mouth. The boy seemed not to notice.

"Mr. Vonosovich," Kroc asked, "are you not feeling well?"

Von's eyes snapped open. "Hunnnmmm?"

Kroc raised his hand to his own mouth and tapped his index finger under his nose. "Are you all right?" he asked again, trying to alert the boy to the obvious. "Your nose is bleeding."

"Oh—oh!" Von said, suddenly understanding. "Yeah, sorry. That's nothing." He pulled a yellow bandanna, already stained with dried blood, from his pants pocket and dabbed absentmindedly at the discharge. "I'm okay, really," he said, from behind the bloody linen, literally waving away the concerned looks of his classmates. "It's nothing, no big deal. I—" Von looked at Jacobson, as if noticing him for the first time. "Hey, Jake," he said, "where you been? We were starting to think you didn't like us any—nnghhhh . . ."

Von doubled over, clutching at his stomach like a man trying to contain his innards after a disembowelment. Eugene Kroc was already on the intercom, calling for help, by the time his body hit the floor.

Chapter 41

Von could not remember exactly when the muscle cramps had started, but he could pinpoint unequivocally when the first cluster headache had struck. His digital alarm clock was displaying 4:42 A.M. when he had awakened from a deep sleep on Sunday morning with his cerebral cortex feeling as if it was literally going to explode and spill out of his ears. His cries woke his mother, who had rushed downstairs to find him prone on his bed, lathered in sweat and afraid to even move, lest he bring on another pounding swell of agony.

She had waited at his bedside, applying cold compresses to his forehead and waiting for the *Amerge*, her own prescription migraine medicine, to shrink the swelling blood vessels in his brain. He had fallen back asleep, mercifully, after an hour of the most intense pain he had ever known. When he had risen from a fitful sleep later that morning, he found his mother slumped in a chair beside his bed, her eyes vacant and resigned, like those of a shell-shocked refugee in an aid station.

He had managed to talk her out of a trip to the hospital, but after hearing of his collapse in homeroom on Monday, his mother had him in Dr. Harlan's office that night, for a complete physical. He could hear the two of them talking, of course, behind the closed door of the examination room and he knew just what to say when Harlan started in with the questions. No, this was the first of the headaches (the truth). No, he hadn't taken a nasty blow to the head in Friday's game (the truth). No, this was the first and only nosebleed (a lie). Yes, he felt just fine now (a lie). He thought that he had smoke-screened the doctor pretty thoroughly, but the old quack had still prescribed two days off of football practice and ordered a CAT scan along with a barrage of blood-work.

Luckily, the Imaging Center under his mother's HMO was booked solid for the next two weeks so he could buy himself some time, and with any luck, blow the whole thing off entirely.

The blood-work was his real concern, though.

Von sat outside the school nurse's office, fingering the note from Dr. Harlan, wondering if this would be his last week in a RedHawks uniform. The results from ISAC were due back any day now. If those came back dirty, God only knew what a complete work-up would reveal.

He would not allow it. He would hightail it out of town before he would subject himself to that kind of scrutiny.

Nurse Kremer motioned to him through the half-open door, and Von put on his best happy face as he walked in and handed her the note.

"What have you got for me, Von?" Nurse Kremer asked, taking the note from his hand. She smiled at him, a coy smile that put his senses on code red. Her pupils were markedly dilated when she looked at him.

Von looked her over. Teresa Kremer had to be pushing the mid-century mark, but she was smiling like a schoolgirl melting under her first kiss. "Get out of jail free card," he said. "I'm cleared to go back to practice today."

"Oh," she said. "Good for you." She swiveled in her chair, on the pretense of getting a pen from her drawer, giving him a good look at her legs, sheathed in nurse's white sheer. "How are you feeling?"

"Like a million bucks," Von smiled. What, now all of a sudden you're a doctor? Just sign the release so I can get to practice.

"Okay, hon," she said, initialing the release and handing it back to him. "You're all set."

Von took the form, letting his finger touch hers during the exchange. He felt the hot flash through his fingertip. A cheap thrill, it evaporated with the stinging inaccuracy of her words. "Am I now?" he asked, tiring of the flirtation. He suddenly found her very old and repulsive.

Von turned on his heels and walked out of the nurse's office. The day's final bell sounded, filling the main corridor with freshmen and sophomores scrambling for the exits with the frenzy of a jailbreak. Von walked unimpeded through the crowd, the lower classmen giving a wide berth to the Big Man on Campus.

He sensed a change in the air the moment he opened the door to the locker room. The frenetic energy, the anticipation that normally lingered in the air, was gone, replaced by a troubled calm, not unlike the quiet that fills a courtroom as a jury files in after a long deliberation. They all looked up when he entered, their faces as solemn as old friends gathered at a colleague's funeral. Von's eyes darted immediately to the coach's office where Lally and Steponic sat slumped with their heads hung low, opposite Coach Mangan and Coach Minot. At their feet were their equipment bags, stuffed hap-hazardly—hurriedly—with their gear. Mark Steponic's helmet and huge, oversize shoulder pads looped through the drawstring, balanced precariously atop his bag. The equipment toppled to the floor as the boys rose from their seats and turned to go. Steponic bent to straighten the gear but Mangan waved him away with a sad gesture of resignation.

Von swallowed hard. The test results were back.

Coach Minot looked up and saw him standing there. Von could not read the coach's dark eyes, as the man motioned for him to come inside, but that alone gave the boy some hope.

Lally and Steponic shouldered past him as he opened the

door. Von could see the tears welling up in Mark Steponic's eyes despite the huge lineman's refusal to look at his teammates. Frank Lally's pig-like little eyes flashed only anger.

"Jake's a dead man," he said softly but clearly.

Von entered the small glass cubicle and closed the door behind him. Coach Minot sat behind the scarred oak desk (in Coach Houghwat's chair); and Coach Mangan was flanked to his left on the ratty old couch where Coach Houghwat would sometimes grab a quick catnap between all-night film breakdowns.

"Sit down, Von," Minot said, his face impossible to read.

Must be a hell of a poker player, Von thought as he settled into the folding aluminum chair.

"Frank Lally and Mark Steponic are no longer members of the Ridgewood RedHawks football program. They tested positive for several banned substances, including Sustaton and Finajet, a drug that is illegal in this country. Both will receive counseling and attend a substance abuse intervention program if they want to graduate."

Von felt as though he might be sick.

"You, however, are clean." Minot's poker face gave way to an easy smile that vanished so quickly Von thought he might have imagined it. "One hundred percent clean," Minot emphasized, unable to keep the sense of wonder out of his voice. "Coach Mangan and I would like to commend you for the hard work you have put in to reach this level without resorting to the temptation of anabolic steroids. Hopefully this will indicate that steroid use at Ridgewood is spotty and isolated—not the widespread epidemic that has been reported in the local press."

Von wanted to jump out of his seat. The elixir had gone undetected through his bloodstream. He fought to maintain an even keel in front of Coach Mangan. "I have to admit I'm a little relieved. I mean, of course I knew I was clean, but these tests—you never know . . . you know what I mean?"

"Of course," Minot said, nodding at Coach Mangan. "There is always room for error even in the most advanced tests—which these were. Now," Minot asked, the smile back in full bloom, "you ready to put on the pads and hit someone?"

Von smiled his best *gee whiz* smile. "You bet, Coach."

"Good. You've got a lot to catch up on." He turned to Mangan. "We got a couple of holes to plug and some personnel to evaluate in the next few days. I want to make sure we got everyone on this team maximized to full potential when we hit that field Friday night." Minot checked his watch for effect. "Coach, we're runnin' a little behind. Can you get the guys through calisthenics? I need a word with Von."

Mangan bristled but stood to go. He was getting tired of playing second fiddle to this NFL bust-out hotshot. "Sure, Coach." He clapped Von on the shoulder. "Good to have you back, kid. Don't forget to give Coach Minot your medical release," he said, eyeing the form in Von's hand. "We wouldn't want to violate any procedures here."

Minot watched him go. The bitter tone in his assistant's voice did not go unnoticed. He waited until the door closed behind the big man before turning his attention to the enigma sitting across the desk from him.

"All right," he said looking Von dead in the eye. "Let's put all our cards on the table here. You don't play football until you come clean with me." He softened his tone, not wanting to destroy the trust, the rapport he had built up with the boy. "You can trust me, Von. Nothing you say leaves this room. I promise."

Von swallowed the lump rising in his throat. Von believed him, he really did. But how much would this man—this man he had come to love as a father, be willing to believe?

Chapter 42

"Time!" Mike Minot shouted through the driving rain that had started at the two-minute warning of the first half and hadn't let up since. "Time out! Time out!" he motioned frantically to the field judge, forming a "T" with his hands. The zebra caught the gesture and blew his whistle, stopping the clock with 4:46 left in the third quarter and Ridgewood down 21–10. Naperville Central had just crossed midfield on a quick slant in the flat that Central's tight end had popped for a twenty-yard gain.

Sergei Vonosovich blinked through the maddening pink-ponking of rain off his headgear, only dimly aware of the whistle blast.

"Von!" Ryan Amberson reached across the huddle and grabbed his arm. "Von—Coach called *time*. Time out! You all right? C'mon, man . . ."

Von's head snapped around. Coach Minot was waving him in. *Damn!* "Yeah, yeah . . . I'm fine," he lied. He looked around the huddle at the scared faces of his teammates peering at him through eyeblack and birdcage facemasks.

"I—*damn* . . . hang on."

Von broke away from the huddle and trotted to the sideline, fighting off the cramping in his gut. This was a hell of a time to get sick . . . *Walter Payton had a 103-degree fever on the day he gained 275 yards against the Vikings—suck it up! Don't be such a wuss. . . . Don't—*

Mike Minot grabbed his facemask and yanked it violently. He pulled the boy close, their faces separated only by the tubular rubber and steel.

"What's your responsibility on the 32 flood zone?" Minot demanded.

Von struggled to recall. "I come up, no—I provide corner support on the strong side if—if the quarterback drops back ... unless the tight end is in motion, then I have the option to blitz . . ."

Minot thunked him on top of his helmet with his metal whistle. "That's *Monster* flood 46! We haven't played any Monster since the first quarter when it became apparent your head wasn't in this game! You *have* no options!" He fought to regain his composure. "Are you all right? You want out? I got a friend—a scout from Fresno State in the stands. He flew all the way in from the coast to watch you play. You let me know."

Suck it up—don't be a wuss . . .

Von felt something pop in his lower abdomen and then a rush, like an internal flow of liquid near his groin.

"Yeah," he said, through gritted teeth. "I just got a touch of the flu. I'm good to go." He looked his mentor in the eye. "Don't take me out . . ."

Minot considered his options. The kid was way out of his game and his head was squarely up his ass, but he was still better than anything they had riding the pine. "Okay," he said. "Don't let me down. Listen . . . you listening?" The coach rapped his clipboard atop the boy's helmet to insure that he had his full and undivided attention. "Watch the fullback, number forty-two. You can read him like a billboard. If they're going to run, he leans forward in his stance, his ass high in the air, all his weight on his down hand. If they sweep or go off-tackle, he leans to the right or the left—they prefer the right. Now here's the key: if it's a pass, he lays way back in his stance—ass low, on his heels, and no weight on his hand. He always stays back to block—always. He has hands of stone, so don't worry about him as an option if they go to the air. Don't bite on the play-action. Just watch the fullback. Got it?"

Von nodded furiously. Ass-high—run. Ass-low—pass. "Got it!"

"Attaboy," Minot said, bringing his hand down hard on the boy's shoulder pad. "Listen up. *Monster*, forty-four, dog-*Z*. I'm reinstating your license to kill. Don't let me down."

Von sprinted back to the huddle, ignoring the pain in his lower back. He did not know it, but his pelvis was expanding to accommodate the gradual, but steady, lengthening of his vertebrae. "Okay, listen up," he said to his teammates bending low around him. "Keep an eye on the fullback. His high ass is made of stone."

"What?" Donny Musconi asked, unsure of what he heard through the driving rain.

Von blinked, trying to unscramble the idiotic nonsense in his brain. "No, no. Number forty-two. His *hands* are made of stone. His ass is a *billboard!*" He smiled triumphantly. "How's that, horse-face?"

The peal of the referee's whistle cut though the steady downpour. On the other side of the football, lying ominously at the thirty-eight yard line, Naperville Central broke from their huddle with a crisp, unified, handclap.

"Von!" Owen Daniels yelled. "What's the formation?"

Von looked at him stupidly. "Huh? Oh . . . oh! Monsterdog forty-four Z."

"What the hell is a *monsterdog?*" Tim Halloran asked.

Jason Jankowski spoke up. "He means Monster, forty-four, dog-Z. Let's go."

"You screwing Haley?" Von asked Jason, forgetting where they were. "You know, I have a license to kill."

"Screw this!" Ryan Amberson said in a panic. Central was trotting to the line of scrimmage. In another moment they would be in their stances, set in their formation, and catch them with a quick snap. "I'm taking over. Stack high, six-pack, red dog. Ready—break!"

The Ridgewood defense broke from their huddle in a mad scramble, foiling the intended quick-snap command from Bruce Bucz, the Naperville Central QB. A tall and rangy quarterback with a cannon arm and a sharp mind, he opted to go with the long count, eyeballing Ridgewood's dreaded free safety. The kid was traipsing around in the secondary like a guy that just got off a bus at the wrong stop. Bucz knew the stands were loaded with college scouts with their binoculars trained on Vonosovich and decided to take full advantage of the situation. He audibled out of the deep-post that his coach had called during the RedHawks time-out and called for an option, shuffling the formation of his backfield to a wishbone with the clock winding down at three seconds and counting. The snap went off with one tick left on the clock and Bucz ran to his right, never even considering a pitch to either of the two running backs that flanked him as he rounded the strong side.

The RedHawks line, weakened by the departure of Lally and Steponic, crumpled under the double-team blocking made possible by Central's pulling left guard. Ryan Amberson reacted quickly and flowed to the ball. The big linebacker shed the token block of the Naperville wide-out and shot the gap a split-second before it closed behind him in a thunderclap of high-impact plastic and Kevlar. He drew a bead on Bruce Bucz but did not commit, anticipating the pitch to Gordon Graunauer, Central's all-conference half-back.

Bruce Bucz saw the linebacker closing in and extended his long arm, the football exposed and frozen in mid-pitch. He waited until the last possible moment before yanking it back in to the cradle of his ribcage and cutting inside. He lost his footing for a moment on the wet turf, but recovered in time to see the linebacker bite hard on the fake and commit to Graunauer sweeping wide around the right corner. Bucz burst into the secondary, greeted by a sight that normally would have struck fear in the heart of any ball-carrier.

The kid named by the *Chicago Tribune* as the most dangerous high school football player in Illinois since Dick Butkus was the only obstacle between him and the end zone some thirty yards downfield. Bucz saw the flash of yellow fire in the safety's eyes and wondered for just a moment if he hadn't made some horrible mistake. His doubts vanished as quickly as the strange glow in the free safety's eyes, leading the lanky quarterback to believe it was a trick of the stadium lights. There was no menace there, only a mask of pain and confusion that grew clearer with every galloping stride. Scholarships and headlines danced through Bruce Bucz's mind as he lowered his head and charged straight ahead, directly into the path of the most feared football player in the state.

A wet plop, like the splat of a water balloon on concrete, followed the initial crash of padding as the bodies collided on the seventeen-yard line.

Sergei Vonosovich left his feet in a graceless backwards somersault, only vaguely aware of the quarterback's cleats stabbing his abdominal wall before bouncing off of his facemask. Bruce Bucz sprinted into the end zone unimpeded, waving the football high above his head, playing to the Naperville faithful before casually flipping it to the referee in a calculated display of good-sportsmanship. A hideous footprint of mud and blood stained the exposed stomach of the vanquished gladiator sprawled out on his back in the wet grass.

The mad cheering from the visitors' stands fell away, replaced by a nauseating silence that gripped the entire stadium.

The body lying prone on the hash mark at the fourteen-yard line was not moving.

Chapter 43

"How's he doing?"

Lorelei Vonosovich looked up, startled by the sudden intrusion on her misery. Her first thought upon seeing Mike Minot standing directly in front of her was that she must look a sight. Already soaked to the bone from sitting in the driving rain, her eyes were red and swollen from crying, their inherent sparkle extinguished forever by tears wrenched from the very core of her being.

"Oh . . . Coach Minot. Hi! Excuse me—I . . . he . . . he—" Lorelei shook her head furiously. "They don't know. They don't know," she stammered. "I've just . . . I've just been sitting here!"

Mike Minot hoped that his poker face was able to stifle the initial shock he had felt when Mrs. Vonosovich looked up at him. The woman had aged ten years from the last time he had seen her, which was just last week at the Hubbard game. Lorelei Vonosovich was a damn good-looking broad and Mike had always made sure to dust off his best smile when acknowledging her.

"I'm sorry," he said. "I wanted to come right away, but I had to stay. I had to stay and—hang on . . ." The coach turned and plucked a crisply folded towel from a laundry cart being maneuvered through the drizzle of traffic in the narrow corridor. "Here you go," he said, draping the towel carefully over Lorelei Vonosovich's wet head rather than just handing it to her. There was an odd but comforting familiarity to the gesture that actually made her smile.

"Thank you," she said. "I'm sorry. I must look a sight."

"You look fine," Minot lied. "So what exactly did the doctor say?"

"I haven't seen a doctor yet," she said, patting down her wet hair. "They had him in Emergency when I got here and then . . . there were, there were at least four interns standing around him at one point. I don't think any of them knew what they were doing. Finally, they wheeled him out. I saw him—saw his face. He looked at me . . . but I—" Lorelei swallowed hard. "I don't know if he knew who I was. And he looked . . . he looked . . ." She left that last thought unfinished. "Anyway, they brought him up here. I haven't seen him since. That was about an hour ago."

Minot looked around. *Up here* was the Infectious Diseases Isolation Ward.

"Hmmm," he mumbled, taking a seat next to her on the vinyl bench. "Well, I guess all we can do is sit and wait."

"Yes," Lorelei said, nodding blankly.

An awkward silence threatened to descend. Minot sensed it and broke it before it could take hold and corrupt any sense of intimacy he was trying to establish.

"He's a good kid. You should be very proud."

"Yes," she replied. "Yes, he's everything to me."

"Must be hard raising a boy in this day and age on your own," Minot said, edging in a little deeper. "Working with these kids, I see what it's like out there. Different world from the one you and I grew up in. Faster, more temptation. Sports are a good diversion—keeps them off the streets, but it all starts at home. You did a hell of a job. Von is an exceptional young man—and I'm not just talking about what he can do on a football field."

"Thank you," Lorelei said. The simple acknowledgment boosted her spirits, however briefly, more than she would have thought possible. "Oh," she said, suddenly remembering, "what happened with the game? Did you win?"

"No. We lost. Thirty-five to seventeen."

"I'm sorry," she said again.

"It's only a game. Only a football game. The only thing I care about right now—the only thing anyone at Ridgewood cares about right now—is Von."

As if to underscore his point, the doors at the end of the corridor burst open and Haley McBride and Jason Jankowski rushed through. A hospital security guard, very fat and very out of breath, was waddling behind, hot on their heels.

"Mrs. V," Jason said. "Coach . . ." He nodded to Minot, surprised to see him there. "How is he? What happened? We got here as quick as we could . . ."

Haley stepped out from behind Jason. She did not—*would* not look at Coach Minot.

"Hello, Mrs. Vonosovich," she offered meekly. "I'm . . ." Haley's lower lip crumpled like an over-stressed scaffold, pulling the rest of her face down with the collapse. She stood there unsure and unable to say exactly *what* she was.

Lorelei extended her arms to the girl. "Ohhh . . . come here, honey . . ." She pulled her son's first true love close and held her tight, knowing, as women do, things that no man could understand or impart.

Mike Minot and Jason looked at each other and shrugged.

"They don't know yet," Lorelei said, breaking the clinch and wiping away fresh tears. "They're running a bunch of tests. I haven't seen him since they brought him up here. No one will tell me anything."

"Hey!"

They turned to look at the wheezing security guard. "You can't all be here," he said, catching his breath. "This is an ICU floor. You two," he glared at Jason and Haley. "Where are your passes?"

"We need passes?" Jason asked, playing dumb. "I'm sorry. We didn't know."

"That's because you ran up without checking in," the guard snapped. "If you would have stopped at the front desk, you . . . anyway," he said, looking at Haley and softening the tough guy stance, "you're going to have to wait downstairs until the passes become available."

Minot looked at the wheezing guard. "Can you give them ten minutes, officer?" he asked, giving him his best man-to-man.

"Sorry," he said. "I don't make the rules. I only enforce them."

Jason slipped an arm around Haley. "It's all right. We understand." He looked at Lorelei. "Hang in there, Mrs. V, I'm sure Von will be fine. I'll check in with you tomorrow."

Lorelei smiled at Jason. He was such a good kid. "Thanks, Jason. I'll probably be—I'll probably be *here*," she said as if realizing it for the first time. "Here," she said, rummaging through her purse for a pen, "here's my cell phone number. Haley, you call too if you want. Maybe by tomorrow, he'll be out . . . or at least out of the Iso ward," she added hopefully.

Jason took the number and folded it into his pocket. "Don't worry. Von's a tough guy. He's going to be fine." He looked to Haley for confirmation, but she remained strangely silent. It was like she couldn't wait to get out of there.

"Yes," Haley said finally, "he's going to be fine. I'll call you, Mrs. Vonosovich," she added, lying again.

Jason turned to Minot. "See you Monday, Coach."

Minot nodded solemnly and watched them leave, the fat security guard following a respectful distance behind them. The weird vibe he was getting from Haley McBride put him on edge.

"Nice kids," Lorelei said.

"Yeah," Minot agreed leading her back to the bench. "They are." Their little intrusion had knocked him way off course. Now he had to start all over again. "It all starts at home with the parents. I could tell right away, what kind of homes these kids come from. After you work with them for a while, it starts to become second nature. The ones with no stable family background—you could see it in their eyes. It's like they're looking for something—some guidance. I worked in an inner-city school in Atlanta a few years back," he lied. "I saw a lot of kids come from single parent homes—no fathers, no direction. But a lot of those mothers—they were tough."

Lorelei nodded. "Von was easy. It's almost like he raised himself. He kept to himself a lot but he always kept himself busy. He was a reader—read anything he could get his hands on. And he always had this maddening curiosity about him." She sighed. "He got that from his father."

Minot brightened. At last. "Von never talked much about his father . . ."

Chapter 44

Mike Minot closed the handsome leather-bound journal across his lap and sat unmoving, trying to take it all in. A stein of Sam Adams sat at the side table near his elbow, warm and flat, untouched but for the first sip he had taken, just after pouring it. The sporadic song of the morning's earliest birds and the soft glow of dawn suffusing the west wall of his apartment rustled him from the numb entrancement he had been in since opening Alexei Vonosovich's memoirs just after midnight.

Fascinating.

Minot had found the journal almost immediately after entering the Vonosovich household with Von's own key. When a quick sweep of the boy's room had come up empty, he had glanced up at the drop ceiling and knew before he had pulled the tiles down that he would find it there.

It was all starting to come together now, as bizarre and inconceivable as it seemed.

He'd had his doubts about much of the boy's story early on, but was unable to dismiss any one part in light of the hard evidence he had seen with his own eyes.

He had been standing on the sideline during the Shepard game when Vonosovich went down not ten feet away. He'd *heard* the kid's knee tear like a bed sheet caught on rusty nail. He had seen that initial X-ray clearly indicating the fibula dangling from the ravaged lateral collateral ligament, held in check only by an Ace bandage and sheer luck. He had seen the results of the MRI taken the very next day. He stared in disbelief at the healthy knee and the taut ligament, marred only by a hairline seam so faint, you had to squint to see it at all.

Sixteen months of healing almost overnight.

Von was the most remarkable physical specimen he had ever seen outside of an NFL locker room. The kid possessed a frightening combination of speed, size, strength, and agility unseen in the high school—or college—ranks. Last year the kid had been a skinny benchwarmer, too slow and too timid to even crack the suicide squads.

Best high school football player in the entire country?

Sure.

Shapeshifter? *Werewolf?*

Don't think so.

But still . . .

He drummed his fingers across the pebbled leather cover of Alexei Vonosovich's journal. The kid's father had been a major brain, funded by the most prestigious biochem research lab in the world. His death was shrouded in secrecy and swept under a dirty rug that was rolled up and thrown in a closet already filled with skeletons.

Minot not only believed that Sergei Vonosovich was juiced by a wonder drug—he *wanted* to believe it. Still relatively young at twenty-seven, Mike Minot had never entirely ruled out a return to professional football. The Eagles and the Browns had both given him a long look, as did the Bears, after he had called in an old favor from a friend at Halas Hall.

They all stopped looking when they got to his knee.

The damn knee.

Held together by surgical pins and bone grafts, he was lucky he could walk on it, let alone pass an NFL physical. It would mend, Dr. Fox had told him—with time.

Ten to fifteen years. Years he did not have.

If everything Von had told him was true—hell, if *half* of it was true—he could do it. He could play at that elite level and be part of it all again. The money. The women. The excitement. The fame and the glory.

The former Kansas City Chief closed his eyes. Visions of NFL grandeur splashed across the backs of his lids, the seeds of a sweet dream that would come with the sleep that was a long time coming.

The phone rang, startling him into the realization he *had* fallen asleep. He looked at the clock. It was six thirty in the morning. Minot picked up the phone and pressed the receiver groggily to his ear.

"Hello?"

"Hey, baby." The voice, husky, sweet. It was Sherrie, the leggy dispatcher from Mokena.

"Hey, doll," Mike said, fully awake now. "What's up?"

"Did I wake you up? I'm sorry. But you said to call as soon as I got that file for you."

Mike blinked. "Already? I thought you said it would take a while."

Sherrie laughed. "That's what I thought last night. Turns out, this file has made its way around. Parts of it were leaked before the Feds put the clamps on it. It's got a cult following, sort of like the Jeffrey Dahmer file, but on a smaller scale. It's been photocopied and faxed to departments all over the country. The pictures are a little hard to make out. This is like a third- or fourth-generation photocopy—not the best quality. Still, I think it will help you out."

"You're the greatest," Minot laughed. "When can I pick it up?"

"Well," Sherrie giggled. "I'm getting off work in ten minutes. I thought I could swing by and drop it off. You're not too tired for some company, are you?"

"No," he said, "come on by. I just got a second wind."

"Mmm . . ." she purred. "I'll be there in forty minutes."

"I'll be waiting," Minot said. "Oh—and baby?"

"Yeah?"

"Bring your handcuffs."

Chapter 45

The scent rolled in on the southeasterly breeze that stirred the early morning fog blanketing the moors, rousting the beast from its logy torpor. The creature stood erect like a man, its long snout pointed skyward. The wet nostrils quivered on the end of the leathery black nose, pinpointing the source of the smell, separating it from the myriad cluster of odors assaulting its olfactory senses.

That the beast was damaged, there could be no question. Ratty tufts of thick brown fur sloughed off its hindquarters with every step through the waist-high foliage, exposing the scaly, raw corruption of the creature's skin. Worse than the defoliation of its once majestic hide was the incessant pounding in his head and the churning turmoil racking its internal organs. The pain was getting progressively worse. Von could feel the distress in his bones, could feel the perversion of his anatomy, as the molecular integrity of his body spun into a free-fall.

The scent, more pungent, closer now, kindled the fire within him. If he could kill, if he could eat, he could grow strong. He could be complete.

The beast stopped. His canine ears twitched. Nothing . . . and then . . .

The voices again—so far away. But so close—in his own head?

. . . *never seen anything like it . . . extremely rare . . . triggered y enzyme defects . . . acute attack . . .*

A sharp stabbing pain tore through his lower abdomen, bringing him to his knees. Von recoiled and clutched at his stomach, fully expecting to feel a gaping wound from a gun-shot that he did not hear.

Initial diagnosis would indicate cutaneous hepatic porphyria . . . the skin becomes thin and dark—see there? The hirsute growth of hair on the face . . . careful, don't touch the open sores . . . in time it will affect his central nervous system . . . mania, auditory and visual hallucinations are not uncommon . . . a boy this size . . . check those restraints . . . he was actually growling earlier this morning . . .

Were they talking about him? Good God . . . sounded awful.

The sun broke over the moors, burning through the cloud cover that had held off the coming of dawn. Von-wolf rolled onto his back to ease the cramping in his abdominal wall and felt the warm kiss of the sun on his scarred face.

. . . sometimes due to a recessive gene . . . I'd heard the blood work is all over the place—they're sending it out to Johns Hopkins—yes! . . . thinks the facial lesions and ulcers are due to photosensitization . . . has already advanced . . . attacking the cartilage and bone . . .

The sunlight, too hot now, burned through Von-wolf's closed eyelids, turning his world into a searing panorama of orange fire. He turned his hairy face from the sky and tried to bury it in the dew-drenched long grass when the scent, over-powering now, attacked his olfactory nerves once again.

The food source was near—within striking distance . . .

. . . see? Oh God, what a shame! You know I saw his picture in the paper a few weeks ago. Such a good-looking kid. You wouldn't have believed it. Careful—he's stirring . . . maybe we should call . . .

Sergei Vonosovich opened his eyes, nearly blinded by the surgical lamp hovering inches over his face. He bolted up-right, so confused by the hospital surroundings that he did not notice the implosion of the light bulbs and the shower of metal and glass. Von's powerful jaws clamped on to the nurse's arm and held fast, unmindful of her screams, wanting only to feed, to be strong and whole again.

The thing thrashing about in the bed bit down hard and tore a ragged mouthful of muscle and tissue from the woman's narrow forearm. Nurse Stringer spun, nearly pulling free from the jaws. Her ragged arm sprayed the walls with blood and pieces of bone. A scaly claw broke free from the leather restraint that had held it to the bed and pulled her close as she tried to retreat. The candy striper in the corner could do little but scream as the monstrosity yanked the night nurse onto the bed and brought its horrible hairy head down into the nape of the woman's neck.

Nurse Stringer's thrashing and screaming stopped with the shocking and abrupt finality brought on by the kill-strike. She lay motionless, her life blood pouring from the wound and painting the sheets dark red, oblivious to the champing and sucking sounds emanating from the beast feeding on her shoulder.

A guttural moan welled up from the obscene coupling and the demon raised its head, a slack-jawed grin of contentment on its ruined face. Fire flashed anew in its yellow eyes upon spotting the tender meat cowering in the corner. That look sparked the last ember of self-preservation in the girl's soul and she made a break for the door, colliding with Greg Bauer and Danny Egan, the first two orderlies to arrive on the scene.

Were he in his right mind, Sergei Vonosovich might have admired the way the tiny nurse's aide split the seam between the two large men and ran for daylight, nearly catching up with her screams echoing down the tiled corridor.

Greg Bauer was not so lucky. Rooted to the spot by pure fascination and fear, he stood transfixed, like a man on the periphery of a dream, watching a nightmare unfold. He did not see his partner turn and run as the thing in the bed threw back one more mouthful of Nurse Stringer and tossed her lean carcass on to the floor.

Suddenly it was on its feet, exploding from the bed in an eruption of tattered, bloody linen and overturned monitoring devices. With agonizing deliberation, the demon rose from its crouch, not stopping until the wild crown of hair (fur?) atop its head towered seven feet above the puddle of blood soaking its taloned paws. IV tubes and shunts dangled wildly from the beast's outstretched arms, complementing the long, wispy, tufts of fur sprouting haphazardly from its scaly skin. Even in this bastardized state of transition, the creature might have imparted a sense of savage majesty were it not for the ulcers and oozing sores dotting its hide.

The stink of the beast's corruption sifted through the wall of shock that had immobilized the big orderly's defense mechanisms, bringing with it the startling realization that he was in some deep shit. A womanish scream welled up from his lungs, cut short by the clammy grip of the dervish's claw around his throat.

Greg Bauer forgot all about the fresh *Born to raise Hell* tattoo on his bicep that had been itching like crazy all afternoon. He forgot about the big bag of dope that he had stashed in the glove compartment of his Chevy Malibu, and the waitress at O'Leary's with the killer rack.

He felt himself being lifted off of the ground. He felt the warm sensation flowing down his leg as he lost control of his bladder.

He remembered his mother telling him how important fresh underwear was when he was a little boy—how important it was to be clean "down there."

The demon pulled him close and his world was swallowed

by the beast's gaping mouth, a cavernous maw, ringed with ivory butcher knives.

He remembered the nuns at St. Nicholas and their seemingly eyewitness accounts of the agonies awaiting the sinner in the subterranean labyrinth of hell.

Yes, yes, he agreed as the felt the cleansing liberation of the first bite. *They were right . . .*

Lorelei Vonosovich's eyes had opened a full second before she had heard the screams. She knew, before looking, that they were coming from her son's room and she had barely stirred when the nurse's aide bolted past her down the hall, her face twisted and her eyes wide with terror. Lorelei stood, surrendering at last to the horror and walked calmly toward her son's room, unmindful of the frantic hospital personnel rushing back and forth all around her.

Lorelei was second-generation Moldavian Gypsy and knew of all the room for incongruity in the uneven corners of the physical world. She had thought that the last years she had spent with Alexei would have prepared her for any horror this side of heaven or hell. What she saw when she stepped into ISO room 504, however, gutted the last vestiges of her sane mind.

The thing that had been her son stood splay-legged in a pool of carnage, cradling the mutilated carcass of something that looked vaguely like a man. It took respite from its feeding upon hearing her enter, pausing like a glutton interrupted midway through a pie-eating contest. Lorelei Vonosovich's only son lifted his gore-flecked face from the dripping husk of Greg Bauer's chest cavity and looked into his mother's eyes.

Time froze in that room for one polarizing moment, as two human souls screamed silently from within the flesh and blood vessels that imprisoned them.

The thing that had been Von dropped what remained of Greg Bauer and spun away from the damning eyes of its mother. The creature hit the window at full speed, showering the room with shards of storm pane and its own molting flesh.

Lorelei stood unblinking but did not see her son land on the river-rocked surface of the roof two stories below. She did not see his mad dash through the maze of heating and air-conditioning ducts or hear his howls as he leapt over the coping onto the street two stories below.

Chapter 46

Mike Minot awoke of his own accord Sunday evening and shambled from his bed toward the bathroom. He relieved himself, smiling as he took note of the eyeliner case resting on the vanity.

They always left something.

It was a cheap but clever ruse employed to necessitate a return visit or another encounter. He shook his head in wonder and admiration. Men should be so subtle.

Mike finished and shuffled into the living room. He plopped onto his black-leather recliner and fingered the remote control, but did not switch the television on. His thoughts drifted inevitably back to Sergei Vonosovich and his father's "Elixir of Life."

The stuff was definitely the most potent juice Mike had ever seen and he had seen some real rocket fuel in his time. It increased muscle mass throughout the body proportionately without sacrificing the integrity of the skeletal system or stressing the ligaments and tendons. It increased blood circulation and lung capacity to better fuel the increased demands on the host system. It not only accelerated the healing process, but also regenerated tissue that was stronger and more resilient than what it had replaced. It heightened the senses, and improved your vision, your sense of smell. It quickened your reflexes, sharpened your instincts.

It was designed, Von had told him, to maximize the potential of the human animal.

How absolutely perfect.

But the side effects. Good lord.

The Vonosovich kid was pretty messed up right now—no doubt about it. Mike had seen his face—had seen the degeneration of the tissue. He remembered the shudder that went through his body when he pulled Von's helmet off on the sideline last night and saw the layers of skin that sloughed off as the headgear came away.

But still, there were extenuating circumstances—that whole issue of him being descended from an ancient line of Romanian shapeshifters.

Shapeshifters.

He supposed it could be possible. Mike Minot was no Nobel candidate biochemist but he wasn't stupid. He'd comprehended most of what Alexei Vonosovich had left behind in his journal.

Chromosomes, cells, genes—all that stuff. It was all in the arrangement. And if you could program—if you could control . . .

The phone rang.

He had intended to let it ring, glancing sideways at the LED display on the caller I.D.

No indication. Star-7.

Damn, he hated that. Could be Sherrie, wanting to pillow-talk—the last thing he needed right now—or it could be Andy Freeman with a job. He almost let the answering machine get it, but he relented and picked up.

"Hello."

"Mike?"

Damn, it was Sherrie. She was working the swing-shift tonight at Mokena P.D. How come the caller I.D. didn't catch that? He really didn't want to talk to her so soon after being with her.

"Yeah, hey, babe . . ."

"It's Sherrie."

"Yeah, I know. What's up?" He tried to sound sweet and keep the annoyance out of his voice.

"I'm on my cell phone," Sherrie said, no music in her voice. "I didn't want this call on record at Dispatch."

Damn. This was no kissy-cuddly call. "What is it?"

"I heard some of the guys talking in back—Esposito and Sergeant Tully. They didn't know I could hear. I was in the chicks' john, sneaking a smoke."

Mike caught his breath. Esposito was heading up the Melanie Houghwat investigation for the South-Suburban Task Force S.I. unit.

"They were talking about that girl—the one from your school, Melanie Houghwat, the coach's daughter."

Mike felt his stomach knot up.

"Your name came up," she said flatly. "Big. An eyewitness placed her car in your apartment complex the night she turned up gone."

The knot in his stomach tightened.

"Mike?"

He said nothing for a moment. "Yeah, so?"

"You weren't sleeping with that schoolgirl, were you?"

Mike feigned indignation. His mind was racing. "Come on, Sherrie. Give me a break! Of course not. I mean, give me *some* credit. Screwing Melanie Houghwat? Tom Houghwat's daughter? No way."

There was a brief silence on the other end of the line. "I believe you," Sherrie said, sounding relieved. "But I had to ask—and I won't be the only one asking. What was Melanie Houghwat's car doing in that lot?"

"How the hell should I know?" Mike asked, going on the defensive. "Am I the only one that lives here?"

"I don't know, Mike. But you can bet they'll question everyone who does live there."

"I miss you already," he said, laying it on thick. "Can you keep me posted?"

"Save it, Mike," Sherrie said. "I just called to get some peace of mind—not as a favor to you."

"Well, I appreciate it anyway, doll," he said backing off a bit. "Geez, that's creepy. I've never been under investigation before." He cut to the chase. "Who placed me at the scene?"

"Another student," Sherrie said. "Haley something— Haley McBride. Didn't hear any details."

"Haley McBride, huh?" Mike asked casually. Von's girl-friend. "Thanks, babe. I'll be in touch."

"Don't call me," Sherrie said, and then hung up.

Don't worry about it, Mike thought, cradling the phone. Damn, this changes everything.

He knew a crack-addict in the Heights that would swear under oath that she was with him that night. Hell, she would testify that they were both in church that night if you fed her enough junk. She would do in a pinch if it came down to it.

Haley McBride, now she was another story.

Mike pulled on a pair of sweatpants and padded to the kitchen. He pulled a Sam Adams from the fridge.

How much did she know? What had she seen that night?

It had been a simple matter; stealing Melanie's body out of the apartment and stuffing it rudely into the trunk of her car. Driving down the main drag, along 183rd Street, in her Escort GT with the *MELNS X* vanity plate was a bit nerve-wracking, even though he had waited until after midnight when most of the high school kids that populated the strip were tucked away in their little beds. He had, as far as he could tell, avoided detection and made it safely to the old American Motors stamping plant, skirting the edge of town along the banks of the Cal-Sag. On the bank of the channel, he had propped her up behind the wheel of her Escort and peeled off his clothes before slipping in the passenger seat.

He punched the accelerator and steered for a high point on the bank. They had to be doing a good forty miles an hour when they hit the water. Melanie's window was already rolled down and it was a simple matter for him to slither over her and out of the rapidly descending metal coffin. The car had rolled a bit upon entry, and a moment of panic had set in when he couldn't tell up from down without the benefit of daylight on the surface. He had forced himself to remain perfectly still in order to regain his vertical bearings and saw the hulk of Melanie's Escort dipping below, off to his left. In a moment, it was gone, swallowed up by the darkness and Mike had swum in the opposite direction as fast as he could. It came as a surprise when his head broke the surface seventeen seconds later, so black was the starless sky above.

He had dressed and walked the twelve miles back to his apartment (he had checked Melanie's odometer). On the long walk he had thought about Friday's game plan and the leggy dispatcher from Mokena that he had been meaning to call. The whole sordid turn of events had come off so clean he had given it little thought until now.

He hoped that the McBride girl had just happened to spot Melanie's car in the lot that night and that was all. He would really hate to have to kill her.

Mike fished a mug from the icy depths of his freezer and carefully poured a Sam Adams, topping the head off at just over an inch.

But of course, he would if he had to.

He shuffled into the living room and switched on ESPN. The Packers and the Bears were locking horns in the late game, and Mike had laid a C-Note on the Bears to pull an upset on Favre and the heavily favored Pack. The former Kansas City Chief settled in to watch the big boys and contemplate the very nasty situation he had suddenly found himself in. The Bears were on the move in Green Bay territory when the doorbell rang.

Damn. Now who could that be?

Mike lifted himself out of the chair too quickly, a twinge in his lower back reminding him of his own playing days. He flicked the intercom switch, making no attempt to hide the annoyance in his voice. If it was somebody selling something, he swore he would go down there and rearrange his nose.

"Who is it?"

The voice, barely recognizable, crackled through the box.

"It's Von. Let me in, Coach. Please. I think I'm dying."

Mike Minot smiled. Sometimes the solution came right to your door.

Chapter 47

Dan Jacobson wheeled the mop bucket into the utility closet and pulled the apron off over his head. He tossed it in a heap of dirty restaurant linen, where it landed with a wet thud that made him wince. The cockroaches that had scattered when he had flicked on the lights grew bold again and scurried across the floor in plain sight, fat and living high on the hog. He had never imagined just how filthy a restaurant—where they served people *food*—could be. Jake pulled the chain dangling from the naked overhead bulb and fumbled up the steps in the semidarkness.

Dennis Powers, the night shift manager, was waiting for him at the time clock.

"You remember the men's bathroom tonight, Daniel?" he asked. "You missed it last night, you know."

Jake seethed. This squirrelly little wimp was the type of guy he used to eat for lunch. Yeah, pinhead, Jake thought, I cleaned your bathroom. Would you like me to show you? Maybe I can shove your head into the urinal so you can get a real good look at it.

But he didn't say that.

"Yeah, Dennis, it's clean."

"Great, thanks," Dennis smiled and moved away from the time clock. "See you tomorrow, Daniel."

"Good night, Dennis."

Jake pulled his timecard from the rack and positioned it under the stylus. Ten fifty-eight. If he waited two more minutes he could get four hours even. If he punched out now, he would lose ten minutes.

Dennis Powers glared at him. "Good night, Daniel."

267

Jake swore silently to himself and punched his ticket. " 'Night."

From big man on campus to busboy—just like that. His father would not have him lying about the house after school and had made him take this godforsaken part-time job. Better get used to working, son, he had told him, I don't think your *grades* are going to open any college doors for you.

Great advice, Dad. The bitter truth—and this was the hardest part—was his father couldn't stand to look at him.

Dan Jacobson was far too dim to have envisioned the wretched turn his life would take after selling his soul to that reporter from the *Tribune*. His days of playing football for the RedHawks had been finished anyway, thanks to Kroc and the golden boy, Vonosovich, but he had never dreamed his social status could plummet so far.

In the last two weeks, Jake had become a pariah, an outcast trapped within the very world that had banished him. He was not welcome at the lunch table with the guys. Conversation grew stilted, then came to a halt whenever he drew near. The girls, whom he now realized merely tolerated him before, did nothing to mask their revulsion; giggling or rolling their eyes behind his broad back. The scout from Libertyville junior college, the only real scent he had caught of a college ride, would not return his calls.

So complete was his misery that even Friday night's loss, a crippling blow to Ridgewood's chances for a state title, had brought him little joy. They would find some way to blame him.

Jake walked out to the parking lot and gasped—a sound like a little girl would make upon seeing a mouse run between her legs.

Mike Minot's Corvette was parked next to his Camry.

The black window powered down, pulling the reflected

starlight with it down into the low-slung door. Coach Minot peered at him; his face dappled in shadow and reflected dash lights.

"Hey, Jake," the coach said. "You got a minute?"

Jake looked around. The lot was nearly deserted. The Hitching Post Steak House was a dive on the outskirts of the Chicago Heights shipping yards. The only time the lot was full was for the lunchtime "fashion shows" that brought in the railroad workers and the dockhands.

"Come on, Jake," the coach said. "I'm not going to bite you."

Jake shuffled over to the Corvette and stood his ground by the Toyota's rusted passenger-side door. "Coach . . . what's up?"

"You like your job, Jake?" Minot asked. His voice held the promise of a proposition.

"No," Jacobson said. "This job sucks."

Minot laughed. "Of course it does, Jake. Working for a bunch of pencil-necked, sweaty, grease slingers. I imagine it does suck. Look at it this way though, if you stay here long enough, you might make assistant manager some day. Would you like that?"

Jake shook his head. "I won't be here that long, Coach."

Minot stared straight ahead. "No," he said. "No, you won't."

Jake pulled his keys from his pocket. "Is there something I can do for you, Coach?"

"No, Jake. But there's something I can do for you." Minot twisted the key and the 'Vette's LS1 engine growled to life with the subdued revs of a turbine at idle. "You play ball with me and you'll be back in football pads next fall. I have a friend at Slippery Rock College downstate. Take a ride with me, Jake." The Corvette's power door locks popped, the soft click almost seductive in the night air. "Unless you got something better to do."

Never one to think on his feet, Dan Jacobson made the last mistake of his life.

"No," he said, stuffing his keys back into his pocket. "I ain't got nothing better to do."

Jake settled into the passenger seat and closed the door. Minot continued to stare straight ahead.

"You got a death wish, Jake?" he asked suddenly.

Jake looked at him, his eyes all at once filled with fear.

"Fasten your seatbelt, son," the coach grinned. "Buckle up."

Minot pulled out of the gravel lot, accelerating when the tires bit into the blacktop of Route 83.

Jake shifted his bulk in the bucket seat and clicked the belt. "So, what you got on your mind, Coach?" he asked, finding his voice again.

"I do some work, Jake," Minot answered. "Some work for the local police districts. I clean up the garbage that slips through the cracks from time to time. We got a screwed-up system, Jake. This is the greatest country in the world—make no mistake about it. But we're lame when it comes to dealing with our own criminal element. We have bleeding hearts like the ACLU, crying about everyone's civil rights and lawyers in their Lexus SUVs, springing child molesters and rapists on technicalities and then laughing about it over lunch." Mike Minot's lip curled in real disgust. "It makes me sick."

Jake looked mutely at his former coach, his face a mask of bewilderment.

Minot sighed and pressed on. "Well, sometimes the police—the guys out there risking their lives—say *enough's enough*. That's where I come in. For a small fee," he continued, spelling it out for the boy, "I will administer the justice that the system has failed to provide. It's street justice. The only justice these scums understand."

Jake was grinning like the village idiot. Coach got paid to beat the shit out of people! And the cops *paid* him! How awesome was that?

Minot smiled that quirky secret smile. "You understand where I'm going with this, Jake?"

"Yeah, Coach," Jake said, very pleased with himself. "I follow you. Where do I come in?"

"Good question. I got a case that just came up. Perp was a seventeen-year-old kid—has a rap sheet that started sometime back in kindergarten. Anyway, he pulls a B and E one night in a retirement village—whacks the old guy that lives there on the head and puts him in a coma."

Jake whistled. "Holy cow."

"That's not even the bad part," Minot said, laying it on a little thicker. "He goes into the bedroom and finds the guy's wife hiding in the closet. Eighty-three-year-old woman, scared to death—and he rapes her."

"Holy shit!" Jake almost shouted.

Minot nodded solemnly and turned off 83 onto the fireroad that skirted the Cal-Sag channel. They were buddies now. Comrades again. "Yeah, ain't that a bitch? They nailed him two days later trying to fence their VCR at a pawnshop in Oak Lawn. The kid makes an initial confession—everything matches up, and then his lawyer shows up and the next thing you know they're screaming police brutality. Anyway, the old broad is too shook up to I.D. this piece of garbage and the old man isn't talking. Make a long story short—he walks."

"Man," Jake said, noticing for the first time they had turned off the beaten path, "that sucks. What about DNA testing? He raped her, right?"

Minot grumbled. Moron was destroying a perfectly good

story. "Eh, DNA tests were inconclusive. That happens, you know."

"No," Jake said, "I didn't know that. I thought—"

"In any event," Minot said, cutting him off, "the old folks just happened to be the parents of a lieutenant with the Midlothian P.D."

"Wow," Jake said. "Big mistake. And they want you to beat this guy up?"

Minot turned pensive. "Let's say I was approached," he said pulling into the lot of the old American Motors stamping plant. "I don't like messing around with minors." The irony of the statement was lost in threads of the story being woven. "I thought I might vend this one out."

The car came to a halt in front of the chain-link fence. "You interested?"

"Hell yes," Jake answered. Visions of an exciting and lucrative future danced through Jake's stunted mind. He and Coach Minot could be partners! Like Butch and Sundance. Like Crockett and Tubbs. Like—

"Jake," Minot barked. "You interested? I could give it to someone else . . ."

"No!" Jake stammered. "I mean, yeah, I'm interested. But why me? I thought you didn't like me."

Mike Minot cranked it up a notch.

"I got nothing against you, Jake," he said contritely. "The whole steroid thing . . . ? It needed to be done." Mike opened the car door and stepped out into the gravel lot, motioning for Jake to follow. He pulled a flashlight, the longest Jake had ever seen, from the trunk and turned it on. Its wide beam was the only light aside from the moon and the stars. "Those kids were killing themselves. I've seen what steroids can do to a person long-term. Look what happened to Von."

Jake fell into step beside the coach, walking the length of

the chain-link fence. "What *did* happen to Von?" Jake asked incredulously. "Did he really kill those people? It's all anyone in school can talk about. Hey—where are we going?"

They came upon a run-down section of fence. Minot pulled the chain-link away from its post and ducked through. "I don't know, Jake. I wasn't there. But there are two dead hospital workers and Von is missing. Come on," he said, waving Jake along. "I got someone I want you to meet."

Probably the *inside* guy, Jake thought. Just like in the movies.

They skirted the plant entrance and walked along the corrugated steel side of the building, to the back of the plant. "Von is a prime example of a life ruined by steroid abuse," Minot said, continuing to preach the gospel of clean living. At the rear of the building, they came upon a battered fire door. The doorknob and lock had been punched out. "Don't get me wrong," the coach said, pushing the door open and stepping inside. "There's nothing wrong with a getting a little edge using modern science, but the keyword here is *abuse*. Von took it too far. He had a good thing going and screwed up. He overdid it."

They walked along a narrow passageway that led out to the main floor of the plant and took a sharp left up a flight of wooden stairs. Mike Minot continued to talk, imparting his wisdom to the youngster, a tool for the boy to utilize during the last remaining minutes of his life. At the top of the staircase, Minot elbowed open a rickety freight door and motioned for Jake to follow.

"Uh—where we going, Coach?" Jake asked.

"This is the old Quality Control room," Minot said, shining the light around the vast space. "Last checkpoint before shipping, which is where we are headed. Watch your feet."

Jake looked down and saw the steel rails, like a railroad crossing, although much narrower—more like a roller coaster, inlaid in the concrete floor.

"Freight track," Minot explained to his young charge. "The stamped parts would come through here in steel tubs along these rails. Come on. We're almost there."

They passed though a portal and Jake found himself inside a covered bridge.

"You're not scared of heights, are you, Jake?" Minot asked, shining the flashlight at Jake's feet. Through the slats in the track ties Jake could see that they were a good fifty feet off the ground.

"No, Coach," Jake lied. "Just snakes—I hate snakes."

Minot grinned. Something in his face made Jake very scared.

"I knew Vonosovich was juicing," Jake said, following his coach along the track. He was starting to babble now. If they were meeting someone here, how come there were no other cars in the parking lot? "But nobody could figure out what he was on. Geez, Coach, do you really think he killed those people at the hospital?"

They reached the swinging doors at the end of the tunnel. Jake could see the faintest hint of dim light seeping out from under the wooden door of the repository. Coach Minot stopped at the door and stepped aside, positioning Jake at his elbow.

"Between me and you," Minot said, opening the door, "yeah, I think he did it. But why don't you ask him yourself?"

Jake's slow reflexes, a burden throughout his football career, sealed his doom. An arc of white light whirled across the ceiling and exploded into a rainbow as Minot brought the flashlight down hard against the crown of his skull. The light faded altogether, then reappeared in sporadic bursts from above, like sunlight viewed from the bottom of a lake.

Jake heard a door slam shut somewhere above, and behind him, the hissing of snakes. He blinked back into consciousness, unsure at first if the darkness around him was real or imagined. A soft light emerged from a far corner of his tomb—a Coleman propane lantern, fizzing on its dimmest setting, not the snakes that he had feared so. More light, starlight, filtered in through the slats of the boarded-up window, high—too high—on the far wall.

All at once he realized that he was not alone.

Why don't you ask him yourself?

A wet noise, like gelatin being freed from a mold, spiked the hair on the back of his neck. Jake looked around wildly, his eyesight returning just as his wits were retreating. The shape in the far corner, away from the lantern—at first he thought it was a large piece of furniture—was moving.

The shape of the thing became more discernible as it gathered itself up, backlit against the sifting starlight. It was humanoid and larger than he had first thought; moving in a crouch, as if wary, or disturbed.

Jake froze, hoping his stillness would render him invisible to the thing. The sudden realization that he was in the more illuminated part of the room nearly caused him to cry out. When the thing turned its misshapen head in his direction, he saw the eyes, so familiar, lock on his own.

Jake blubbered, the sound foreign and comical in his ears, a prelude to the tears that began to fall as the thing lumbered toward him out of the darkness.

It stepped into the fuzzy light, moving slowly, but with a purpose that was undeniable. Tufts of hair sprouted from the creature's head, an appendage that seemed to sprout directly from its reticulated torso without the benefit of a neck. Razor-sharp nails extended from the webbed claws at the ends of its stubby, powerful arms, a mirror image of the endless rows of teeth set back in the horrible, twisted mouth.

It was only when that mouth opened wide and the thing somehow uttered his name that Jake began to scream.

Chapter 48

Lester Lesko waited, as he always did, for the sun to drop behind the skeletal tree line rimming the Creekside Forest Preserve, before turning down the Venetian blinds dressing the long bank of windows on the west wall. The white plastic slats shut out the purpling twilight and threw back the crisp illumination of the fluorescent overheads, bathing the room in the antiseptic light that Lester found so satisfying.

This was his favorite time of day, his time alone in the Ridgewood High Computer Learning Center. The halls were empty and silent, void of the juvenile barbarians that herded through with no purpose or direction, like Neanderthals suddenly deposited in a modern maze of brick and glass. Only the steady whirring sounds from the rows of Dell desktops and colorful iMacs and the hum of the mammoth IT server played in the background, sweet and airy as the holiday Muzak piped into the stores at Christmas time. Lester felt most alive when working in this room, like a man secure in the knowledge he was doing what he was born to do. Lester had built his first computer when he was in fifth grade, an IBM/Hewlett Packard hybrid made from spare parts that his father, a network specialist with GemTech International, had brought home from work. He had breezed through the computer classes in elementary school and had been assisting Mr. Bettis, Ridgewood High's computer dean, since midway through his freshman year.

Truth be told, Lester knew more about computers than Mr. Bettis could ever hope to know. By Lester's junior year, Mr. Bettis was quite content to let Lester handle all aspects of the Computer Learning Center—from ordering software and selecting operating platforms, to consulting with vendors and instituting new curriculum. It was Lester who suggested to the school's financial board that they write to the various software manufacturers and request Beta copies of developing software. Most companies, eager to get outside feedback from a sequestered environment other than their own R&D labs, were quick to comply. Although Lester's strengths lay in IT and programming, he left no stone unturned, helping to insure that Ridgewood's computer program ranked with any in the state. It was Lester who pushed for the iMacs and the G4s for the graphics programs, knowing the prevalence of the Mac platform in the design and animation fields.

Lester oversaw the maintenance and upkeep of all the machines as well as troubleshooting the IT server and the development of the OutReach E-mail system (a free Beta version from VizionToolz, a fast growing software firm in nearby Buffalo Grove). Lester was swapping out a corrupted hard drive from one of the Dells after deciding it could not be saved, when he suddenly realized that he was being watched.

Lester turned and gasped. Coach Minot was standing in the doorway smiling at him.

Coach Minot's imposing frame never failed to instill a sense of dread in Lester. He could tell—he could just tell—that men, grown men (and weren't they all at one time just young bullies?) looked down on him, thought less of him, for his slight build and his lack of physical prowess.

Lesko! You run like a goddamn girl! Anyone ever tell you that?

Lester! Le—esster! Pick it up, son! You're bringing down the whole team!

"Hey, Les," Coach Minot said, looking around the room. "This is some set-up you've got here."

Lester nodded and then found his voice. "Um, thanks, Mister—eh, Coach."

"Damn nice," Minot grinned.

He did seem genuinely impressed.

"I've been meaning to get up here . . . but the season—well, you know how crazy it's been. Geez, is it almost November already?"

"October 25, Coach," Lester said. Jesus, what a stupid thing to say. Of course he knew what day it was.

"Like I said, I've been meaning to get up here. You did a nice job, Lester." Mike Minot eased his muscled torso out of the doorway and strolled into the room. He looked around, eyeing the equipment with admiration. "Nice to see you have some Macs to go along with the PCs. I suppose you're comfortable with both . . ."

Lester nodded, surprised and pleased that the man would know the difference. "Yes, both have their advantages but I prefer the Macs myself. Of course the Windows operating platform has made leaps and—"

"Hell of a job putting this together, Lester," Minot interrupted. "You should be commended."

"Well . . ." Lester said, almost blushing, "Mr. Bettis actually oversees the—"

"Bettis oversees two things, Lester, *diddly* and *squat*. And you know it." He winked at Lester, a sly, just between you and me, wink that filled Lester with joy. "You're the man, Les. Pocket-protector types like you will inherit the world and guys like me will come crawling to seek your counsel—like now."

Lester beamed. "You need my help?"

Minot nodded. "Big time, Les." He pulled a chair out and eased himself in behind one of the active Dells. With one push of the mouse, the fish on the aquatic screen saver disappeared and the screaming RedHawks logo appeared on the monitor. "I'm trying to organize a benefit for Coach

Houghwat at this year's sports banquet and I need to get a letter out to every student participating in a varsity sport. I figured this OutReach program of yours would be the just the ticket—you know, save the trees and all that."

Lester nodded. "If you get me a list I can create a database and you can do a mass mailing. Piece of cake."

Minot tapped his temple with his index finger. "Great minds think alike, Les. I was doing that very thing. However, I ran into a problem. A couple of the names keep popping up as *unavailable*. I figure no big deal. I can do a separate mailing for those few names. But when I try to delete those names and send the e-mail to the names the system *does* recognize, my computer freezes up and crashes. I was down for two hours last night."

"Could be your PC," Lester mused. "You try to send it from another machine?"

Minot nodded. "Yeah, that's what I thought too. I tried the one in the coach's office. Same thing—froze up."

Lester's forehead scrunched up. "Hmm. Must be a glitch in the system." He took a seat next to his new friend and powered up. "Do you have a list of the names that are coming up as invalid?"

"There's just two," Minot said. "Jason Jankowski and Haley McBride."

"Hmm. That should make it easy," Lester said. "Let me see if there is a problem with their individual accounts." His fingers click-clacked over the keyboard in a blur. "I just need to pull up their passwords . . ."

Chapter 49

"You know, Haley," John McBride said to his daughter over a forkful of teriyaki steak, "none of this is your fault."

Haley looked up from her untouched plate. Her face was void of expression. "I know, Daddy."

"The boy got caught up in something and he got in too deep. Steroid abuse is no different than any other form of drug abuse—and the goddamn pressure they put on these kids nowadays to succeed . . ." John McBride let that thought trail off, perhaps thinking of the lavish praise that he himself had showered on the boy. Damn it. Why couldn't he see it coming? He had let his daughter date a violent sociopath—*a killer*. "He obviously couldn't handle it. Some people are just hard-wired with addictive tendencies—if it wasn't steroids it would have been something else. In any event, the boy was not in his right mind."

"Von didn't kill those people," Haley said. "That wasn't Von."

Jenna McBride looked at her husband across the table. "Haley," she offered, "I want you to think about going back to see Dr. Leggio. I know it's a bit of a drive back to the city but—"

"I don't need to see Dr. Leggio, Mom," Haley said, a little too harshly. "I—I'm sorry. Yeah, maybe that's not a bad idea." She pushed a forkful of food around on her plate. "We'll see. But not right now, okay?"

"Sure honey," her mother said. "Maybe we could set something up on Saturdays . . ."

"Maybe," Haley said. She had to admit, going back to Dr. Leggio was not such a horrible idea. She wasn't crazy. It's not

281

like she needed a shrink, but it was nice to have someone to talk to other than her parents. And besides, she really liked the old guy. "We'll see, okay? Can I be excused?"

John McBride looked at his daughter's plate. "You hardly touched your food."

Haley looked apologetically at her mother. "I know. I'm just not hungry right now. I'll wrap it up and take it to work."

Her parents looked at each other.

"I don't think that's a good idea, Haley," her father said. "That—*he's* still out there. I want you to stay home. The Jacobson boy has been missing for two days now." John paused and looked at his wife. "Everyone knows there was bad blood between him and Von. The police haven't ruled out—"

"Jake ran away, Daddy," Haley said. "He had a *lot* of enemies. The whole school hated him."

"His car was parked outside the restaurant where he worked, Haley," her father countered. "Where did he go?"

Haley pursed her lips and swallowed hard. The tears were not far behind.

"I want to go to work," she said, her voice cracking. "I can't sit around and think about it. I have to keep busy."

John McBride relented. He was the same way. "Fine," he said. "But I'm going to drive you."

Haley groaned. "So we're back to this, now? Living like refugees in a DMZ? Afraid to go out at night? Geez, Dad . . ."

"And who put us there!" John McBride slammed his fist down on the table, rattling the place settings and startling all three of them. "Damn it, Haley!" He cursed himself under his breath, ashamed that the tension had finally managed to snap his last nerve. "I'm sorry."

"No, Daddy," Haley said. "*I'm* sorry." It was true. She had put her family in jeopardy. Again.

"You can drive yourself to work," her father said, going against his better judgment, "but make sure the guard walks you out to your car on your way out. Understand?"

"Yes, Daddy. Can I be excused?" she asked. "I have some homework to finish before I leave."

"Sure, honey," her mother said. "Go ahead. I'll wrap it up for you."

Haley padded up the short flight of stairs and into the room she had called her own for only the past ten months. She had done all she could to make it seem like home, but for whatever reason—perhaps because she was going off to college in the fall—it seemed foreign and temporary. Haley sat down at her workstation and noticed the mailbox icon in the corner of her monitor had a letter peeking out of it.

Haley logged on and keyed in her password to the Ridgewood Intranet system, delighted to see an e-mail from Jason. They had grown close over the last three weeks, brought together by the steady deterioration of a friend they had both loved. She had suspected that Jason was gay, and he had confessed as much to her one night last week. It was an offhand confession that began as a joke over an order of curly fries in the back booth at Schoop's, but quickly evolved into tears. It was the first time he had ever said it aloud and Haley suspected the actual vocalization was a confirmation of sorts that had finally broken a lifetime of denial.

She knew that people at school thought she was latching on to Jason on the rebound from her break-up with Von. They had her tagged as a first-class tramp, jumping into the arms of a guy's best friend after ripping his heart out.

If they only knew the truth—God, they would die.

Haley managed a smile as she double-clicked on the flashing envelope.

Haley:

Have big news on Von. Meet me at the old American Motors plant tonight at 10:00. It is on RT83—about three miles west of Cal-Sag road. Take fire-road off 83 near Harlem and you will run right into it. Go around to the back of the plant. I will leave the light on for you. And most important— do not tell anyone about this!

xxx

Jason

Haley read it three times. The cold, clinical tone of the letter disturbed her more than the cloak-and-dagger nature of the message that it conveyed. Jason didn't talk like that and he didn't write like that—or sign off with little *xxx* kisses.

Maybe he was in a hurry. Maybe he was just trying to be funny.

Haley continued to stare at the letter on her screen. She was not laughing.

Chapter 50

The man slumped low in the seat, his long frame cramped in the confines of the Corolla's cockpit, and waited for the cloud cover to stifle the last light of the moon. His eyes fixed on the unimposing façade of the Regent Extended Care nursing home, hiding a monster within its walls like a gilded jewelry box containing a severed thumb. He might have smiled at the irony of it all, if not for the ugly work that lay ahead.

He thumbed the latches on the briefcase resting beside him on the passenger seat and popped the lid. The knife lay beneath the memos and ungraded term papers, its broad, flat blade absorbing the scant remaining moonlight like a sponge. The man lifted it gingerly before wrapping his deceptively strong right hand around the handle, an ornate carving of the god Baphomet. It was an ugly thing in spite of its intricacy, a grotesque goat head with a snake for a tongue, looping all the way down to the hilt, an unpleasant reminder of the "bad times" when the Order had become inundated with traitors and pagans. He slipped it beneath his long coat, flat against his chest, close to his heart.

Haley McBride was preoccupied with the time and was checking her watch. She did not see the man in the long duster slip quietly through the door at the end of A wing and glide like a shadow down the corridor before disappearing into the room she had emerged from only moments before. It was coming up on quarter past nine and although time was growing short, she had wanted to check on Von's grandfather (one final time?) before she left for her clandestine rendezvous with Jason Jankowski.

The old man was sleeping, but it was not a restful sleep. She had seen it before, so many times since working in this house of slow death. It was the sleep of the short-timers, the respiration hitching and labored, as if each precious breath might be the last. Von's grandfather might be dead before morning but she had seen them hang on for weeks, without so much as a detectable pulse, refusing to die, as if waiting for something or someone.

The old man was waiting for Von.

She choked back a tear and hurried down the hall to the nurses' station.

Drajac Vonosovich felt the knife at his throat before he opened his eyes. The film of the cataracts and the impending dementia could not hide the intent in the knight's eyes and the terminal wolf knew who he was before the man uttered the words.

"My name is Eugene Mathaus Kroc, old one. I have come here to kill you."

The old wolf smiled; it was a hideous, toothless smile that made the knight's blood run cold.

"What took you so long?" the old man wheezed. His lips were parched and cracked, and a viscous film coated his tongue, making it difficult for him to speak. Drajac motioned for the plastic tumbler that lay atop the bed cart.

Eugene Kroc eased the knife away from the monster's throat but did not relax his grip on the handle. "The trail was cold," Kroc said, "almost two centuries and an ocean away. We had to be sure." With his left hand he poured a splash of ice water into the cup and tendered it beneath the creature's knobby chin.

The beast strained to lift its head off the pillow, the gauzy wisps of dirty-gray hair atop its speckled cranium clinging

stubbornly to the pillow. The wrinkled mouth found the offered straw and latched on like a leathery barnacle finding a
ship's hull.

There was something about the way the thing sucked on
the innocuous straw that made the knight's stomach turn. He
pulled the cup away, unable to mask his disgust.

"Before I kill you," he said, pressing the flat of the blade
against the fold of Drajac's throat. "You will tell me why you
did it."

The old man settled back onto his pillow, a dribble of
water glistened in the corner of his wizened maw. He closed
his eyes for a moment, and when he opened them, the film
was gone and Kroc could see, in the watery depths, something that may have been a human soul.

"The year was 1827," Drajac began, "when I killed your
great-grandfather Jan Kroc, and his wife, Marie Saskova, but
the *troubles*, they begin at least two generations before."

Kroc bristled at the mention of his ancestor's name, surprised by the beast's recall and clarity.

"The bloodline—and this was a *noble* bloodline," Drajac
stressed, "as courtly and patrician as any line of kings dating
back to Solomon—you need to know that before I continue
story."

Kroc drew the blade away from the old man's throat, realizing he was in effect, hearing a deathbed confession.

"This bloodline, this lineage that began with the mother of
all men, and stay pure for centuries, had become polluted by
the very restraints imposed for its sanctity. As often happens
with royalty, the Sons of Irad fell victim to a limited gene
pool." Drajac rolled his bulging eyes. "It is early on in the six-
teenth-century that first mutated births appear on record."

Eugene Kroc opened his coat and tucked the long blade
into a deep inside pocket. The old man was talking about in-

breeding. Outside in the hall, a med-cart rolled by on squeaky wheels. He guessed he had another fifteen minutes before it made its way back. Kroc reached around and eased his frame into the boxy chair beside the nightstand.

"Most were still-born, half-man, half-wolf—sometimes . . . *other* things," Drajac frowned. "But some were born *alive* and breathing . . . monstrous things, mewling and howling, their tiny jaws snapping at very arms that hold them." His cracked lips curled at the thought. Kroc thought he saw a tear in his one bulging eye but it could have been a trick of the light. The old man steeled himself and continued. "Our philosophers, the alchemists, they do little but shake their heads and wait for the mutations to die—which they did, as there was no way to feed them. Their teeth were too sharp to suckle, you see . . ."

Kroc shuddered.

"These were old-times," Drajac explained. "The alchemists knew nothing of genetics and *DNA* and chromosomes, but they knew of the *transmutational* properties of alloys and fluxes and the hermetic arts. They knew of our history and the Fruit from the Tree of Life. Knowing these things, our philosophers began their quest for the Forbidden Fruit stolen by the Mother of all Men at the behest of the Serpent so long ago."

Kroc leaned forward in his chair.

"The mutated births stopped eventually. These were brilliant men after all, and very skilled. However, their cures were cosmetic at best. The real pollution still lingers in the blood and although we walk as men in daylight and as wolves at night, our souls still bear the stink of the corruption. The Sons of Irad, the splendid breed that fight alongside your order, the Templars, as mercenaries in the great Crusades, had become . . . tainted. Yes—that is the word."

Drajac paused, pleased with his explanation. "In the fall of 1799 there are many unprovoked attacks in the village of Kitebsk outside of Bukovina. The clan seek refuge in the forest in shadow of the Carpathian Mountains. They hold tribunal and make rogue wolves accountable for atrocities. They claim no recollection of attacks but admit their guilt." Drajac looked at the lanky knight seated at his bedside. "The memory is like shadow-play when the fever overtake you," he explained. "In all my life—and you know it to be long life . . . I never taste human flesh until . . ." Drajac stopped there. "You know rest of story."

Kroc nodded solemnly. "When did you make the crossing? I know my father almost had you in Strasbourg."

Drajac nodded, recalling the close encounter. "In 1939 we escape to America. Is truly land of free. We settle in wild land of Minnesota—far from temptation of human flesh."

Eugene Kroc checked his watch. He had but a few minutes.

"You must know," Drajac said, sensing the knight's impatience, "that I always carry the sin with me and we never stop looking for cure. It was this very search for sanctity that killed my only son."

Kroc stood and nodded glumly. "And Von—Sergei? You know he is infected also . . ."

The old man gasped. The words hitching in his throat. "The boy can still be saved!" he insisted. "Sergei is good wolf. His blood is pure! He—"

The slice was so clean and easy across the papery folds of the old man's throat that only the copious flow of blood confirmed the severing of the jugular. Eugene Kroc stood and watched, waiting for the last light of life to vanish from the bulging, filmy eyes. A discernible chill coursed through the room as the monster's soul escaped the withered husk that had held it for so many years.

The knight wiped the long blade clean and tucked it back into the folds of his duster. He felt none of the satisfaction he had expected upon completion of such an arduous hunt, only a sense of dread for what lay ahead.

There was still one more.

Chapter 51

Eugene Kroc slipped into the hallway and closed the door behind him with a soft click. It would have been so much cleaner—so much easier, to suffocate the beast, or simply unhook him from his life support devices.

But that was not how it was done, was it?

He peered around the corner and scanned the nurses' station, surprised and delighted by what he saw there.

Haley McBride was hurrying into her coat and bidding a hasty goodbye to the floor nurse even though it was only nine forty. Kroc knew Haley worked till eleven o'clock on Tuesday nights. He knew she was never late for work and that she never left early. He had learned an awful lot about Haley McBride in a few short weeks.

Kroc ducked back down the hallway and bolted through the A wing door into the parking lot. Haley's car was parked around the other side by the main entrance. With any luck—and Eugene Kroc believed a man made his own luck—she would lead him right to the boy.

He waited until she had pulled into the flow of traffic on 183rd Street before initiating pursuit, staying four to five car lengths behind Haley's blue Neon until the girl took a sudden left at Cal-Sag road. Kroc made the yellow and followed well behind, just keeping the Neon in sight amidst the busy mall traffic. The clusters of stores diminished and the thoroughfare narrowed into a twisty two-lane, snaking through the Cook County forest preserves. The Templar Knight cut his lights and motored up three car lengths behind the girl, the speedometer climbing toward seventy-five. Kroc frowned at the reckless driving habits of today's youth, hoping Haley didn't flip the Neon before leading him to the wolf.

She slowed abruptly, the stop sign at the Route 83 inter-section apparently taking her by surprise. Haley blew the stop and spun the Neon around in an arcing right-hand turn, crossing well into the oncoming lane of Route 83. Kroc ex-haled though his teeth, thankful for the lack of semi traffic on the usually busy road. He followed, backing off a bit as she slowed at the flashing red light crowning Harlem Avenue. Haley idled at the intersection, as if unsure of her next move, before hooking left and turning onto an access road, splin-tering off 83's eastbound lane.

Kroc waited before following, frowning at his own care-lessness. He had never even thought to check the abandoned American Motors plant, largely because of its distance from the hospital, the last place Von had been seen alive. If the boy was holed up here, he had some outside help. The wolf was in no condition to make it here on his own.

Kroc pulled up behind the tree line masking the plant en-trance and ditched the Corolla, covering the remaining fifty-or-so yards on foot. Haley's Neon was parked at the main gate, a towering chain-link affair, topped with razor wire spun around elliptical crescent spikes. A Chevy Beretta sitting just a few feet away from the Neon was the only other vehicle to be seen. Kroc guessed that Haley knew the car, parking in such close proximity to it, and surmised that she and at least one other person were in league, protecting the wounded wolf.

The industrial chain-link of the front gate had been cut clean and spread wide, making for an all-too-obvious and in-viting access onto the shuttered grounds.

Staying low in the dark shadows cast by the massive plant, Kroc made his way along the fence and looked for an alter-nate point of entry. He was not one to go loping into the front door of hostile territory—school kids or not. The knight followed the meandering fence around to the back of the plant and immediately noticed the dim light burning in the second-story window. It was a gaslight—most likely a lantern, almost imperceptible from his vantage point—as if it were set low on the floor of the room.

Kroc stepped back and took note of the configuration of the plant. The room from which the light burned rested atop a skeletal gantry, connected to the rest of the plant by a covered bridge, probably housing a freight track or conveyer belt of some kind. It jutted out over the lip of the channel before ending in an abrupt amputation of steel and cable. Kroc guessed the missing appendage was the cargo belt leading down to the waterway where barges would be loaded with stamped metal to be shaped into AMC Pacers and Gremlins upon their arrival at the end of the line in Saginaw, Michigan.

The Templar Knight smiled to himself, recalling the old Javelin he had tooled around in as a kid back in the seventies. It was American Motors' sole entry in the muscle car market and not a bad hunk of iron when you got right down to it. He had taken on his share of Camaros and Barracudas, before the transmission—which had probably shipped from this very plant—dropped one night while racing a Dodge Charger for twenty dollars and local bragging rights. The smile vanished quickly enough, joining the memories of long ago times, when he had never dreamed he would grow to be a man preparing to kill a seventeen-year-old boy.

Wolf—he reminded himself as he followed the fence all the way to the end of the embankment overlooking the channel. The ground was loose here and Kroc grabbed hold of the chain-link and skirted along its length, looking for a quick way in. The girl had been inside for almost fifteen minutes now and her trail was growing cold. Kroc could feel the fence starting to give under his meager weight and realized that the ground over the embankment had eroded to the point where it could no longer contain the support posts. He pushed forward with all his strength and clung tight as the steel mesh collapsed beneath him. With his section of fence lying almost horizontal on the crumbly soil, Kroc leaped over the crown of razor wire and landed neatly on the other side.

He was in.

The knight crouched as low as his long legs would allow and dashed across the open terrain to the near wall of the plant, cursing the naked landscape and the bright light of the waning moon. He came upon a freight door and saw the bottom panel had been removed—rather hastily from the looks of it—and shimmied underneath it.

The plant was vast and dark as a tomb. As the knight's sharp eyes adjusted, he could see the structural remains of the assembly line scattered about in various stages of tear-down. Eugene Kroc was almost to his feet when he realized, a split-second too late, that he was not alone.

He whirled, and the blow, which would have been lethal had it struck home, glanced off his shoulder, knocking him back down to the concrete floor. The knight rolled and turned to face his attacker only to be blinded by the powerful beam of the flashlight that had almost crushed his skull. Reflex squeezed his eyes shut and the bright orange fireballs erupting on the surface of his lids exploded into stardust as the heavy rubber sole of a Nike cross-trainer crashed flush into the side of his head. Fighting to stay conscious beneath the shower of pain, the knight was braced by anger and disbelief upon hearing his tormentor's voice.

"Well, look at this!" Mike Minot crowed. "The *English teacher* has decided to join the party!"

Kroc stumbled backward, feigning disorientation as the football coach advanced on his wounded prey.

Keep talking, Kroc thought, scrambling backward, waiting for his vision to return. *Just keep talking . . .*

"You should have stayed home with your Chaucer and Longfellow, teacher," Minot barked, swinging the flashlight back for the kill-strike. "You might have lived to—"

Kroc spun around in a full three hundred and sixty-degree arc, his long legs sweeping Minot off his feet. With a quick back flip, the Templar Knight was up and in his combat-stance, blinking the last of the pain from the corners of his eyes.

"Hot-damn," Minot said, unable to keep the surprise from his voice. "The Stork can fight!" He scrambled to his feet and squared off against the spidery man in the long duster. "You took me by surprise teacher, but that was your one shot. Now you're going to taste some real pain."

Despite the bravado, Kroc could see, even in the dim star-light filtering in through the high windows, the uncertainty in the man's eyes. He felt the knife, heavy and at-the-ready, in the pocket of his greatcoat as he raised his arms. Kroc smiled and waved him in.

Minot charged, intending to tackle the gangly man and bring the fight into close quarters where his superior strength could take the day. Kroc misjudged the man's speed but still managed a sidestep move that brought his knee directly into Minot's hard belly. Three more quick blows rained down on the back of the former free-safety's head before he hit the ground in a heap.

"You will tell me where the boy is?" Kroc asked, snatching the flashlight off the ground next to his fallen adversary. He shined the beam into the coach's face. He couldn't help but relish the anger and confusion he saw there.

Minot blinked away from the beam. The skinny school-master had given him all that he could handle. As much as it pained him, as much as he wanted it, he chose not to go in for another round.

"You win, teacher," Minot said, lowering his head. "I'll give you the boy. Quit shining that damn light in my face. I can't take you to him if I can't see."

Kroc moved the beam out of the coach's eyes and pointed it at his chest. He saw the glint of the gun just before the orange flash exploded from the shiny blue barrel.

Chapter 52

The report from the .22 snub-nose, louder than it had any right to be on the cavernous floor of the assembly plant, reached Haley's ears in the repository above as a muffled pop. The sound, no more menacing than the first kernel exploding in a bag of microwave popcorn, had nevertheless jarred her from the merciful state of tranquility brought on by shock. She screamed again upon seeing the soupy carnage that lay before her.

Her screams had jolted Jason and he turned to her, his mouth sealed with duct tape, his eyes wide with terror, pleading with her to . . . *please be quiet!*

The thing in the corner moved.

Haley squeezed her eyes shut and strained against her own bonds, pressing herself against the post to which they were both bound, trying to raise herself from her seated position on the floor. A moist, sticky sound rose up in the silence followed by a rude expulsion of air, stinking of rotten meat and things long dead. Jason's scream, stifled by the duct tape, rang only in his own ears as the monstrosity hefted its segmented trunk off the creaking floorboards and inched forward out of the darkness into the dull light cast by the Coleman lantern.

It still had Von's eyes.

That was the worst part of it—the part that had made it so unbearable to look at. Sergei Alexei Vonosovich, who had walked all too briefly as the greatest and most noble of wolves, had devolved into little more than a gelatinous grub. Limbless and pale, it slithered through the tattered, bloody clothing and undigested body parts, leaving a slick mucus-like sheen in its slimy wake. It stopped a short distance in front of Haley, its eyes, all too human—all too *Von,* and looked away as if ashamed.

And then it regurgitated.

The truncated torso of Lester Lesko, mummified and horribly intact, spilled from the beast's gullet onto the floor, just inches from Haley's sneakers. Haley McBride screamed to wake the dead. Lester's head rolled within the oily membrane enveloping the halved corpse, his mouth open in lost protest. He stared at Haley in perpetuity through hollowed eye sockets, unseeing, black, and rotting.

Spurred by its own debasement, the slug roared with shame, exposing the fan-like row of razor-sharp teeth nestled deep within its stinking maw. The howl of outrage fell to a whimper as the beast's eyes (Von's eyes) suddenly looked beyond Haley and filled with fear.

A peal of laughter, even more horrible than the monster's pitiful whimpering, rose up behind her.

"Oh," Mike Minot cracked, barely able to contain his glee. "Someone is having trouble keeping their food down."

Minot backed into her field of vision, pulling the limp body of Mr. Kroc, her English Lit teacher, behind him. Mr. Kroc's beautiful, curly hair was matted flat with blood. Minot stopped a respectful distance away from the thing that used to be Von and let the limp body fall to the planking.

"Dead too long, I guess," Minot said, stepping around Lester Lesko's grisly remains. "Our boy likes *fresh* meat. He's having a little trouble keeping his food down, but I'm sure he's still hungry, not a lot of meat on our friend Lester, anyway."

Haley's stomach did a slow roll. Lester Lesko's broken eyeglasses lay off to her left in a puddle of brackish slime.

"Same with this skinny bookworm," Minot said, "but there's more to him than meets the eye!" He kicked Mr. Kroc in the ribs, eliciting a moan from the prone body.

He wasn't dead. Haley held on to a last shred of hope. Judging from the looks of Mike Minot's face, it looked like the English teacher had gotten in a few licks of his own.

Minot stepped over his body, clutching a cattle prod duct-taped to the end of a broomstick. The thing that used to be Von backed away instinctively.

"Go on, ya ugly mutt," Minot laughed, waving the electric prod at the frightened beast. "You want some more of this? Huh?" The coach grinned at Haley, not the dazzling smile that made women melt, but a leering sardonic grin, teetering on the edge of madness. "He knows who's boss," Minot winked at Haley. "He knows who is boss!"

"Leave him alone!" Haley screamed. "Leave him alone! Why are you doing this?"

Minot feigned indignation. "Why am I doing this? *Why am I doing this?* Well, let's see: Number one, I'm doing it to beat a *murder* rap. I don't know how you connected me to Melanie Houghwat but you should have kept your mouth shut. When the cops get here in the morning and find this ugly bastard along with your remains, I'll be the furthest thing from their minds. It's going to make quite a story, don't you think? Teen love triangle spurs betrayed monster to eat unfaithful lovers! I can't wait to read it.

"Number two, I think our boy here was really onto something before he got too carried away with it—something that's going to get me back to where I belong, back to the top of my game—back in an NFL uniform." He glared at Haley. "Pretty tidy, wouldn't you say, Haley?"

Haley started to laugh, a mocking, haughty laugh, full of contempt.

Mike Minot looked at her, amazed. "What the hell are you laughing about? You're going to be dead before the sun rises.

Do you think that's funny?"

She had him out of his rhythm. She took her best-shot bluff. "Not as tidy as you think. You don't know much about teenage girls, do you? Melanie kept a *diary!* She let me read it. Some very lengthy passages about you. I'm sure it's only a matter of time before the police find it. I phoned them before I drove over here . . ."

"Liar," Mike Minot growled, stepping around the sedentary giant slug. "Lying little bitch! I'll kill you myself! I'm going to feed you to your boyfriend piece by—"

The Von-slug's head shot out three feet from its thorax as if spring-loaded, clamping its jaws firmly around its former coach's calf. Mike Minot howled in pain, as the beast pulled its head back into itself, dragging him through the slime staining the wooden floor.

"Get him, Von!" Haley shouted above Minot's screams. "Kill that son-of-a-bitch!"

Kicking and struggling to break free, Mike Minot felt his leg being sucked perilously close to the circular row of teeth deep in the monster's throat. He spun around on the floor, his eyes burning from the foul secretions leaking from the beast's underbelly. Still clutching the cattle prod, he swung the broomstick in a wide arc, hoping to catch the beast in its hindquarters.

There was the sound of broken glass as the electric prod smashed the propane lantern. The room went black for a split-second before exploding in a wall of white light.

The toxic excretions from Von's chemical breakdown ignited in a flashpoint, engulfing the room in orange flames. Before Haley could blink her singed eyelashes, Minot and Von were swallowed up by the inferno, an unholy coupling, shrieking and whirling across the burning floorboards.

Jason kicked at the burning floor, bucking in vain against

the grip of the duct tape holding him tight to the pole. Haley, succumbing to the smoke, resigned herself to her fate and took what comfort she could from the fact that Mike Minot would die along with her. A flash of blue steel in the corner of her eye yanked her from the brink of unconsciousness.

Mr. Kroc on one knee, slicing through her bonds.

Haley felt the tight embrace of the duct tape loosen and fall away altogether with each rapid swipe of the Templar Knight's sharp blade.

Jason, in her ear now, yelling at her to stay low, her hands burnt and blistering from the heat. The floor, popping and sparking like kindling in an October campfire. A scream—her own scream—in her ears as she fell forward into nothingness, the floor giving way beneath her next frantic step. Strong hands pulling her up and free from the splintery jaws of the flaming floor. A mad scramble, Jason pulling her, pushing Mr. Kroc, through the doorway onto the blessedly cold steel of the freight tracks.

"Come on!" Jason yelled, grabbing her hand. "When the fire hits this tunnel it's all over! The backdraft will—Haley! Come on!" Haley stole one last look into the smoking inferno, her eyes clouded with soot and tears, not knowing what she had hoped to see.

"It's better this way, Haley," Mr. Kroc said, his hands on her shoulders. He turned her around like a man helping a blind woman across a street. "He will find peace in the beyond. He will be a man again."

Haley looked at Mr. Kroc, his bloodied face otherworldly and beautiful in the glimmer of the firelight behind her. He looked like a wounded angel standing there in his greatcoat—yes, that's what he was, an archangel sent from the Army of God.

"Can you carry her, Jason?" the angel yelled. "I think she's in shock. I don't have the strength." The angel touched his head where Lucifer had struck him. Angels bleed.

Haley felt herself being scooped up. Jason—Jason from school. Such a sweet boy—too bad he was gay.

"Let's go," Mr. Kroc said. "We've got twenty—maybe thirty yards. You think you can make it?"

Jason could see the ground below them through the slats in the wooden ties. It would be the only light in the dark tunnel as they made their way to the other side. Jason reaffirmed his hold on Haley. "Yeah, let's go."

Kroc nodded. "You go first. I'll stay behind." He pointed to their feet. "Be aware of the spacing of the ties, but don't—"

The bridge groaned beneath their feet, a great wrenching shudder that shook the walls around them.

"Go!" Kroc shouted. "Now!"

Jason turned and ran stagger-step across the ties, not bothering to look down. He was still twenty feet from the hatchway to the main plant when the bridge buckled in a tortured squeal of timber and steel. He fell on top of Haley and Mr. Kroc fell on top of him. Remarkably, Haley was the first to her feet.

She stood tall and ramrod straight as Kroc and Jason hunkered on their knees. Haley turned and stared silently as the repository disintegrated behind them. The floor went first, an incandescent web of orange and yellow flame, startling and oddly beautiful against the night sky. It folded into itself upon collapse, following the howling fireball of Mike Minot and the thing that used to be Sergei Alexei Vonosovich into the murky depths of the Cal-Sag channel fifty feet below.

Chapter 53

"I think we're just about done here," Special Agent O'Mara said, flipping his tiny notebook shut. He shot a sideways glance at his partner, the heavyset man to whom Haley had taken an instant dislike.

Special Agent Bukich raised a fat finger on his meaty fist as if to make a point, then thought better of it. "If there's anything else you can remember—"

"Please give us a call—when you're feeling better, of course," Special Agent O'Mara interrupted. He rose from the bedside chair and extracted a card from his rumpled suit coat. He attempted to hand it to Haley, forgetting for a moment her heavily bandaged hands. He grinned sheepishly and placed it on the stand next to her bed. O'Mara nodded to Haley, his bright-blue Irish eyes smiling sadly. "Take care of yourself, Haley."

Haley managed a smile. Special Agent O'Mara's face blurred for a moment and then flickered back into focus. The morphine drip was really starting to kick in.

"He was a hero."

Special Agents O'Mara and Bukich stopped at the door.

"What's that, Haley?" O'Mara asked, his fingers fumbling for the notepad inside his suit coat.

"He was a hero," Haley said. "Von. He saved us all."

Special Agent Bukich rolled his eyes. "Sure he did, Haley," O'Mara said, motioning his partner out into the bustling hospital corridor.

"A hero," Haley mumbled.

But the FBI agents had already left.

"A hero . . . tall, and strong, and handsome . . ."

Haley drifted into the waiting arms of Morpheus, who carried her, limp and unresisting, to a gentle place—far away from all the pain, and heartache, and death.

Von was waiting there for her, standing on a rock, in a forest by a stream. Tall and strong and handsome, just as she had insisted.

Just as she would always remember.

Epilogue

"Freshen you up, sweetie?"

The man at the counter looked up from his newspaper and smiled at the waitress. "Just a splash," he said, nudging the half-empty cup a few inches closer to the pot of coffee she had poised and ready to pour.

"There you go, doll," she smiled. She poured a quick but perfect refill, an eighth of an inch from the rim of his cup. "You need anything else, just whistle."

"Just the check, please," the man replied.

"Sure hon, coming right up," she said, clearing his plate from the counter. She sounded disappointed.

The man watched her walk to the tiny window that fronted the grill and pluck his check from the tin wheel hanging there. There was a little extra sway in those hips and it was there solely for his benefit. He ran his finger self-consciously along the side of his face. Smoother than the week before. Smoother than yesterday.

He adjusted the napkin dispenser on the counter, turning it so that he could check his reflection in the shiny metal surface.

So odd to see another face staring back.

Not his old face, but a handsome face nonetheless—a face that still had waitresses hovering over him like a visiting dignitary while coffee grew cold in the cups of those around him.

"There you go, babe."

The waitress, Shelly was her name, slid the check along the counter to him, bending in low and close. The smell of frying eggs and corned beef hash wafting from the kitchen could not mask the scent of her heightened arousal. The man helped himself to an eyeful of her breasts, all the more accessible after she had casually unfastened just one more button on her blouse.

"Thanks, Shelly," he said, giving her a thrill.

He rose and dug his wallet out of his pants pocket, fishing a five-dollar tip out for Shelly and her sweet-smelling cleavage. The man glanced at the photo on his new Missouri driver's license. His face had already changed, ever so slightly, since the photo was taken just last week. He thumbed the bogus I.D., admiring the craftsmanship. Tom Kitna was his new name. Tom had been his middle name. It wouldn't take that long to get used to it.

He paid at the register and walked out of the greasy spoon into the early morning sunshine. The smell of fuel from the idling Greyhound was nearly overpowering but he lingered at the side of the road, taking in what he could of the perfect spring day before boarding.

He breathed deeply, blocking out the exhaust fumes. The faint smell of lilac hung in the air and he found he could differentiate it from the crabgrass and Creeping Charlie scouring through the gravel at his feet. A dog (pregnant) had recently relieved herself not far from where he stood, and he whiffed out a clutch of pheasant nesting in the cornfields across the road.

So much he could smell now. So much he could see.

"All aboard, Mac." The Greyhound bus driver nodded at him from his perch high behind the wheel. A hiss of the hydraulic doors accentuated the driver's point.

The man took one more deep breath of fresh air, the last before being confined in the stagnant, conditioned atmosphere inside the bus. He hitched the strap of his bag snug across his broad shoulder (he would not let it leave his side) and bounded up the short, choppy steps, noting the twinge in his calf where he had lost so much tissue. It was just a tingle, not unlike the phantom itch an amputee might feel where a lost limb had once been. He settled in, setting his bag next to him in the seat closest to the window. He stretched his legs, feeling the tight harmony of the musculature, and the twinge was again just a memory.

He waited until the bus had picked up speed and the few other passengers were secure in their own seats before pulling back the zipper on his duffel bag. He fished the leather-encased med-kit from the depths of the bag and carefully removed the vial of elixir, his grip as sure and careful as a parent holding a newborn. He raised it to eye-level, marveling at the way it caught the stubborn rays of the sun filtering in through the Greyhound's tinted window and made them its own.

It was almost two-thirds full. That would be more than enough if he had made any sense at all of the journal lying at the bottom of his duffel bag. Besides, he had seen first-hand what too much of the stuff could do. It made the long-term side effects of anabolic steroids look like the chickenpox.

Certainly didn't want that.

No, he was careful. He wouldn't let the juice destroy him as the kid had done. He used it sparingly, wisely. He would not succumb to the temptation—to the rush of the fast-fix. He knew his body, knew what it could take and when it needed more.

He knew he was strong now. Stronger than he had ever been. Faster than he had ever been. Better than he had ever been.

Open try-outs—scrub days, the established veterans had called them—for the Oakland Raiders started next week.

Mike Minot always liked the way he looked in black.

About the Author

Joseph J. Curtin lives in a small suburb on the outskirts of Chicago. Having recently completed his first screenplay, he is working on his third novel. You can email the author at razorbldesmile@comcast.net.